Love's Trusting

By
Maryann Jordan

Love's Trusting

Copyright © 2015 Maryann Jordan
Print Edition

This book is a work of fiction. Names, characters, places, and incidents either are products of the author's imagination or are used fictitiously. Any resemblance to actual persons, living or dead, events, or locales is entirely coincidental.

Cover Design by: Kari Ayasha, Cover to Cover Designs
covertocoverdesigns.com
Editor: Shannon Brandee Eversoll

ISBN: 978-0-9864004-1-4

Dedication

I dedicate this love story to my husband, Michael. We met in high school and went our separate ways. We met in college and once again went our separate ways. Then we met one more time…and that was it. It was the right person at the right time. And we've been married for thirty-three years.

So to all the enduring loves, the second chances, the one-more-times. This book is for you.

Acknowledgements

First and foremost, I have to thank my husband, Michael. Always believing in me and wanting me to pursue my dreams, this book would not be possible without his support. To my daughters, MaryBeth and Nicole, I taught you to follow your dreams and now it is time for me to take my own advice. You two are my inspiration.

My best friend, Tammie, who for eighteen years has been with me through thick and thin. You've filled the role of confidant, supporter, and sister.

My dear friend, Myckel Anne, who keeps me on track, keeps me grounded, and most of all – keeps my secrets. Thank you for not only being my proofreader, but my friend.

Going from blogger to author has allowed me to have the friendships and advice of several wonderful authors who always answered my questions, helped me over rough spots, and cheered me on. To Kristine Raymond, you gave me the green light when I wondered if I was crazy and you never let me give up. MJ Nightingale and Andrea Michelle – you two have made a huge impact on my life. Anna Mychals, EJ Shorthall, Victoria Brock, Jen Andrews, Andrea Long, A.d. Ellis, ML Steinbrunn, Sandra Love, thank you from the bottom of my heart.

My beta readers kept me sane, cheered me on, found all my silly errors, and often helped me understand my characters through their eyes. A huge thank you to Denise VanPlew, Sandi Laubhan, Barbara Martoncik, Vanessa Spradling, Jennifer Alumbaugh, Anna Mychals, Danielle Petersen, Shannon Brandee, Leeann Wright, Lynn Smith, Kelly Williams and Tracey Markin for being my beta girls who love alphas!

Shannon Brandee Eversoll has been my editor for the past three books and what she brings to my writing has been amazing. She and Myckel Anne Phillips as my proofreader gave their time and talents to making Love's Trusting as well written as it can be.

My street team, Jordan Jewels, you all are amazing! You volunteer your time to promote my books and I cannot thank you enough! I hope you will stay with me, because I have lots more stories inside, just waiting to be written!

My Personal Assistant Barbara Martoncik is the woman that keeps me going when I feel overwhelmed and I am so grateful for not only her assistance, but her friendship.

This is the sixth book cover that Kari Ayasha from Cover to Cover Designs has created for me and her talent is evident in every detail. Thank you for working with me.

As the owner of the blog, Lost in Romance Books, I know the selflessness of bloggers. We promote indie authors on our own time because we believe fully in the indie author community. I want to thank the many bloggers that I have served with, and who are assisting in promoting my series.

Most importantly, thank you readers. You allow me into your home for a few hours as you disappear into my characters and you support me as I follow my indie author dreams.

If you read my books and enjoy them, please leave a review. It does not have to be long or detailed…just that you enjoyed the book. Reviews are essential to indie authors!

Author Information

Maryann Jordan

I am an avid reader of romance novels, often joking that I cut my teeth on the old bodice rippers. I have been reading and reviewing for years. In 2013, I created a blog, Lost in Romance Books, to promote and showcase indie authors. In 2014, I finally gave in to the characters in my head, screaming for their story to be told. From these musings, my first novel, Emma's Home, The Fairfield Series Book 1 was born.

I am a high school counselor having worked in education for thirty years. I live in Virginia, having also lived in four states and two foreign countries. I have been married to a wonderfully patient man for thirty-two years and am the mother to two adult daughters. When writing, my dog or one of my four cats can generally be found in the same room if not on my lap.

Please take the time to leave a review of this book (on Goodreads). Reviews are the lifeline for indie authors.

Feel free to contact me, especially if you enjoyed my book. I love to hear from readers!

Facebook:

www.facebook.com/authormaryannjordan

Facebook:

www.facebook.com/lostinromancebooks

Booktropolous:

booktropoloussocial.com/index.php?do=/profile-1765/

Email:

authormaryannjordan@gmail.com

Blog:

www.maryannjordanauthor.com

Prologue

"**A**RE YOU SURE?" he asked while sliding into the back seat, trying to maneuver her so that she was more comfortable.

Her blue eyes held his as a nervous smile played about her lips. "Yeah," she whispered. "I'm ready." *I've loved you since I was thirteen years old. And every day for the past five years I have thought of only loving you.*

Both settled into the back of his parent's old SUV that had been given to him when he went off to college. They suddenly looked at each other nervously. Reaching across the seat, he slid his hand around the back of her neck then gently pulled her forward until their lips met. The kiss was like so many they had shared over the past several years – soft and sweet, but this time there was more urgency, knowing that something life-changing was about to happen.

He slipped his hand up under her shirt and pulled it over her head. The lacy bra shimmered in the moonlight. *This is new. She must have just bought it.* Knowing that she was as anxious for this night to go as they had always planned made him smile. He'd grown up with this beauty and knew that she had been in love with him for a long time. But it wasn't until she turned fifteen that she had really caught his eye.

They'd been together ever since, throughout high school and now into his first year of college, but had never had sex. They'd promised each other they would wait until she was eighteen, and that was today. Or rather tonight. After the family celebrations, they drove to their place by the river under the large old tree that had seen many a lover under its branches.

Raising her hand to cup his cheek she asked, "Where'd you go?"

"Oh, baby, I'm right here with you," he assured her as he unsnapped the front closure on her bra. Her pale, rosy-tipped breasts spilled out and he leaned his head down to capture her nipple in his mouth, sucking deeply.

"Ahh," she moaned as he lapped and sucked first one and then the other. She could feel the juices begin to flow and knew what he would find as soon as he slid his finger up her skirt. *Which I wish he would do…now.*

As if on cue, he slid his hand along her thighs seeking the prize that lay waiting. Quickly discovering that she was as wet as he anticipated, he thrust his finger inside. Moving it around with his thumb on her clit, it only took a moment for the orgasm to roar over her as it milked his finger.

When he slid his finger out, she watched as he brought it to his mouth, swirling his tongue around, sucking her juices off.

Jesus fuck, I could come in my pants right now. Determined to not make their first time be a disaster he slid her skirt down over her legs and dropped it onto the floor of the backseat. His dick was screaming for him to get on with it and he was losing the battle of trying to take things slow. Barely able to hang on to his control he pulled his shirt quickly over his head and maneuvered out of his jeans, pulling a condom out of his pocket.

She looked at his beautiful body. Boys hate to be called beautiful, but it was the only word she could think of to describe him. Tall, blond, slate-blue eyes, with a body that made every girl envious of her boyfriend. They'd been naked before but held off of sex. Until now. Until tonight.

The backseat did not afford them very much room, so he had the forethought to put the seats down so they could make a little bed. He lay her on her back, his hand skimming from her cheeks down her long neck to her breasts and then lower. Pulling himself over her with his weight resting on his arms, he kissed her as his legs nudged hers apart.

Trying to be careful, he slid the end of his cock into her entrance watching her luminescent blue eyes widen in momentary distress.

"Just go quickly," she encouraged. "I've read that makes it less painful."

Nodding, he plunged in to the hilt, but her gasp halted him as he saw tears slide down her cheeks. *Oh*

Jesus, I've hurt her. He stilled but his dick was unhappy and the desire to move was almost overwhelming.

She lay panting for a moment trying to acclimate to the sharp pain and intense fullness that she felt. It finally eased and she looked at his strained face.

"It's okay. You can keep going," she said softly.

"I'll stop if you want. I'll do anything for you," he vowed.

Smiling up at the man that she loved more than anything in the world, she nodded. Needing no more encouragement, he slowly slid in and out, allowing her body to continue to accommodate his girth. Her juices began to flow making the friction burn less and delight more.

She hadn't been allowed to date until she was sixteen, but for the past two years since then he had not had sex with anyone else. At nineteen, his college friends teased him mercilessly about his abstinence, but for him it was her. Had been for years. And would always be. When he went away to college, he vowed to her, "You can trust me. I'll never betray you."

But now, his dick was screaming in delight and he wasn't going to last. "Baby, are you good?"

She had read the magazines and romance novels about losing her virginity but had no idea how it would feel. But this…this was amazing. As he pumped in and out, she could feel herself becoming wound up like the old clock her grandfather kept on his mantle. Tighter and tighter. Suddenly he dipped his head down and sucked hard on her nipple and it was as though the tightness in her entire body exploded and she swore she could see stars behind her closed eyes.

With only a few more thrusts, he felt his balls tighten as he powered through his own orgasm, pouring himself into her tight pussy.

They lay there for a long time in the bed of the SUV, limbs tangled, panting, fogging up the windows, creating their own little world. He continued to thrust a few more times as his dick finally calmed down. It was a bit later that he pulled out and tossed the condom to the side.

Looking up into his blue eyes as she cupped his face with her hand, she said, "I love you. I've loved you for the longest time."

Smiling down at the beauty whose dark hair and blue eyes proclaimed her Irish heritage, he said, "I love you too, doll. I'll always love you, till the end of time. You can trust in that."

Chapter 1

(four years later)

"I NOW PRONOUNCE you man and wife. You may kiss your bride."

The wedding was beautiful and as Suzanne stood in her jewel-blue bridesmaid's dress at the front of the church, she looked on as her boss and good friend was finally married to the man who had swept her off her feet. Suzanne was a veterinarian technician for Annie's clinic in the city of Richland. The small apartment over the inner-city clinic that Annie used to live in was now hers since Annie and Shane had moved out to the suburbs. It was an old, tiny apartment, but Shane had made sure it was safe for Annie; it now gave Suzanne a chance to be near work and save on rent.

Glancing to her side was her good friend and fellow bridesmaid, Lily, in a pale blue dress that highlighted her blonde hair. She saw Lily and her fiancé, Matt, making eyes at each other, their happiness obvious to everyone.

Happy for her friends, she could not help the longing that twisted deep inside. The desire to love and be loved. To find the one that would never forsake her.

No matter what...*Stop. Don't go there. Not today.* Reminding herself that this was Annie and Shane's day she smiled back at the happy couple.

Soon the reception was in full swing. Sitting at the table with Lily and Matt, she saw Lily looking around as though desperate to find someone.

"Who are you looking for? Matt's going to get jealous if you don't pay attention to him," she joked.

"I'm trying to see when BJ comes in. I can't believe that you two are so close to me, but I haven't been able to introduce you to each other since you're never in the same place. He had to miss the wedding but will be here for the reception and I'll finally get you two together."

The light dimmed just a little in her eyes as she admonished gently, "Lily. Don't try to fix me up with someone. You know I'm not interested."

Lily speared her with a sympathetic look. "Honey, I know you were hurt a long time ago. And I know you grieve for something lost. I just want to see you happy."

Smiling at the couple in front of her, she gave a little shrug as she whispered, "I had happy once. But when it's broken, there's no getting it back."

She stood and then kissed the top of Lily's head as she said, "I'm going to go mingle with some old friends. You two have fun." Winking at Matt, she floated away.

One table in particular caught her attention. Four large, handsome men sat around the table, as comfortable in their suits as they would be in a biker bar. Tony Alvarez ran a security company that had helped save Annie when she had been kidnapped earlier in the year. Gabe, Vinny, and Jobe sat with him with one chair empty. Having all served in the military together, each man brought their own special skills to their new civilian careers. Tony had been the squad leader and maintained that position in his new business. While they all seemed like brothers to her, she knew that the table full of hard, handsome men would catch the eye of any single women at the wedding…and probably a few married ones as well. They all stood as she approached and Gabe leaned over to give her a hug and a brotherly kiss on her cheek. Greeting them, she nodded toward the empty chair. "Who's missing?" she asked.

Vinny, always the ladies' man, jumped up to pull the chair out for her. "Why you, of course."

Laughing, she punched his shoulder as his twin Gabe responded, "It's for BJ. He's on his way from a family event."

Raising her eyebrow at this news, she had the feeling that BJ's co-workers and friends were just as anxious for her to meet him as Lily was. "Hmmm, well we'll see if he shows."

Giving each man a hug, she made her way over to another table. She saw some old family friends from Fairfield, the town she grew up in, so she moved over to greet them. Emma Campbell had been her high school counselor and had married her brother's best friend, Jake. Along with them was Carol and Tom Rivers, another one of her brother's best friends.

The two couples couldn't believe that the beautiful woman in front of them was so grown up.

After hugs and greetings, Emma kept her arm around her, pulling her in tightly. "I miss you so much. Your mom's bakery was never the same after you left home. But I'm so proud of what you've accomplished. Are you happy?"

"I love my job and working for Annie," Suzanne effused. "I'm thinking about going back to school to become a veterinarian nurse. It would allow me to do a few more things than I can do right now. The animals are great and our clinic...well, I can't think of a better place to work."

Emma exclaimed, "Your enthusiasm for your job is overwhelming. But that still doesn't tell me if you are happy."

Suzanne found herself scrutinized by Emma's thoughtful gaze. "I'm happy enough," she replied, her smile not quite reaching her eyes.

"Do you ever see..." Emma began.

Shaking her head, Suzanne's eyes widened. "Nope. And no, I'm not talking about it."

Emma patted her shoulder before pulling her in for a tight hug. "It's okay."

Giving a small smile, Suzanne was just getting ready to turn away when Lily came over to her. Besides

Annie, Lily was her closest friend.

"Sweetie, come with me," Lily said as she linked her arms through Suzanne's.

"He's here, right? Oh Lily, you know I hate this."

"Come on. It's just an introduction. All the guys at Tony's really like him and you know how much he helped me last year." Lily had stumbled across a prescription fraud scheme and BJ had helped her with the software codes that contained the evidence they were looking for.

Suzanne allowed Lily to tug her through the crowded reception hall then heard her name called. She turned around to see Leon waving at her from across the room. He worked as a vet tech with Annie as well and was there with his wife. Behind her she could hear Lily say, "BJ, I'd like you to meet…"

Suzanne turned around and stared into the eyes of the man she had been avoiding for four years. Gasping, she saw his eyes widen.

"BJ?"

"Suzy?"

Oh no, not him. Not now. Opening her mouth like a fish, she found that nothing came out. Just as he looked like he was going to say something, she quickly turned. "I have to get out of here," she said, pushing her way through the crowd. Making her way out of the reception hall, she ran into Annie and Shane. Giving them fast hugs and congratulations she explained that she was getting a migraine and had to cut the reception short.

"Oh honey, you're going to miss the bouquet toss," Annie said.

With tears in her eyes, Suzanne just shrugged. "I need to go, but please don't worry about me. Just enjoy your honeymoon. It'll be nice to have a few days off anyway."

With a last hug, she hurried out of the hall towards her car.

LILY LOOKED AT the retreating back of her best friend before turning around to BJ, who she noted was watching Suzanne as well.

"BJ? Why did she call you Brad?"

"Bradley James Evans. BJ was a college nickname and it just stuck." Looking down at Lily's concerned face, he gave her a hug. "It's not your fault she left. We have a…history. It goes back to high school."

Standing there for a moment as the rush of emotions washed over him, he remembered the last time she ran away. Anger replaced the surprise as he thought about his Suzy. *His Suzy? I wish. She hasn't been my Suzy for years.* Taking a deep breath before letting it out slowly, his determination settled in.

"Goddammit. I let her walk away once before. Not again." Kissing Lily on the head, he turned and walked back out of the reception hall.

Matt came up to Lily, seeing from across the room

that she was upset. She quickly told him what had happened. Pulling her into his embrace, he said, "Babe, nothing you can do about it now. They're not teens anymore. They gotta figure out what they want to do." Tugging her back to the dance floor, he began to twirl her gently.

She couldn't help but stare at the door her friends had disappeared through.

SUZANNE BARELY MADE it to the parking lot before the tears began. Stumbling as she wove amongst the cars she didn't care if it looked as though she were drunk. By the time she found her car she stood next to it with her hands on the top of the door, her head hanging down as she choked on the sobs.

Hearing footsteps behind her, she didn't turn around. She knew who it was. She could feel him. *This is why I haven't gone back to my hometown when I knew he was there.*

"Suzy?" he called softly.

Shaking her head, she pressed her fingers to her lips, trying to stop the trembling. "Don't," she croaked. Clearing her throat, she whispered, "Don't call me that. I'm not Suzy anymore. I haven't been for a long time."

With that, she jerked open her car door and quickly got in. Starting her engine, she was about to pull out when he was suddenly right by her window.

"Suzy, please don't do this. Let's talk. Please," he

begged.

She allowed herself a glance. Just a glance up at his face. Ravaged. *Just like mine must look like.* Holding his eyes, she mouthed, "I can't." Then she drove away leaving him standing there.

His eyes never left her car until it was out of sight. Moving his hand up to his chest, he absentmindedly rubbed it trying to ease the ache.

"You wanna tell us what you did that made our Suzanne cry?" came a growl from behind. Turning, he saw Gabe, Vinny, Matt and Lily standing right behind him.

With a tight jaw, he answered, "Nope. No one's business but ours."

Gabe took a step toward him, "Wrong answer, man."

Lily quickly intervened, stepping in front of Gabe. "BJ, I just want to help. Is there anything I can do?"

He looked down at the pint-sized beauty strategically placed between the men. He would have laughed at her attempt to keep grown men from pummeling each other, but he knew that Matt had his cold eye on them. No one would hurt Lily, but just in case anyone was going to lose their cool, Matt would make sure Lily was safe. Both he and Gabe took a step back.

"Don't know what to tell you. I loved her. I lost her. She won't let me in and hasn't for the past four years."

"You the reason she only goes home to visit her

parents sometimes?" Gabe demanded.

Sighing deeply, BJ nodded. "Yep, I guess so." Looking over at Lily, he said, "Could you check on her? Make sure she's all right?

"Of course, we'll go," Lily answered. "But I have to tell you that she's very private. I don't think she'll talk to me."

"I just want to make sure she gets home all right."

She stepped up to him and placed her hand on his arm. "Of course. Maybe she'll talk. But…" she said looking around at the men standing behind her. "I think you all need to take BJ out for a drink. He needs a friend too."

Gabe nodded although he watched BJ warily. Vinny stepped in slapping BJ on the back. "Come on, guys. The bride and groom have left. Let's go get a drink."

BJ left with the brothers and Matt walked Lily over to his truck. She pulled out her phone and called Suzanne. The call went straight to voice mail. "Honey, I just wanted to come by and see if you are okay."

She looked over at Matt, but her phone rang before she could figure out what to say. "Hello?"

"Hey Lily, it's Suzanne. I got your message, but I'm really not up for company. I took something for my headache and I'm going to bed. I'll talk to you later."

"Well, if you're sure," Lily agreed. "You know you can always talk to me, don't you?"

"I do, Lily. Thank you…for everything."

HANGING UP, SUZANNE made her way up the stairs to her tiny apartment, barely one foot in front of the other, until she made it through her front door. Locking up behind her, she stood with her back to the door, surveying the room. A new sofa and television graced the living area to the right, surrounding a throw rug that pulled the colors of the walls together. The distressed wooden table and chairs sat in the dining nook next to the kitchen.

Walking over to the wall where she had a couple of family pictures, she stared at one in particular. It was taken at one of her family's huge Thanksgiving celebration with friends. There she was with her parents, her brother Rob, and in the background, just in the left corner of the photo, was BJ. She tried to reconcile the boy she had loved with the man she saw today. He was taller. Definitely broader. And if possible, much more handsome. The cute boy had become a gorgeous man.

But the love by a girl that was once there was gone. At least she tried to tell herself that.

Moving away from the visual memories, she walked to the tiny bedroom kicking off her shoes. Stripping out the bridesmaid dress, she turned on the water in the shower allowing it a few minutes to get warm. Looking at herself in the mirror, she stared at the reflection. Long, silky, black hair flowed down across her shoulders. Clear skin. Nice curves. Blue eyes, belying her Irish heritage. As she stared into her eyes, she saw the sadness. The pain. The grief.

Sighing, she entered the shower. As the hot water sluiced over her body, her hands roamed, ending on her stomach. Memories came back, flooding her mind and forcing their way to the forefront.

Growing up together, our families were good friends, and I still remember when I first fell in love with Brad. It was the summer that I was fifteen and he had been gone to football camp for most of the time. My mother ran Bernie's Bakery and allowed me to work in the store. My cheerleader personality and smile made me the perfect waitress and tips were good. But, with my mom right there I couldn't even flirt. And with my older brother being a firefighter and former college football player, his eyes were everywhere. No dating. But it didn't really matter since there was no one who captured my attention.

Until he walked in. Brad Evans. Somehow over the summer during football camp he'd changed. He definitely looked at least six feet tall. And bigger. And broader. And totally gorgeous.

I remember when he first appeared in the bakery. His eyes met mine and the rest of the world fell away. He had smiled, but I couldn't seem to catch my breath. Or smile back. So like an idiot I turned and ran into the back. When mom came to look for me, I made the excuse of not feeling well but she just smiled her knowing smile.

During the rest of the summer he'd managed to come

in almost every day that I was working and when he finally asked me out, I hated having to tell him that I couldn't date yet. Smiling down at me, he'd simply said, "Then we'll just hang out."

When school started, all the girls began vying for his attention, but he waited for me after class and walked me to the bakery after school. Friday night football games gave me a front row seat as I cheered and he played. Begging my parents to let us date, dad kept saying that any man worth having would wait.

The water cooled and she exited the shower, drying off with one of her soft, extra-large towels. Pulling on one of Brad's old t-shirts that she slept in, she crawled into bed trying to force the memories from flooding back, but the dark, quiet night was perfect fodder for her overactive mind. She thought back to the first time her trust was broken.

All of the kids were able to go to the bonfire out by the river after football games. Except me. I finally thought I had convinced my parents to let me go but as soon as my brother Rob found out, he put his foot down.

"I know what goes on. Drinkin' and makin' out," he stated emphatically. "The nice girls don't go and the ones lookin' to score are there."

I had pleaded and pouted to no avail. So after the winning game Brad, feeling the peer pressure of celebrating with the other jocks, headed off and I went home. We'd made no promises to each other. We were officially just friends hanging out, but he'd done everything to make me feel as though I was his girlfriend.

The rumors abounded by Monday morning in school. Stacey Luckell, known for letting the boys get lucky, had been seen with Brad at the bonfire. Coming around the corner of my first period class, I saw the guys slapping him on his back and congratulating him on 'getting Lucky'. My eyes flew to his as he turned around. The smile on his face had left immediately when he saw me and when I saw his face through my own tear filled eyes, I thought I saw regret.

I remember the pain slicing through *my heart as I turned and ran down the hall, desperate to get away from the stares of everyone.*

It took weeks of Brad coming around to the bakery before I would agree to see him. "Suzy, I'm so sorry, I know I fu...messed up. It's you and only you I want. I don't care how long we have to wait."

"We never made any promises to each other, so it's not like you cheated on me," I said softly, trying to hide my hurt.

"I let them get to me...the other guys. I wasn't man enough to not follow the crowd. But I've learned my lesson, Suzy. Nothing is ever worth seeing that look on your face. I wanna be the kind of man you'd be proud of. Not some dumb-ass jock that can't stand tall and go my own way. I want to take care of you and I don't care how long we wait."

As he held me close, I looked up into the face that I was falling in love with, listening to his promise, "Baby, I'll never hurt you again. Trust in that."

Chapter 2

THE MEN SAT in the back of a small family bar, Vinny and Gabe nursing their beers and waiting for BJ to talk. Each had taken off their suit jackets and ties and had their dress shirt sleeves' casually rolled up. The waitress couldn't help but look…the trio sitting in front of her was every woman's dream. All tall, all built, and all looked like they knew their way around a woman. But the owners frowned on waitresses bothering the patrons, so she just kept her eye on them, determined to keep the beer flowing.

BJ looked up at the almost identical faces in front of him trying to decide what to say. How much to say. If he should even say anything. *They know her. They know what she's been like. They know the Suzy that's turned into Suzanne.*

"You gonna finally open your mouth for something besides drinking?" Gabe asked.

BJ sat tight lipped, frustration coursing through him.

"Look man, we're not asking for you to tell us your life's story. Just help us understand how you fit into Suzanne's life, 'cause that girl's been sad since we met her."

BJ leaned back in his chair taking a deep breath. "We grew up together in Fairfield. I was a year ahead of her in school. By the time she was fifteen, we'd started hanging out. Her parents wouldn't let her date until she was sixteen so we just mostly hung out. Our parents were close so we were practically raised together."

He grew quiet, tossing back more of his beer. Setting it down on the table, he glanced around seeing the stares of the other men still on him.

"What the hell, guys? What else do you want?"

Vinny piped up, "Maybe the reason why that woman has a hurt so deep it shows in her eyes every fuckin' day."

"Jesus," BJ bit out. "We dated in high school and when I first went to college. Then we had some problems, which…" he paused while giving each man there a hard look, "I will not be going into. I wanted to stay together, but she didn't. End of story."

"Hardly," Gabe growled.

After one more long pull on his beer, BJ slammed the bottle down on the table. "Look man," he said as he leaned forward staring directly at Gabe, "I'd have stayed with her forever. She was it for me. Maybe that's fucked to you, but I knew when I was sixteen years old who I wanted to be with."

"So what happened?" Vinny asked, his voice softer.

Rubbing his hand over his face, BJ leaned back in the chair. "Some things just can't be forgotten." He looked off into the distance for a moment, his face ravaged. "Sometimes grief…just makes everything black."

Pushing his chair back, he stood stretching his tall frame. Giving the men a nod, he walked to the door heading out into the night.

Vinny and Gabe finished their beers before following BJ out.

Gabe spoke first, "Lot more to them than just high school lovers."

Vinny nodded, "Yeah, but whatever it is, they've got to work it out themselves."

"I'm still keeping an eye on Suzanne."

"I figure we'll keep an eye on both of them."

With that, the two brothers left the bar.

GOING INTO HIS apartment, he stalked into the kitchen and snagged a bottle of water. Downing it in a couple of gulps, he tried to allow the liquid to cool his fevered mind. Ever since he had seen those blue eyes staring at his in the middle of the wedding reception he could not get her out of his thoughts. Not that she had been very far from his mind these past four years.

Suzy had just been a scrawny little girl in the neighborhood, one who'd been at all the family gatherings playing with her dolls when I was off tossing a football with her older brother. But I remember her that summer she was fifteen and I returned from football camp. Me and my buds had headed into Bernie's Bakery after practice, planning on meeting up with some girls later in the day. Bernie greeted us and as I turned around to get my drink I almost ran into…Suzy? Same dark hair, same big blue eyes…but now the whole package was a complete blossoming woman. Where did that body come from? As I was checking her out, I noticed she was drinking her fill as well. Giving her my best smile, the one that had the other girls in town hoping for a date, I was surprised when eyes-wide, she fled into the kitchen.

"Way to go Romeo," one of my friends joked.

Staring at her retreating back, I just grinned, knowing that would not be the last of her. Weeks later, after seeing her at the bakery every day, I was disappointed when her parents wouldn't let us date until she was sixteen, but I was ready to be patient. At least I thought I was, but being a sixteen year old thinking with his dick almost cost me everything.

That fall I royally screwed up. The bonfire out by the river was the place to go after a big game and I was disappointed when she couldn't go, but decided to go with my buddies anyway. Several girls were there with their boyfriends and as my judgment became cloudy with beer I barely noticed Stacey Luckell coming on to me. The other guys egged me on and I didn't want to look like a punk in front of them. She and I wandered off behind the trees where she boldly pulled her t-shirt up, showing that she wasn't wearing a bra. My dick didn't listen to my brain and it didn't take long for her pants to come off and mine *to go down around my ankles. I didn't even have a condom but thankfully she pulled one out of her jeans. Losing my virginity to Lucky Luckell was not even memorable. In fact, it made me feel like shit.*

But as I stumbled back to the bonfire, I was greeted with hoots and hollers about 'getting lucky'. It was supposed to make me feel like a man, but inside all I could see was a blue-eyed, dark-haired beauty in my head.

The next Monday at school as the rumors bounced around, I saw those blue eyes staring at me. Hurt. Pain-filled. Sad. Jesus, I never wanted to see that look again.

My dad and I were close, so I talked to him. I spilled the story as I was working for him one afternoon. He'd listened while we stocked the bar.

"Son, I've worked in bars my whole life. Seen a lot from this side of the counter. But I can tell you from my own experience and from those years of lookin' at others…you want easy? Not hard to find. Any bar, any night will get you easy. You want a woman that'll love you and last…now that ain't always easy. Not easy to find. Not easy to keep. But when you do, you be the kind of man that lives up to what that woman needs."

"But dad, I hurt her. I screwed up."

"Then you learn from that, son. It's not the mistakes a man makes that shows us who he is. It's the way he learns from those mistakes and changes…that's the true measure of a man. Seems to me you've found your woman. Now become the man that she deserves."

It took weeks of showing her how truly sorry I was before she warmed back up to me. And as soon as she would have me, we began to date. By then I was a goner. How can a boy of sixteen know that he'd found the one? The everlasting love? I didn't know, but she was it. Promising to never hurt her again, I vowed that she could trust me always.

But some hurts can't be easily fixed and some broken hearts can't be mended. At least that is what he had always told himself. Staring in the bathroom mirror, he wondered if he had been wrong.

THE NEXT DAY at work, BJ arrived at Tony Alvarez Security. He had been hired right out of college to do computer programming for them and given free rein to be as creative as he needed to be to get the job done. Considering the Richland Police Department occasionally used their services, it was nice to be able to operate outside of the traditional limits.

Entering the building from the underground parking facility, he made his way to the conference room. Nodding to the other employees, he took his place at the table. Ignoring the stares of the others, he pulled up his laptop.

With military precision Tony walked in and brought everyone up to speed on the most recent cases. Since his crew had helped Matt rescue Lily when she had been kidnapped by drug dealers, his business had increased to the point that they could pick and choose the cases they wanted. Gabe and Vinny had recently been used to escort several high profile persons while they were in Richland, including several millionaires, as well as some actresses.

Jobe preferred doing surveillance and several of the others, including Tony, were experts in security systems. Lily had recently joined the firm as a computer software engineer, designing many of the programs they needed. Now that Lily was taking over a lot of the computer programing, that allowed BJ to learn more of the diversity of the security business.

With the meeting over, they dispersed and Lily cornered BJ. "So, what gives?"

Raising an eyebrow, he looked down at her in question.

Slapping his arm, she admonished, "Don't give me that look. You know exactly what I'm talking about. I want to know why both of my friends are sad and now I know that it's because of your history. Two people that sad should surely get together and be happy."

"There are a lot of assumptions in there, Lily. And you should know that life doesn't always wrap things up in a nice little package."

She nodded, keeping her eyes on his. "Yeah," she said softly. "You're right." Reaching over, placing her hand on his arm, she continued, "But you know if you ever need anything, I'm here."

ANNIE AND SHANE only took the weekend off for their honeymoon since they planned a longer vacation together later in the year. That Monday morning she and Leon found Suzanne already in the clinic getting things prepared for the day.

She was bustling around the clinic in her dog-print scrubs, a fake smile plastered on her face, looking nervous. Leon and Annie shared a look.

"So, Suzy huh?"

Suzanne's eyes cut sharply to his. "Suzanne," she declared firmly.

His eyes warmed as he walked over to give her a hug and kissed the top of her head. "I know doll. I'm sorry. You'll always be Suzanne to us."

The sting of tears hit her eyes and she blinked quickly to keep them at bay. Looking over at Annie, she said, "I suppose that Leon told you."

Annie nodded but said, "We don't really know anything sweetie. Is there something you want to talk about?"

Shaking her head, she admitted, "My high school boyfriend was Brad Evans. We broke up four years ago and went our separate ways. I decided that Suzy was too childish so I started going by my given name of Suzanne. I don't know when he started going by BJ, but I had no idea that he was Lily's friend."

Sensing that they were about to ask more questions, she put her hand up quickly shutting them down. "Guys, I know you're worried and I know you love me.

But that's it. That's all I'm willing to tell."

Annie and Leon smiled and nodded. Annie clapped her hands together and said, "All righty then. Let's get the day started."

The clinic opened with a flurry of activity. By the time the morning surgeries were over, Suzanne was up to her eyeballs in wellness checks. With her training, she was able to do all of the pre-assessments before Annie had to come in. Walking into the exam room, she recognized one of their regulars with his small dog. Mr. Marcelli had a distinguished, old world charm and always kissed her hand when she entered the room. He had brought the dog in for treatment of dog bites the week before. Cleaning the wounds and checking his stitches, she looked into the owner's worried face and assured him that Chaucer was doing fine.

"I will tell you that I'm concerned about the dog attacks recently. You're the third client who has come in with these cases. Tell me again exactly where this happened."

"Chaucer and I were walking early in the morning. It was just before dawn, but I've always felt safe. A large dog, I suppose it looked like the pit bulls you see on TV, came from the alley down by my apartment and before I knew what had happened, it jumped on Chaucer. I beat it with my cane and it finally ran off."

"Mr. Marcelli, I am going to call the police to report this. I just don't like the fact that it is occurring more often. We report it to the animal control, but I've got some friends on the police force that I want to alert."

He patted Chaucer and then turned his look to the pretty lady in front of him. "You're a good lass. You report to whoever you need. And if you need me, I'll make a statement too."

After he left, she grabbed Annie before she went to the next exam. "Do you mind if I call Shane or Matt to check these dog attacks? I know it's not their thing, but maybe they would have some suggestions. I called animal control, but they are overworked and understaffed. I'm just afraid there are some vicious dogs around this area."

"I think that's a good idea. Shane is picking me up after work, you want to talk to him then?"

"Yeah, that'd be fine."

A little while later, Shane and Matt walked through the door. While Shane greeted Annie, Matt walked over to Suzanne. "Hear you may have some dog problems?"

She looked up in surprise. "I thought that Shane was coming by after work."

"Annie called and asked us to come by earlier."

Raising her eyebrow, she stood with her hip cocked. "Are you sure you aren't just checking on me?"

Smiling, he gave her a hug. "Lily is worried, honey. We both are."

She sighed as she looked into his face. Pulling her lips in for a moment as though weighing heavily what to say, she finally admitted, "It was a shock to see my old boyfriend. We didn't part under the best of circumstances, but that was a long time ago."

"Appears to me that you haven't really moved on."

Looking up sharply, she grimaced then admitted, "Well, some things take time."

Shane walked over, his face serious. "So what's up, Suzanne? Annie says you've got concerns?"

"I just had another case come in where a loose dog attacked someone's pet on a leash. I'm afraid of there being some vicious dogs in the neighborhood and animal control can't always get to us. Annie though that maybe a call from you all would go further."

"Got any details?"

Looking disconcerted, she replied, "Not really. The last two clients who we had to treat for bite wounds had been out walking with their owners when a large dog came running from an alley and went after the other dog."

Pondering for a minute, she continued. "It's interesting that neither owner gave similar descriptions of the dogs so that would mean there's more than one. But that's also scary since there are elderly dog owners as well as a lot of children around here."

Nodding, Matt and Shane promised they would call animal control themselves and ask that the patrolmen in the area step up their vigilance when driving around. Matt gave her a kiss on top of her head as Shane said goodbye to his wife before they left.

Watching them walk out of the door, she jumped when Leon came up to her.

"Oh, you scared me," she exclaimed. "Did you need something?"

"Nah, I just want you to be careful that's all."

"Careful?"

"Yeah, you now live upstairs in this run-down neighborhood. If there are vicious dogs out I don't think you should be running or going out unprotected."

Patting him on the arm, she just smiled. "I'll be fine, I promise." As she turned and walked toward the back of the clinic, she called over her shoulder, "And I don't need protecting."

Annie and Leon shared a look. "She protects her heart so much she thinks it will keep her from getting hurt. I worry about her, Annie."

"I know. I'll ask Shane to make sure he has the patrolmen go by here more often as well."

With that they headed back to the next examination room.

"BJ? IT'S MATT. Just wanted to know if you'd like to meet me and Shane for a beer tonight?"

"Look guys, I've already had one interrogation. Don't think I'm up for another."

"No interrogation man. Just got some things we want to let you in on."

Sighing heavily, BJ agreed.

Later that evening as he arrived at the bar, he noticed not only Matt and Shane, but Tony's group as well. Matt was a handsome man who sported a wicked scar across his forehead from breaking up a fight years before and Shane, equally handsome, but with the rugged looks of a man who had lived hard and rough. The men were casually gathered, some playing pool and the others watching with beers in their hands. Greetings all around were said, and he headed over to the table where the two detectives were sitting.

"Gentlemen," he acknowledged, sliding into a chair while nodding at the waitress for a beer. "What's going on?"

"We had a talk with Annie and Suzanne today."

At the mention of Suzanne, BJ's attention was captured. "Are they all right?"

"Yeah, just have some suspicious activity they're noticing. We're on it but thought you'd want to know also," Matt began.

"You know that Annie used to live above the clinic? Before she and I bought a house," Shane asked. At BJ's nod, he continued, "Well, Suzanne lives there now." He paused to take a pull on his beer. "I made sure that the apartment had a good security system, but it's in a part of town that can be rough."

At this BJ set his beer down on the table. "Rough? Define rough."

Shrugging, Matt said, "You know the area. Old

houses, old apartments. Many of the inhabitants are elderly folks on pensions and some of the homes that have been renovated have families. But there are sections around them with pimps, prostitutes, strip joints, and drug dealers."

Sitting up straighter, BJ looked between the two men, his protective feelings ratcheting up. "You telling me this for a reason?"

"Seems to me that no matter what happened years ago, you've got feelings for her," Shane answered.

Matt chimed in, "Plus there's some suspicion of dangerous dogs in the area. She called us to let us know there were some clients in the area who had their dogs attacked."

BJ reared back, "What the fuck?"

"We talked to her. Warned her to be careful and not go out after dark. We've also stepped up the patrol cars around the area and put in a word to animal control. But," Matt continued, "we just thought you'd wanna know."

BJ sat there for a moment, his jaw tight with anger, staring at his beer. Looking up, he saw the two men staring at him. "You want to know what my deal is? I'll tell you the same thing I told Gabe and Vinny. We dated in high school and she was it for me. She left me. Wasn't my choice, but she left me."

Shane leaned in, hands on the table. "Let me tell you somethin' BJ. You shoulda never walked away. A man's got a woman that he knows is it for him, you never let that go. You were young so I get that you didn't know that then. But you're a man now and you gotta know – you find somethin' in life so precious that you can't think of breathin' without it, then you do not let that walk away."

The desire to snap back was strong, but BJ knew Shane was right. Rubbing his hand through his hair he sighed. "I wasn't entirely honest. What we went through broke us. Broke her. I can't go into details, but I couldn't fix what broke." Pain sliced across his face as he looked away.

"Looks like she wasn't the only one broken," Matt said quietly.

"Yeah well, I'd have taken all the pain myself if it would have kept it from her."

"That sounds like the kind of man she deserves," Gabe said from behind.

BJ turned his head, seeing Gabe, Vinny and Tony standing behind him. Leaning back in his chair he said, "So what do you all suggest? What if being with me just makes her pain greater?"

"It's been four years, bro. If that pain was going to go away, it woulda already gone. I'd say that the only two people who can fix what was broken is the two of you," Tony piped in.

The noise from the bar faded to the background as the silence between the men spoke volumes. Pushing his chair back, BJ stood up. Tossing a couple of bills on the table, he nodded to the group and began to walk out.

"So whatcha' gonna do?" Shane called out.

Turning his head in the direction of his friends, he replied, "I reckon I've got some old business to take care of." With a smile, he walked out of the bar. He never heard the laughter or saw the nods of approval from the others, but it didn't matter. He knew what he needed to do. For him. And for her.

Chapter 3

THE NIGHT SHADOWS crept along the walls of her apartment as the lights were turned down. Sometimes she kept the lights off, letting the sliver of illumination from the street lights filter in. The dark could be comforting. Or sometimes painful.

Deciding to head to bed, she heard a knock on her door. *Who on earth can be knocking this late at night?* With her door facing the alley, she carefully peeked out of the security hole that Shane had installed. *Brad?*

She stood still, peering out of the hole at the face that haunted her, holding her breath as though that would keep him from knowing she was looking.

"Suzy? I know you're in there. I also know you're looking at me right now. Open up. I have to check your security system."

She cracked the door, leaving the chain on. "What do you mean?"

Glad that she opened the door to him even if it was just a little, he said, "Tony had your system installed and said it needs to be checked."

"In the middle of the night? I hardly think it needs to be done now."

"I'm not gonna lie to you. Matt and Shane told me that there had been some problems with dogs in the area and Tony told me that it needed to be checked. No matter what happened between us, I want you safe."

"Why didn't he send Gabe?"

Jealousy shot through BJ as he thought of Gabe here with her. "Don't know, but if I know Gabe, he's out chasing skirts tonight. Anyway, Tony must have thought I was the man for the job. Now open the door so I can do my job."

Huffing, she closed the door to take off the latch and then opened it again. "Well, make it quick. I was heading to bed." With that, she turned and walked back into the kitchen area.

He watched her walk away, her figure hidden within the folds of an old robe; but her hips swayed delectably as she moved. Her bare feet padded softly to the sink where she stood quietly, not looking at him.

BJ walked into the room, stunned at the tiny apartment and wondered if her family had ever visited. It was clean and neat, decorated simply. *But this neighborhood? Sure, the vet clinic was downstairs, but that was only open during the day and had others around. Her brother, Rob, would have had a fit if he saw where she was living.*

She turned and glared at his back as he walked over to the security panel by the other door, the one that led down to the clinic, and began his checks. Her eyes followed him as he made his way around the room, checking the camera and the doors.

He stopped to look at some of the pictures on her wall. Pictures of family. Old times. Fun times. Times long ago when life was less complicated. And memories were less painful. *Just keep working.*

His eyes landed on the picture of a Thanksgiving at her parent's house many years ago. Suzy, as he remembered her when she first got on his radar as more than just a little girl. And he was in the background of the picture, his eyes always close on her. "How's the family?" he asked casually, looking at the pictures without turning around.

Silence greeted him. "They all doing okay?" he prodded.

"They're fine."

"Rob still working at the fire station with your dad?"

"Brad, I know you go back to visit some, so you must know that he is."

He turned, his eyebrow lifted. "So you know when I go to Fairfield? I thought you must since you're never there when I am."

Irritated that she gave away that amount of information she pursed her lips, returning to silence.

Finishing the security checks, he walked over to the small kitchen and leaned against the counter effectively blocking her in. His eyes raked over her body, noting that the robe had parted at the top, showing the worn t-shirt she wore. With a closer look, he discerned the faded words *Fairfield High School Football* on the shirt. *Mine. That was mine. She still wears my shirt.* Not overtly sexy, it still had his dick standing at attention just seeing her in his shirt. *But then she could always do that to me.*

"I was wrong to leave, Suzy."

She gasped, her eyes darting around desperate to look at anything other than his face.

"I was young and foolish and didn't know how to fight for what I knew was best. For what I wanted."

Her eyes finally rested on the floor as she slowly shook her head. *Please don't do this.*

"Suzy, look at me. Please. We have a history. We had good times and maybe you don't want to remember them, but baby I can't forget them."

Her eyes lifted, the pain replaced by anger. "My name is Suzanne. I left the childhood name back in Fairfield."

He took in her rigid stance and defiant look. One he had seen years before. But this time was different. As a young man, he viewed it as the end. Now he realized it was self-preservation. *She still yearns after all these years. She still hurts. She still grieves. That means she still feels.*

Leaning over, he kissed the top of her head whispering, "You'll always be Suzy to me. And get used to it, baby. This time I'm not giving up." With that, he turned and walked to the door saying, "I want to hear the deadbolt after I leave."

Memories slid over her as the third glass of wine was beginning to take effect. Tonight they were sad. The ones that moved in even when she didn't want them to and threatened to pull her under…

I stood next to his old, beat-up SUV that was packed to the hilt with everything he was taking to college. He was leaving and I had one more year of high school. I was terrified about being left behind. There were so many women at college who would take one look at Brad and want him for themselves. We haven't even had sex yet. He wanted to wait until I was eighteen, but that was seven months away. Sighing, I looked over as his mom and dad were saying goodbye. His mom was tearful, but both parents were so proud of him. I am too, but I wish…

Suddenly he was standing in front of me, holding me close. No matter how much I tried to stop them the tears still came.

"Shh Suzy. We'll get through this just fine. I'm yours, you know that. And nothing will ever be able to tear us apart. Not distance, not college, nothing. We're meant to be, baby. You can trust that we're strong enough to face anything."

Pushing herself up from the couch, she walked into the kitchen to toss the wine bottle and rinse out her glass. *Trust. Yeah, right. I believed him. I believed that we were stronger than anything. I just had no idea how bad it could get.*

BJ FOUND HIMSELF driving around town before going back to his apartment, the dark of the night penetrating his truck, the only illumination coming from the dashboard and occasional street light. A country song played on the radio, its words soulfully reminiscing about a lost love or a new love. He couldn't really tell. He just knew it opened up the flood-gates of his memories.

I can still remember looking from the sidelines of the football field and seeing her in her cheerleading outfit. I only had eyes for her. And she made me feel as though I could conquer the world. Jesus, she used to say that I was her knight in shining armor and could rescue her from anything. How fuckin' stupid I was to think that was true.

Once in college, I never looked at another girl. Not with Suzy back home, waiting on me. Believing in me. I thought we could make it. I never thought of the possibility that we wouldn't.

Her words echoed in my mind when she pushed me out of her life. It got ugly. I was mad and she wouldn't talk to me. Wouldn't let me in. Wouldn't let me help. She just pushed and pushed, until I climbed back into my old Explorer and headed out of town. Pissed. Angry. And...heartbroken.

Pulling into the parking lot of his apartment building, he sat for a moment throwing his head back against the headrest. He had tried for four years to block out the pain of losing everything. Grimacing, he remembered how he had tried to block it out. Alcohol, frat parties, girls he couldn't even remember their names or faces. Rubbing his hand across his face, he realized that while he was out trying to be a big man on campus, she was alone and grieving. Glancing in the rear view mirror, he thought, *Time to man up. Time to get the girl back.*

Chapter 4

THE EMPTY WAREHOUSE was beginning to fill up. The crowd was not as rowdy as they had been when the warehouses were along the riverfront. It was getting harder to find places that the cops would not check, but there were still some areas of the city that no one wanted to venture into. Unless they had a good reason. And the lure of making money was reason enough for some.

The beer was selling along with the easy handoffs for drugs. Marcel stood on a platform high above the mass, scanning the area. His suit looked out of place but for a man in his position, nothing but Italian silk was good enough for him. A tall, exquisite blonde in a classic black dress stood next to him, close but not touching. She knew not to disturb unless he wanted to be touched. A possession was all she was and for the money he spent on her, it was worth it to put up with his rages. She watched him carefully for signs that he wanted her closer...or farther. Not watching for his signs would earn her an arm jerk. Or a slap across the face. Or something worse. She did not want to go back into his stable of women, so whatever he needed was what he would get.

She had no worries on that account tonight though. Marcel was in a good mood. The crowd was growing and the money, drugs, and bets were flowing. He turned his head as another man approached.

Without glancing at the woman, Jorge walked over to his boss making sure that Marcel knew he was coming. Known to slit the throat of anyone who came close without announcing themselves, Jorge approached Marcel carefully.

"We're good to go, boss. Is there anything you need?"

"Not now. Charisse and I are going to be in the back. I'll be out for the count when it's over."

Jorge nodded and walked back down the stairs, passing the hulking guards at the bottom. They stepped aside as he moved between them, no words being spoken. Each man knew his duty and knew that Marcel ran a tight ship. There was no place for screw-ups. Those that did…the rumor was that the bodies were not found.

Jorge dressed well, liking the feel and power that expensive clothes afforded him. He saw the looks a few of the hookers gave him as he walked by, but he ignored them completely. No skank pussy for him. His days of dipping his dick into Marcel's stable was over. As Marcel's right-hand man, he was paid well and lived well. He liked pussy and liked it often, but didn't pay for it anymore. When he went out, ladies came up to him and saw prime cock. And he was willing to take them up on their offers.

Jorge nodded to the men in charge of the fighting ring, indicating that they were allowed to start. The crowd moved closer to the pit, ready to cheer on the dogs they had bet on. He moved around the inner perimeter of the building, checking on the security and the money collectors. Watching them with hawk eyes, each money collector was assigned a rotating security man. Marcel wanted men in place that he could trust, but his trust only went so far. He utilized pairing his people in rotating shifts to keep them from arranging to pocket some of the take.

Jorge blocked out the noises from the ring, immune to the sounds of the dogs tearing each other apart. It bothered him at one time, many years ago as a child growing up in the streets. But now, it was just another money-maker. And Marcel paid him well.

As the blood lust flowed, he nodded to the head of Marcel's stable and the women began to move through the group. Some men slid off, making sure to pay up front while others fucked on the bleachers. Occasionally several men would be so high on lust and drugs that they fought each other to take one woman whether she wanted it or not. Jorge moved to a platform to see enough of what was going on to make sure there was at least chaotic order.

As the crowd thinned out the security began walking through, moving the last of the stragglers out into the night as his workers quickly began disassembling the bloody ring. Several of the less used women were assisting those that were in poorer condition.

Moving through the security wall around Marcel's bookies, he collected the evening's take before walking back up the stairs to his temporary office. Entering the room, simply furnished with a long table and a few chairs, he placed the money bags in the center of the table. Followed by four money counters, each with an assigned security man, they quietly begin to sort the bills and count. The money was independently counted by two of the men watched carefully by their security. Marcel's accountant kept the running total and then presented Jorge with a final accounting.

Looking at the total, Jorge knew that Marcel would be pleased. Not that he cared, but life was easier when the boss was in a good mood. He left the room after nodding to the head of security, indicating that the money could be taken to Marcel's financial wizard. No one knew how he did it, but the money was appropriately laundered and Marcel's legitimate businesses and off shore bank accounts grew respectively.

Knocking on the door, he heard "Enter" called out and he moved into the room occupied by Marcel and Charisse. She was sitting on Marcel's lap, her dress off of her shoulders exposing her bountiful breasts. She was a stunner, but Jorge kept his eyes off of her. Marcel looked up as Jorge entered and jerked his head at Charisse. She stood immediately and moved to the side.

She left her dress around her waist, embarrassed but knowing that Marcel wanted immediate access and did not care who saw her.

Jorge held the paper out to Marcel, seeing his eyes light with approval at the night's total.

"Good, good," he said. Looking back up at Jorge, he asked, "Did everything go all right?"

"It was fine, boss. Good crowd. Stayed under control. Women did a good business."

Nodding, Marcel expressed his pleasure. "Good job. Anything needed to be reported?"

Jorge shook his head, "No, sir. Nothing that cannot wait until tomorrow."

At that, Marcel jerked his eyes up to Jorge. "Never wait on anything in our business. You should know that by now. Whatever seems minor now can blow up and kick us in the ass tomorrow. And I have no intentions of having my businesses kicked."

"Heard some talk. A few owners have been letting their dogs loose and there have been a few attacks on pets on the Mayfield side of town."

Marcel just lifted his eyebrow indicating his desire for Jorge to continue.

"We know of at least two that have taken their pets to a vet clinic there. Just don't want anyone snooping more than they should."

"Do we still have our pay-off live?"

Jorge nodded. "Yes, sir. Got someone at the ER clinic there and someone at Animal Control."

Marcel sat silent for a moment, pondering his next move. Looking back up at his trusted right-hand man, he said, "Keep an eye on things. I want the owners watched. I want eyes on the clinic. And I want to know who the fuck has let their dogs loose. I don't accept mistakes and someone will pay. If they can't keep control of their dogs then they will find that no one will pay them to fight."

"Some of the owners let kids take care of their dogs. That may be part of the problem."

"Then let them know that if they want to fight in my clubs, they keep my business off the streets. Or…" he looked carefully into Jorge's eyes, "I will make sure that there are no fuck-ups."

Nodding, Jorge acquiesced. "Anything else, boss?"

"I want you spending time in the Mayfield area. I want to know the minute we may have a problem on our hands."

"Yes, sir."

Smiling, Marcel glanced up at Charisse, knowing she wanted to cross her arms in front of her chest but wouldn't. "Good girl, Charisse. You take orders beautifully. Perhaps one day we will see if your beautiful sister will take orders just a well," Marcel continued with a sly smile. Keeping his eyes on her breasts he never noticed the flash of fear and anger that flew across her face.

Jorge did noticed.

Chapter 5

THE EARLY MORNING light pierced through the blinds as Suzanne tried to focus her eyes. Glancing at the clock, she was jerked awake with the realization that she had overslept. *Damn, I never do that.* But then remembering her morose thoughts from the night before reminded her of how little sleep she had. Memories, never far from the surface, came slamming back. Memories of a happier, carefree time. Memories of uncertainty and fear. Memories of heartache and grief.

No. I do not have time for this, she told herself as she scurried to the bathroom to get ready. Throwing on her kitten-print scrubs after a quick shower, she pulled her long hair into its usual ponytail and headed out of the door with a piece of toast in her hand. Jogging down the stairs, she entered the clinic just as Leon was walking toward the back.

"Slow down girl," he admonished. "You're about to run me over."

"I overslept," she gushed as she continued to run toward the surgery area to start the preps.

Leon caught her arm as she flew by and gently

pulled her back. Turning her so that he could peer into her eyes, he saw more than she wanted him to see.

"Looks like someone didn't sleep well last night," he observed.

"Must have been something I ate," she mumbled looking down.

"Honey, it feels like you haven't been eating enough," he said as he wrapped her in his embrace.

Before she could respond, Annie came in from the front. "Hey, group hug without me?" Seeing Suzanne's face, she asked, "Are you okay?"

Pulling back, Suzanne plastered the smile on her face that they had seen so many times. The one that screamed, *I'm fine, leave me alone.*

Knowing that nothing more would be coming, Annie and Leon moved away, each of the three getting ready for their day.

"YOUR COOKIES TASTE bad," the little boy said as Suzanne brought his puppy back into the examining room.

"Cookies?" she questioned as she set the puppy onto the table. Annie followed her in to talk to the mother about their dog.

"Yeah, those," he said pointing with a chubby finger to the jar of dog treats that were sitting on the counter.

Suzanne and Annie shot each other a look, trying

not to smile. "Well, um…those are for your puppy, not little boys."

"Oh my God," the mother exclaimed, turning to her son. "You ate one of those?"

"It's okay," Annie explained. "It can't hurt him other than tasting bland."

The harried mother hustled her son out of the room with the puppy in tow when they had finished and Suzanne managed to hold on to her laughter until they had left the clinic.

Several hours later the door to the clinic opened and a couple of boys came in with a bloodied dog. Leon called for Annie and she ran to the exam room. She and Leon quickly began to assess the dog as Suzanne tried to find out what had happened.

"Please lady, can you fix Pepper?"

"Where did you find him?"

The older boy of about twelve looked grim, his mouth in a tight line. "He came crawling back home like that." His dirty blond hair was messy, but his clothes were clean…except for some of the dog's blood that had seeped through the towel that they had wrapped him in.

The younger boy, tear streaks down his face, wiped his nose on his sleeve and said, "We couldn't find him this morning. Pa said he was gone. Musta gotten sick and died." This child had the same dirty blond hair like his brother, but still had the cherubic looks of youth.

Wondering how much to tell the boys, she asked,

"Where are your parents? Do they know you're here?"

"Nah. Momma's gone to work and Pa's sleepin'. He works nights."

"Well, you stay here and let me see what's happening with your dog. Doc Annie is super good and she'll see what she can do," Suzanne assured although from the looks of the dog when she glanced at it before Leon took it, she knew it did not look good.

She left the boys and went into the back room, where Annie and Leon were looking at the dog.

Annie looked up saying, "What did you find out from the boys?"

"They say it's their dog and it was gone this morning. Said that their dad told them it had died but then it came crawling back this afternoon."

"Look at this," Annie said, leaning over the dog whose shallow breathing was labored.

Suzanne and Leon peered at the injured animal. "It looks like it's been in a fight," Suzanne exclaimed. "Just like the ones that have been attacked."

"Yes, but look at the older injuries. This dog has been in fights before."

"What do you think it means?" Suzanne asked. "Are these fighting dogs?"

"I would say so," Annie replied. "I'm going to have to put it down to end its suffering. Is there an adult with the boys?"

"No, they said mom was at work and the dad was sleeping. I didn't get the feeling that anyone at home cared except the boys."

Just then the dog took a shuddering breath and died.

"Damn," Leon cursed softly, smoothing the dogs ruffled fur.

The three, each lost in their own thoughts for a moment, looked up knowing what needed to be done.

"Suzanne, do you want to talk to the boys or call animal control?"

Sighing deeply, she hesitated, tears in her eyes. *Fuck. Why do things have to die before their time?*

Leon looked over then said, "I'll talk to the boys. Annie you call animal control."

Annie agreed and left the area to go to the office. Leon headed to the front to let the boys know that their dog had passed. After a moment, Suzanne walked back up front and sat waiting with the boys, getting angrier by the minute.

She wrapped her arms around the youngest one as he cried while keeping her eyes on the other boy who stood stoically to the side trying not to cry. "Boys, where do you live?"

The oldest one choked out an answer of a neighborhood not too far from the clinic.

Suzanne told Annie and Leon that she was going to escort the boys home to make sure they got there safely.

"Girl," Leon said softly, "I don't know if that's wise. Why don't you let me take them?"

"It's fine. I'm going to just drive there and drop

them off and then I'll be right back."

"Make sure you stay in your car then and come right back," he advised.

Nodding, she turned to the boys. "Okay guys, let me take you home." They all shuffled out of the clinic door and headed to her car. Making sure they were buckled, she got into the driver's seat and put their address in her phone's GPS.

As she started down the road, she realized that the boys had passed by the ER vet clinic.

"Guys, why didn't you stop here with your dog? It's closer than where we are."

The oldest boy answered, "They were closed."

She glanced in the rear view mirror and saw his face looking back at hers. *Closed? They don't close in the middle of the day.*

"Are you sure? Did you try the door?"

"We tried it, but it wouldn't open, then I saw a sign next to the door that said they were closed for lunch."

Closed for lunch? What the hell? They don't close for lunch. Determined to get to the bottom of the story, she just smiled and nodded. "Well, I'm glad you found us. Doc Annie is very sweet and even if she was unable to help your dog, she will make sure he's taken care of. By the way, my name's Suzanne. What's yours?"

"I'm Chuckie," the younger boy answered. "He's Dwayne. Chuckie and Dwayne Johnson."

After just a couple of minutes, they pulled up in front of a dilapidated, older home. Bicycles were scattered in the front yard and the fence gate was broken on its hinges.

The oldest boy was getting out of the car and turned to help his brother. Looking up at her, he said, "Thanks, miss."

Glancing around, she asked, "Is your dad home?"

Before his brother could shush him, the younger one answered, "Yeah, but he's grouchy today."

Grim with determination, Suzanne answered, "Well so am I," and proceeded to get out of the car. Walking up to the front door, they were met by a man coming out of the house. He was big, but more belly than brawn. He needed a shave and his eyes were bloodshot as they glared suspiciously at her.

"What'd my boys do?" he growled.

"Sir, I'm just bringing them home. They came to our vet clinic with their dog that was injured and –"

Before she could get another word out, the man turned to the boys questioning, "Dog? Told you that dog was gone."

"Pa, it came back this morning and was all messed up," the younger one answered.

Stepping up to be closer to the boys, Suzanne spoke, "Mr. Johnson, the dog was injured. It looked as though it had been in a fight and they wanted our vet to see it."

At the word 'fight', he turned his narrowed gaze back to her. "Don't know nothin' about no fightin'. Boys shouldn't have bothered you." Before giving her a chance to speak, he growled, "You here to get money outta me for the dog?" He rounded on the oldest and barked, "You had no business taking that dog to the vet. I ain't got no money for that."

"Sir," she said softly to try to diffuse his anger. "I'm not here for money. I just wanted to make sure the boys got home safely."

At that, he quieted a little but continued to stare at her suspiciously.

"Because the dog died, the boys were upset and I didn't want them walking back home by themselves. Plus, your dog had been in a fight and I just wondered if you had seen anything?"

"Ain't no dogfights around here," he said quickly. "That dog wasn't fightin'. Musta been in an accident. Probably got hit by some car."

Knowing he was lying, she feared for the boys if she kept questioning their dad. Plastering a smile on her face, she said, "I'm sure you must be right, sir." Looking down at the boys, she said, "It was nice meeting you. You were very brave to try to get help for your dog."

Backing down from the steps, she made her way over to her car, shaking with anger. A master at hiding her emotions she waved good-bye as she pulled away from the curb, not seeing the dark car that had followed her from the clinic. Or the eyes that followed her. Or the smile that curved his face.

"Dr. Ketchum? This is Suzanne McDonald from Cranston and Donavan Veterinary Clinic."

"Suzanne? It's good to hear from you. How're things with you? I haven't seen you in a while."

"They're fine. Um…the reason I'm calling is that we've had some strange things being said by some clients about the ER clinic and well, I just wanted to talk to you about them."

Without skipping a beat, he replied, "I know I spoke with Annie last year about some dog attacks in the area. Is this still happening?"

"Yeah, it is. I was wondering if you had some time when we could talk?"

"Can we make it over dinner? I could drop by and pick you up."

"Um…sure," she replied biting her lip. Not wanting to have dinner with him, she couldn't think of an excuse quickly enough.

"Great. I'll pick you up at the clinic about five p.m.," he replied cheerfully.

She turned around in her chair seeing Leon leaning against the doorframe. "Setting up a hot date?" he joked.

Before she could answer, Annie walked in from the back and looked between the two of them. "Hot date? With who?"

"It's definitely not a date, guys," Suzanne answered

glumly. "I called Dr. Ketchum to ask about these dogs and his clinic and he wants to talk over dinner."

Annie walked over placing her hand on Suzanne's shoulder. "Sweetie, he's really nice. Dinner out could be really good for you."

Suzanne looked up at her friend and said, "First of all, I'm not interested in dating. Second of all, he wanted you, Annie, before Shane came along."

"Oh, no. We went to dinner a couple of times professionally, but there was absolutely no spark at all. So don't hold back on my account because he's certainly not pining for me."

"Well, I'm not looking for a spark either. I just want to find out what's going on at the ER clinic. Do you want to know what the boys said?" Capturing their attention, she continued, "They went to the clinic and there was a sign on the door saying that they were closed for lunch. Their clinic doesn't close for lunch. And last year, we know the receptionist there turned away dogs that looked like they had been in a fight. On top of that, they didn't report some of those dogs either."

Annie just nodded saying, "Well, I hope you get your answers." Then with a wink she turned, calling over her shoulder, "And if you happen to have a great dinner then that's even better!"

Huffing, Suzanne blew the wisps of hair that had fallen from her ponytail out of her face, as Leon smirked.

THE CANDLELIGHT ON the tables in the small neighborhood Italian restaurant would have made for an intimate dining experience if Suzanne had felt like she was on a date. Looking across at her dinner partner, her eyes scanned him quickly. *Tall, but not as tall as Brad. Handsome, but in a polished way. Not rugged. Not heart-stopping. Not Brad – Stop. Just stop,* she admonished herself.

"Dr. Ketchum, I-"

"Please, you must call me Phil," he said with a smile.

Glancing down at her plate for a second, she raised her eyes back to his and began again. "Okay, Phil. I have concerns which I hope you can answer. Or if not, then investigate because I feel like the integrity of your clinic is at risk."

"Please, let's talk. I want to know what you hear that makes you concerned and I can assure you that Dr. Marker will want to know."

"Dr. Marker?"

"He's retired now, but he is the owner of the ER vet clinic."

"Well, last year when a client came in with a dog that had been attacked, he claimed that he came to your clinic and the night receptionist turned him away. But when Annie talked to you, she was told that you were there in the back and had never been told that a dog came in."

"I did talk to Ralph, our receptionist, after that incident and made sure he knew what the evening and night policy is."

Nodding, she continued. "A little while back, we had another client come in with a dog that had been attacked and he was complaining that when he came to the ER clinic, no animal control report was filed."

At this Phil's smile dropped from his face and was replaced with a look of concern. "Do you have the date of that?"

"I'm sorry, I don't have it with me, but I can email the details to you tomorrow when I'm back in the clinic."

"Is there anything else I should be aware of?" he asked.

"Well, earlier today I had two boys bring in a dog that had been involved in a fight and it looked like it was not the first time the dog had been fighting. The dog died and when I took the boys home, they said that they had gone to your clinic first and there was a sign on the door saying that it was closed."

"Closed?" he repeated incredulously. "We don't close for lunch. There's always at least a tech or vet nurse on duty."

"I know, but that's what the boys claimed," she said watching him carefully.

"Perhaps the boys were mistaken. Maybe they weren't at the ER clinic."

Leaning back in her seat, watching him carefully, "They were very certain. We drove right by your clinic to get to their house."

An uncomfortable silence settled over the couple as their food sat untouched.

"Who were the boys? Did you get their names?" he asked smoothly.

Suspicion slithered over her as she watched his face for clues as to his motive for wanting to know the boy's names. "No, I don't know their names," she lied. "I just dropped them off on their street, so I don't even know where they live." The lie came easily to her as she found herself wanting to protect the boys. From what, she did not know.

"Well, little boys wouldn't know one clinic from another so they probably have us confused."

"Can I ask who was working reception today?" she asked casually as she forced herself to eat a few bites.

"It was Ralph," he said glumly. "But honestly, Suzanne, he's a great receptionist. He loves animals, is always at work and a model employee. I don't think there's anything going on with him. I'll certainly talk to him to verify, but I feel like your concerns are unfounded. He had a natural learning curve when he first started the job, but I have no problems with him now."

What the hell? I point out numerous issues and you defend him? Determined to talk to Ralph herself soon, she plastered a smile on her face. "I certainly hope so, Phil. I'd hate to have to report him to Animal Control for not following procedures."

He leaned over and patted her hand. "I promise to talk to him tomorrow to make sure he is following protocol. But enough about that, let's enjoy the rest of our dinner."

Suzanne managed to choke down several more bites and barely sipped her wine. Finally glancing at her watch, she said, "I really need to leave, Phil. I had a very nice dinner."

He stood as she did and said, "I'd like to have dinner again sometime and we can focus on getting to know each other better instead of all of the other things." He paid for their meal quickly and took her hand as they walked outside. "I'll drive you home."

She glanced at her hand in his. *Nothing. I feel nothing.* Looking back up, she smiled and replied softly, "Thank you for dinner, but I can just walk home."

"No way. Not in this neighborhood," he exclaimed as he ushered her to his car. The ride was only a few blocks, but the silence was broken only by the music.

Once there, she hurried out of the car trying to leave before he could walk around to escort her to the door. "Thanks again," she said as she walked to the clinic entrance. Glancing over her shoulder, she saw his look of disappointment. With a small wave as he drove off, she put the key in the door.

"Have a good time on your…date?" came a voice from behind.

Giving a little scream, she turned quickly to see BJ

leaning against his car parked near the clinic entrance. Placing her hand over her pounding heart, she glared at him. "What are you doing here? You scared me to death."

"I came by earlier to see you but Leon told me you were out on a date."

Narrowing her eyes at him, she just stared. "It was not a date. I was checking on…just finding out…oh, never mind. It's none of your business anyway." Her hand shook slightly as she tried to put the key in the lock.

His strong arm came from behind, placing his hand over hers as he assisted with unlocking the door.

She felt a tingle from her hand all the way up her arm. *I didn't feel this with Phil. I've never felt this with anyone except with…* Jerking her hand away, she tried to pull back but only managed to push her back into his front. His hard, muscular front. Her head slipping easily under his chin and her ass into his…*oh my God.* She tried to move forward, but his other arm snaked around her waist from behind and trapped her against him.

"Oh, no Suzy. You're not getting away so quickly." With the door to the clinic open, he maneuvered their bodies inside and quickly closed and locked the door behind him.

"Brad, let me go," she pleaded, both loving the feel of his body pressed up against hers and fearing the closeness.

He dropped her keys into her purse hanging on her shoulder and deftly removed her cell phone. In an instant, he had his number programmed into her phone and had memorized hers.

Squirming she tried move away but only managed to wiggle her ass next to his crotch.

"Babe, stop," he ordered gently, whispering into her ear. "Your sweet ass is about to drive me wild."

Those words stilled her as the dark silence in the clinic cloaked her flaming cheeks.

"My number is in your phone. Use it whenever you need to babe." With that, he slowly released her and turned her to face him. With his fingers on her chin he lifted her face to his. His eyes burned into hers.

"Why? Why are you doing this, Brad?" came her whispered plea.

"The time for running is over. No more. I was young and foolish when I allowed you to walk away, but at the time it seemed to be the only way I could stop your pain. I now know that your pain didn't end with us ending. We should have stayed together. Should have worked it out."

Wordlessly she slowly shook her head, tears forming in her eyes. "I…," she began.

"No," he said gently, placing his fingers over her mouth. "I thought you'd moved on but now I know you've grieved alone. Not happenin' anymore." Leaning over, he kissed her cheek. "Lock up behind me," he said as he backed away. "I'll see you soon."

She locked the door automatically, then moved through the clinic and up to her apartment as though in a trance. Setting her security alarm, she tossed her purse onto the kitchen counter and reached for a bottle of wine in the refrigerator. Pouring a glass as she hoped to settle her thoughts she noticed her cell phone had slid out of her purse and was lying on the counter.

Reaching for it, she looked down at his number now in her contacts. **Brad.** *Not BJ, the nickname he went by as an adult. Not to me. He'll always be Brad to me.* Closing her eyes tightly to keep the tears at bay, she downed her glass of wine quickly.

Drifting off to sleep hours later, it was no longer the blue-eyed, blond boy that infiltrated her dreams. It was now a man…the one she could never seem to have moved beyond that came to her in her sleep.

OUTSIDE, THE MEN in the dark-tinted SUV sat looking up at the light in the second-floor apartment. Jorge had watched as she came in from her date and then saw the blond man waiting at his car walk her inside. *You're a busy little bee*, Jorge thought before he noticed the man sitting next to him rubbing his swollen dick through his pants.

Knowing how to control his baser urges, Jorge bit out, "Keep your mind on the fucking job. You whack off in my car, it'll be cut off and fed to the dogs at the next fight."

The other man quickly moved his hand away from his dick, fear replacing lust in his eyes.

"You're here to learn. Keep your eyes on the target and make sure you're not noticed. That's it. That's your job. You can't handle it, Marcel will make sure to remove you from his payroll … permanently."

"Yes, sir. I got it."

Jorge's eyes went back to the apartment as the single light was now turned off. "Looks like sleeping beauty is out for the night," he said as he started the automobile. Driving back to report to Marcel, he knew the girl was going to be a problem. Innocent…but a problem.

Chapter 6

"**A**NNIE, YOU KNOW Mr. Charleston whose dog, Petunia, was attacked last year? Well, I have tried several times today and got no answer which is weird. I want to follow up on his dog and also to see if he heard from animal control."

Annie agreed that it was unusual. Leon walked back to the lab where they were discussing what to do next after Suzanne had filled them in on her dinner conversation with Phil.

"Our schedule is light near the end of our day, so if you two don't mind I'd like to walk to his apartment to see if he'll talk to me."

Leon laughed as he said, "That could be our new practice motto. 'If you don't answer our calls, a vet tech will track you down.'"

Smiling, Suzanne said, "Well, Phil made it sound like I had my information wrong. I just want to verify everything before I contact Animal Control again."

Annie agreed, "I think you're right. With one incident from last year, it wasn't such a big suspicion of dog fighting. But with what's going on now, we need to have our information clear and validated before making a complaint."

Leon nodded. "That makes sense. I'll go back through some of our older reports and see if we can find any coincidences."

Heading out into the fall sunshine wearing a sweater over her hamster-print scrubs, she walked several blocks to an old, brick apartment building. Climbing the stairs to the third floor, she approached Mr. Charleston's door. Knocking, she heard barking and shuffling inside.

"Coming, I'm coming," came a voice from behind the door.

It swung open and she saw the smile drop from his face when he recognized her.

"Mr. Charleston," she greeted and then bent to rub Petunia's ears. Standing back up, she searched his face for a clue as to why he seemed so nervous.

"Miss Suzanne, what are you doing here?"

"I just wanted to see how you and Petunia were doing. I've tried to call but since you didn't call back, I thought I would drop by and see for myself."

Visibly relaxing, he answered, "Good. We're good."

"I was also wondering if Animal Control ever came to see you or check in on you after the report we filed several months ago."

"No. Um…no. I didn't hear from them, but that's fine. Well, maybe um…maybe I did. But…um, it's okay. We're good. We're all good. I don't want any trouble."

It wasn't hard for Suzanne to pick up on his nervousness and she wanted to dig deeper. "Mr. Charleston, I don't want to upset you, but why would there be trouble? We just want to make sure that the proper authorities are responding."

Shaking his head emphatically, he continued, "No, no. We're fine. I could have been mistaken."

"Mistaken? Mr. Charleston, how could you have been mistaken about a dog attacking your dog right in front of you on the sidewalk?"

Eyes widening, he began to stammer, "Well, I didn't mean…um…mistaken. Not exactly. I mean that …we're fine."

Realizing that she was making the strange situation worse, she nodded slowly. "Okay, well if you're sure. I'll just leave you then."

Giving the first smile since she showed up at his apartment, he nodded as he said, "Thank you for coming Miss Suzanne. You're very kind."

Deciding to throw out one last comment she replied, "I just hope no other dog continues to attack other dogs or owners…especially a child outside."

Seeing his smile drop at that statement, she turned and walked down the stairs and back out onto the street.

Standing on the corner for a moment, she turned and went in the opposite direction deciding to check on their latest dog attack victim.

She only had to walk a couple of blocks for her to

get to his apartment. Once again, the sound of barking greeted her as she knocked on his door. When it opened, a young man was standing there with Mr. Marcelli in the background. "Well hello," came the smooth voice from the young man. "May I help you?"

"I'm Suzanne McDonald from Chaucer's vet office. I came to check on him."

The young man opened the door slightly so that she could see Chaucer standing next to Mr. Marcelli. A very nervous looking Mr. Marcelli. His eyes kept cutting to the man at the door.

"As you can see my uncle's dog is fine. But how nice for such a beautiful, young woman to make a house call."

His oily words slid over her, making her just as uncomfortable as it appeared Chaucer's owner was. She looked between the two men, seeing no family resemblance and couldn't help but wonder why his nephew was speaking for him. The young man was tall and slender, and she felt an angry roughness pouring off of him. His smile never reached his eyes and the thought that she wouldn't want to meet him in a dark alley washed over her. He was dressed well, but there was something not right about his presence. Forcing herself to look away from him, she settled her gaze on the older gentleman.

"Mr. Marcelli? Has Chaucer had any setbacks since his treatments? Dr. Annie was wanting to know how he was and since I was in the neighborhood, I decided to see for myself."

The older gentleman's eyes cut back to his nephew, as though seeking approval to speak. Suzanne wanted to speak to him alone but couldn't figure out how to separate them.

Clearing his throat first, Mr. Marcelli responded, "Yes, um…my dear. Chaucer is fine. As you can tell…" He stopped speaking as Suzanne pressed forward and knelt in front of Chaucer to rub her hands over his fur.

"You do look good baby-boy. Are you eating okay? Yeah? You playing with your ball?" Trying to keep her sing-song voice from trembling as she noticed the nephew's feet moving next to her, she stood and faced Mr. Marcelli once again.

"Did you get a call from Animal Control yet? We did a report but haven't heard back."

"Um…I'm not sure," he said nervously looking back to his nephew. "Um…maybe. We're out a lot so I really don't know."

What's going on? Why am I being shut out and shut down?

Deciding that she was not going to get any more answers, she plastered her usual smile on her face and touched Mr. Marcelli's arm as she said softly, "Well, if you or Chaucer need anything, and I mean anything, please call the clinic."

Turning back to his nephew, she stuck her hand out and said, "Nice to meet you, Mr. …?"

Not answering her question, he took her hand in

his. Giving it a firm squeeze, "I'll make sure my uncle knows what he needs to do about Chaucer."

As he ushered her out of the door, she glanced back one last time to see Mr. Marcelli take out his handkerchief and wipe his brow. She was just going to give him a smile when the door closed in her face.

Pursing her lips, she headed back down the stairs. *What an asshole his nephew is*, she thought as she trudged back toward the clinic.

THE YOUNG MAN turned to Mr. Marcelli after listening to hear the young woman's footsteps descend the stairs. "You did very well old man. Very well. Now just remember what I said. You keep your mouth shut and I won't have to pay that sweet little piece of ass a visit. Got that old man?"

Licking his lips nervously, Mr. Marcelli nodded. In a shaky voice, he tried to admonish the man in front of him, "You leave her alone. She's a good person. I'll keep my mouth shut, but you need to stay away from her."

A dangerous smile slowly formed on the man's face as his eyes glistened with controlled anger. "Just remember my promise old man," he said as he walked through the door.

Jorge continued smiling all the way to his car. Nodding to the inhabitants of another dark-windowed SUV, they silently pulled away from the curb following the young woman walking back to her apartment.

Suzanne walked briskly down the sidewalk, dodging the few other pedestrians hurrying on their way home. The older city neighborhood was lined with four-story brick apartment buildings with small shops on some of the ground floors. Businesses were closing and the streets were quickly emptying. Looking around, she realized with dismay that the street lights gave off little illumination. Coming to an intersection, her attention was diverted by the sound of dogs growling. Turning to look to her right, she saw a tall, wooden fence where the sounds were coming from.

Cautiously she walked toward the fence, her closer proximity making the barking and growling fiercer. She stopped about a foot away from the fence and leaned in to see if she could peer between the small cracks in the slats.

Suddenly several large dogs lunged at her, their front paws pounding on the inside of the fence, their growls and snarls so loud that she immediately jumped back, her heart pounding. Letting out a scream, she pressed her hand against her chest.

What little she could see, the dogs looked rough as she glimpsed their chewed ears. Their noise intensified and she stumbled back hoping they would quiet. They continued their loud protestations and she quickly moved back to the intersection and began to hustle down the last several blocks to her apartment. Wishing for more pedestrians, she noted the dark and empty streets. Knowing that Annie and Leon would have left the clinic by now, she cursed her decision to make her trips so late in the evening.

The sound of growling could still be heard as she hustled along. *Only one more block to go*, she comforted herself. Her ears perked up as she listened to the noise behind her. *Why does the barking sound louder?* She began to walk faster. The noise grew louder.

Finally turning, she saw three dogs running down the sidewalk toward her, the same growling and snarling emanating from them as she had seen earlier…when the safety of the fence had protected her.

"Oh Jesus," she screamed as she began running as fast as she could the last half-block to her building. Knowing she would never have time to get the front clinic door open, she ran to the back alley and sprinted up the metal stairs to her apartment.

Heart pounding, she tried to pull her keys out of her purse without dropping them. Making it to the top of the stairs as the dogs turned the corner into the alley, she struggled to get the door open. The growling dogs followed her up the staircase and before she could get in the door, one of them grabbed onto her boot as she attempted to kick out on the small grated landing outside her door. *Jesus, help me. Jesus, help me.*

Adrenaline pumping, she stumbled as she continued to kick the attacking dogs. Their powerful jaws were snapping and her kicks only seemed to incense them, not deter them. The sheer size of the dogs was daunting as she desperately tried to keep them from gabbing her legs. Hearing a shrill whistle in the distance, two of the dogs turned and ran back down the stairs, but one continued to pull on her booted foot. Just as the third dog let go and followed the others down the stairs, she lost her balance and tumbled down several stairs before painfully throwing out her arms to stop her fall.

Pain radiated from her body as she looked toward the end of the alley to see a black, dark-windowed SUV stop and the three dogs jump into the back. It slowly continued down the road, leaving her injured, alone on the stairs.

Her ribs were pounding from slamming them on the metal railings, but she managed to pull herself back up a few steps to her purse, where its contents had spilled out over the stairs. *Please let my cell phone still be here.* Finding it she tried to focus on her contact list but the pain made it difficult. Hitting the first one she came across she was surprised when BJ answered.

"Suzy?"

His voice sounded deep. Smooth. Exactly what she wanted at that moment. And she began to cry.

"Suzy, what's wrong? Where are you? What's going on?" his panicked voice bit out.

Her tears drowned out her voice, but she managed to choke out, "Home. Dogs got me. I'm hurt."

"I'm coming now. Are you safe?"

"Gone…they're gone…," she sobbed.

"Don't try to move. I'm coming."

Her head felt heavy as the adrenaline stopped flowing. The desire to lay down on the cold metal stairs and sleep was overwhelming, but she knew she had to force herself to stay awake. She tried to diagnose herself using her vet tech training. *This would be easier if I were a dog…or a cat…or a hamster.*

She lost track of the minutes as she shifted to a different position. Her hip ached as her ankle screamed. Her shoulder was stiff and she had trouble breathing because of the pain in her ribs.

She saw a truck turn into her alley and come to a screeching stop. *Please be Brad,* she prayed.

"Suzy? Suzy girl?" he yelled.

"Brad? Up here," she called, tears returning.

He pounded up the stairs, his eyes on her quickly assessing. Towering over her huddled body, he bent to her, speaking softly. "Baby? What happened? Who did this?"

"D…dogs chased me," she stammered.

His jaw tensed with anger but keeping it in check he carefully lifted her in his strong arms as though she weighed nothing and carried her to his truck. Settling her into the passenger seat, he cursed as he saw her wince.

"It's okay," she said, trying not to groan. "They didn't bite me. Just drug me down the stairs some and then I fell part of the way." Unable to hold back a gasp when he buckled her in, she grabbed her middle.

"Goddamnit," he bit out as he rounded the front and hopped into the driver's side. Starting the truck, he pulled out of the alley and headed toward the hospital. Grabbing his cell, he quickly made a call.

"Matt? Get Shane and meet me at the hospital. I've got Suzy. Suzanne. She's been injured and I'm taking her to the ER. Yeah. Make it official." He slid his eyes to the painful expression on her face, then continued, "Fill you in when you get there. Richland General Hospital."

Clicking the phone off, he watched her face carefully as the lights from the street lamps flashed illumination across her. *In pain and still the most beautiful girl I've ever seen.*

"Suzy girl? We're almost there. Hang on, baby."

"I'm okay, Brad. It's not bad. If I don't move. Or breathe. Or think too hard." She started to smile, then gasped again. "Or laugh," she said through gritted teeth.

He pulled quickly into the parking area for the ER and jumped out. Opening her door, he gently picked her up again then moved inside.

I don't know what the fuck happened, he thought, *but someone's going to pay. No one messes with my woman.* The realization that she was once again his woman flooded over him. Sparing a glance down at the dark-haired beauty in his arms he thought, *now to convince her.*

As she was being wheeled back into her ER room after the x-rays, she was surprised to find the room filled, and the testosterone level was at an all-time high. BJ, Matt, Shane, and Gabe took up all of the space in the small room. Without any pain medication yet, she was in no mood to be interrogated, but the men had other ideas.

BJ immediately moved to her side, bending down to kiss her forehead. "Baby, how ya doing?"

Her pale face showed off the dark circles under her eyes as she looked up into his face. *Why does he have to care so much?* But even as she tried to convince herself that she wanted him gone, her heart felt the familiar pull to have him close. "Everything hurts," she said softly. "But, I'm okay."

The nurse took her vital signs once again and assured her that the doctor would be in as soon as the x-rays were in. "If there's no concussion, then he can give you something for your pain."

Glancing around at the angry faces directed her way, she licked her lips nervously. "Why are you all here?" she asked.

Shane pulled out a notebook as Matt began to question her. "Suzanne, we need to know what happened. Just tell us everything and we'll ask questions as we need to. Okay honey?"

She tried to take a deep breath, then gasped again.

The men, in unison, leaned forward as though to help her before realizing that there was little they could do. She looked up again as she felt the anger pouring off of them. Especially one man. BJ.

Pulling her lips in to ward off the tears, she said, "I told Brad. I was attacked by some dogs. But I'm pretty sure I had seen them earlier."

"In the clinic?" Shane asked, jotting down notes.

"No, behind the fence."

"What fence, Suzanne?" Matt asked.

"The one down the street. Behind Third and Capitol."

"When did you see them?"

"When I went looking for some clients."

"When was that?"

"Earlier today."

Matt rubbed his hands over his face, trying to keep the frustration from showing. Taking a deep breath, he leaned over in her line of vision and said softly, "Suzanne, we're not getting very far honey. Why don't you tell us what happened today, starting from whenever you left the clinic?"

Nodding slowly, she sighed. "Okay. I'm frustrated that some of our clients have had their dogs attacked on the streets and it seems like Animal Control isn't doing enough. So I decided to make some house calls."

Shane looked up sharply. "Annie know you were doing this?"

"Yes. It was daylight when I left and I was only

going a couple of blocks over to see one of our elderly clients."

"So, how'd you end up over near Third Street?"

"I didn't like the answers I got from Mr. Charleston, so I decided to visit another client, Mr. Marcelli, but he lives farther away and it got dark while I was there. But then the creepy man was there too, so I wanted to leave."

Matt, Gabe, Shane, and BJ all shared a look then stared back at the young woman in the bed.

"Jesus, Suzanne," Shane bit out. "You are the hardest victim to get clear answers from. Who's the fuckin' creepy man?"

Tears filled Suzanne's eyes as her chin began to quiver. All at once the men began to apologize.

"Shane, shut the fuck up, man," Gabe growled.

"I'm sorry, darlin'," Shane exclaimed.

BJ slid his arm around her shoulders, gently pulling her into his chest. Cradling the back of her head close to his heart, he rocked her back and forth for a moment giving her time to feel more control.

"Suzy baby, just lay back and tell us in your own words," he paused looking at the others, "without interruption from us, what happened."

Nodding once again, she tried to pull her thoughts together. "Mr. Charleston seemed like he wanted me to leave even though that's unusual for him. He was very evasive when I asked about Animal Control as though he was scared for me to be asking questions. So I figured I wasn't going to get any more answers from him. I decided to walk to another client's apartment. When I got there, another man was there. He said he was Mr. Marcelli's nephew, but he wouldn't give a name. And he didn't really want to let me in, but I pushed my way in any way."

The simultaneous intake of breaths had her looking around at their faces. If they had seemed upset earlier, a drop in the temperature in the room would have clued her into their anger now.

"You did what?" BJ all but roared next to her.

Seeing her chin quiver again, BJ reined in his anger and tightened his arm around her. "Sorry Suzy. Keep going," he encouraged.

Sucking in her lips, she couldn't decide if she wanted to keep talking or not, but the fear of the day won out and she continued.

"Mr. Charleston seemed like he was nervous and then when I saw that Mr. Marcelli appeared uncomfortable as well, I was frustrated. Both men seemed as though reporting anything to Animal Control was the last thing they wanted to have happen even though I had already done it at the time they came in. And Mr. Marcelli's creepy nephew definitely seemed like he was in charge and wanted me out of there."

Sucking in a painful breath, she felt herself lean heavily against BJ, who gave off a feeling of comfort she had not known in a long time while making her wish she could jump up and run away once more.

Just then, the doctor came back into the room. The x-rays had shown that she did not have broken ribs, but she had multiple contusions. "I will give you a pain reliever in your IV and then you will have a prescription to fill for more." The nurse came in with a syringe and immediately Suzanne relaxed, the pain instantly ebbing from her body.

Shane looked at Matt, Gabe, and BJ saying, "We're not going to get anything else out of her tonight."

The nurse looked at the wall of handsome testosterone standing in front of her and said, "Will one of you be taking care of her? The discharge instructions include that she cannot drive nor should she be alone while this pain reliever is in her system which will be for about twenty-four hours."

"She's mine," BJ quickly interjected.

Matt and Shane grinned, but Gabe carefully stared at BJ.

"Just for now or do you mean something more?" Gabe asked.

BJ held Gabe's eyes. "I'll give you that, man. I'll let you question my intentions…this one time and this is the last time." Looking back down at the drowsy Suzanne reclining in the bed, he continued, "She was mine from the time she was fifteen years old. I let her go, but never again." Raising his eyes back to his friends, he said, "So when I say that she's mine…I mean that She. Is. Mine."

Matt slapped him on the back. "Good enough for

me. I'll tell Lily to stop worrying, but she'll probably come over tomorrow to check on her."

Shane gave a chin lift and simply said, "Annie'll come too."

Gabe held his stare for just a moment before the corner of his mouth turned up. "I hope you can get where you want to be with her. She needs you." Then he smiled as he looked at her resting form. "But I think she'll give you hell getting her there." With that, he laughed as he turned and walked out followed by the other two.

Chapter 7

AFTER HAVING CAREFULLY carried Suzanne into the clinic, deftly locking and re-setting the alarm then moving up the inside stairs to her apartment, BJ gently placed her on the bed.

Her face, slack from pain medicine, had a goofy grin on it and he couldn't help but smile. Glancing down, he leaned over to unbutton her jeans. Beginning to slide them down over her hips and legs, he heard her gasp.

"Oh, no-no bad boy," she slurred. "I know what you're tryin' to do. You wanna take at…advanish…advanich of me."

Cocking his eyebrow at her, he grinned. "You think I'm taking advantage of you?" he asked as he tossed her jeans on the floor while keeping his eyes away from her legs. Just to prove her wrong, he pulled the covers up. Walking over to her dresser, he opened a drawer, stunned to find it full of his old high school t-shirts. Fingering the soft, worn material, he grabbed one.

Suzanne looked down at the covers and her face scrunched into a frown. Lifting her eyes back to him, she continued to frown. "You donsh wan me?"

"Baby doll, you have no idea how much I want you," he replied as he lifted her shirt over her head, now forcing his eyes to not stare at her breasts. His eyes dropped to her ribs and saw the dark bruising there and felt his anger flow again. Quickly pulling a t-shirt onto her, he settled her back onto the bed.

Pulling his jeans off as well, he slid under the covers, tucking her body tightly to his, he ordered, "Rest, Suzy. You need it. And tomorrow, we'll deal with whatever you were dealing with that got you in this mess."

The quiet of the night settled around them as her voice washed over him on a whisper. "I always loved you, Brad. I never stopped. That's why I had to leave," she continued to slur. "I dinna wan to, but I left. It was the only way to give you back your life."

The last words came out so softly that he wasn't sure that he heard them. The impact struck him as if she had gutted him once more. *Give me back my life? What the fuck does she mean by that?* Hearing the deep breaths of her sleeping, he knew no more answers were coming that night. *Tomorrow babe. That's it. No more tip-toeing around what's going on in your head.*

Being careful of her bruised ribs, he tucked her back to his front cradling her safely in his arms as he curled his body protectively around her. One arm under her head and the other around her waist, his hand splayed out over her stomach.

SUZANNE'S EYES OPENED slowly to the soft, early morning light filtering in through the blinds on her bedroom window. As she tried to stretch two things became very apparent. One, her body ached as though she had fallen down stairs. The other was that something large was pressed against her back and its arm was wrapped across her body. Her sleep foggy mind suddenly remembered the events of the evening before. She did fall down stairs and *Brad!*

Jerking her body upright, she gasped as the pain sliced through her ribcage. "Auugh," she cried out.

Trying to catch her breath, she felt the bed shift as the other person there moved off and walked around to her side. Keeping her eyes down toward the floor, large male feet came into view.

"Suzy?"

He can't be here. This isn't happening. She could feel the familiar pang of heartache spearing through her knowing that he was near but unable to have him.

"Suzy?" he asked again.

Refusing to lift her eyes, she saw him squat until his face was level with hers.

"Suzy, I'm right here. You can't pretend I'm not."

Slowly she lifted her eyes. Her breath caught in her throat again but not from pain. *How is it possible that he can look this good first thing in the morning?*

"Baby, stay right there and I'll get the pills," he said

as his hand came up to cup her face as he noticed her crystal blue eyes were dulled with pain.

As she stared into his slate-blue orbs, she felt the slight stubble and saw his messy hair – as though he had run his hands through it many times.

She wanted to fight the urge to lean into his palm, but the pull was too great. Closing her eyes for just a second, she allowed herself the luxury of feeling his large hand completely warm her face. As she felt his thumb move over her cheek, she jerked away.

"I'm fine. Really. Thank you for…helping last night. I…um…couldn't find anyone else who could come," she called after him as he walked into the bathroom.

"I'm not going anywhere, babe. You need help and I'm not walking away."

"No, really Brad. I'm just a little sore." She forced herself to look into his face, hoping that he could see the sincerity instead of a lie coming out of her mouth.

He knelt back down in front of her holding out the pills in one hand and a glass of water in the other.

Sighing, she said, "What's the prescription? I don't want to be as out of it today as I was last night."

"It's just prescription-strength ibuprofen. There's another one for codeine, but I knew you wouldn't want that."

How did he remember that?

"Wisdom teeth, Suzy. That summer you had them out, you hated the way codeine made your stomach feel."

She closed her eyes as the floodgate of memories from that summer washed over her.

I was seventeen and he was eighteen. The bonfires, picnics, swimming in the river, hanging out with their friends. Long walks in the woods, each secretly looking for just the right place to start making out. Another growth spurt had him taller and more filled out than the summer before. He always took charge of every kiss, knowing I was shy but that I desperately wanted his mouth on mine as much as he did.

After having my wisdom teeth removed, he came over to my house. Mom opened the door and I could hear him coming up the stairs to my bedroom. "Door stays open," mom called. Brad entered my room, rolling his eyes as he walked over to the bed.

"Hey gorgeous," he said, bending over to kiss my forehead. His arms were filled with flowers, balloons, and a stuffed bear.

My head felt woozy from the codeine and I gave him a goofy, weak smile. We piled up and watched some TV until mom reappeared carrying a tray. For Brad, several sandwiches, chips and a huge glass of milk. For me, jello. Green jello.

"Kids, I have to run to the bakery. Behave yourselves," mom admonished with a smile.

Glaring at him as he shoved down his lunch, I slowly slurped the jello, having to admit that it tasted great. Until…without warning, I threw up. Green juice sprayed all over the bedspread and down the front of my t-shirt.

Mortified, I desperately wished for a black hole to swallow me but no such luck. Nausea rolled through me again and as I dry heaved, blood began to trickle from my lips. Not able to control the heaving and embarrassed at the mess I was making in front of Brad, I began to cry.

He quickly ran to the bathroom to get towels and a warm bath cloth. Cleaning me up while his strong arm supported me, I eased back into him. He took charge and took care of me. Stripping the bedspread off of the bed and gathering the towels, he headed to the laundry room and started the washing machine. Coming back to me, he gently held the bath cloth to my mouth, as the bleeding stopped.

Settling on the bed behind me, he cradled me in his arms. "Shhh," he admonished as I tried to apologize.

"Suzy, we'll have lots of times like this. Times when we take care of each other. 'In sickness and in health.' Isn't that the saying?"

I turned to look at the beautiful face peering deeply into my eyes. Smiling, I agreed. "Yeah, that's the saying."

"And when we get married, we'll take care of each other until we are so old we have to help each other out of bed every day. Or maybe, we'll just stay in bed all day."

I giggled. "I don't think we'll be messing around when we are that old!"

He placed a gentle kiss on my lips as he vowed, "We'll never be too old to mess around."

Settling back into the bed, he continued, "And when we have kids, we'll have to do this for them too."

No. No. Pulling herself out of her memories, she shook her head. "You're right. Just the ibuprofen, please."

BJ looked at her as she swallowed the pills. For a moment, her face had gone soft as her eyes had seemed to focus on something far away, and then suddenly she was right back to pulling away from him again. The wall was back up and it pissed him off.

Standing, he walked back to the bathroom to give himself a moment. *Goddammit. After everything we shared. After everything we went through. How could she have just turned her back on us?* Leaning his tall frame on the sink, he stared into the mirror. *What was it she said last night? It was the only way to give him back his life?*

Turning he stalked back into the bedroom, wanting answers. He saw her wince as she tried to move out of the bed.

"Oh no, Lil' bit. Let's take a look at those ribs before you try to do too much today." Gently laying her back onto the bed, he lifted her shirt carefully to just under her breasts. He could see the dark bruises from the fall and thought his teeth would crack from holding his jaw so tightly. Lifting his eyes, he saw her bright pink face flaming from embarrassment. Lowering her shirt, he leaned down to kiss her forehead.

"Suzy, I'm gonna make you some breakfast and then we'll get comfortable. We've got some things to talk out and now's as good a time as any."

He turned and walked out of the tiny bedroom heading to the kitchen.

She lay there staring at his retreating back. *Talk? Talk about what? Last night? The attack?*

She carefully moved toward the bathroom, quickly taking care of business and running a brush through her long, dark hair. Deftly braiding it so that it hung down her back, she washed her face and brushed her teeth, not having done that when she crashed last night.

Standing at the door of the bedroom, she heard noises coming from the kitchen. The enticing smell of eggs and bacon calling to her. *I can do this. I can walk into the kitchen, thank him for his assistance, and then politely let him know that I'm fine. I can do this. I can do this.*

Walking around the small counter she stopped dead in her tracks. The view in front of her made her breath come unsteadily and it had nothing to do with her injuries. His torso was bare, his back muscles rippling as he moved around the small kitchen area. His blond hair, shaggy and needing a cut had her fingers twitching. His sweat pants hung low on his hips, showcasing his ass which was more spectacular than it had been years ago. He was broader, heavier, more...everything. There was no denying that the Brad of her younger years was now a man in every sense of the word.

Turning around, he caught her staring and he smiled a lazy smile, lifting his eyebrow in question.

"Like what you see?"

She snapped her mouth closed, quickly saying, "Yes, the breakfast looks lovely."

Throwing his head back, he laughed, "Oh baby. You can look at my…bacon all you want."

"Oh, you're impossible," she groused. Moving toward the coffee, she found herself staring directly into his chest as he had moved also. Glaring up, she said, "You so do not want to get between me and my coffee."

His large, warm hand came around and cupped the back of her head, gently pulling it toward him. Placing a kiss on her forehead, he said, "Go on and have a seat babe. I'll get your coffee and serve breakfast in just a minute."

She wanted to lean into him again. Rest her weight into him. Allow him to wrap her in his arms. *Protect. Care. Comfort.*

Jerking back quickly, she sucked in a quick breath. "Yes, um…thank you," she said, moving toward the small dinette table.

The breakfast was simple but filling and she found herself cleaning her plate. Then she watched in amazement as he ate at least three times the amount she had. She started to make a quip about where he put it all, but then couldn't help but peruse his body again. Broad shoulders, muscular build. *He probably needs that much just to maintain that body.*

BJ was doing a good job of pretending not to notice

her as he ate, but it wasn't easy. Her delicate features still showed the dark circles under her eyes, the only marring of a perfect face. *The face that launched my daydreams and haunts my nightmares.*

Quickly cleaning up the dishes, he maneuvered them to the couch, each in their own corner but facing each other.

Taking a deep breath, she began her practiced speech. "Brad, it was really nice of you to come help me out and I apprecia-"

"Not gonna work, baby doll," he interrupted. "We're not kids anymore and I'm not letting you walk away again."

Licking her lips nervously, she looked down at her clasped hands. "BJ," she stammered, "I'm not…um…I can't…I don't…" Clearing her voice as she tried to steady her racing mind, she began again, "It'll be hard…both of us friends with Lily. But…um…we can do this. Friends, I mean. I…think I can."

He moved closer to her on the couch, still not touching her, but close enough that she could feel his presence looming. Crowding. Familiar. She closed her eyes, not able to bear seeing him stare at her.

"Suzy," his voice, gentle and soothing, washed over her. "We can't pretend we don't have a history. We can't pretend we don't have something between us."

Still looking down at her lap, she tried to nod but her heart could not seem to follow. "I…," she stopped, rubbing her head. Her breathing began to falter and the familiar sensation of panic started to flow. Her head began to shake back and forth and before BJ could stop her, she jump from the couch pacing quickly. "No, no. Can't do this. Can't have you here. I can't deal...can't take this."

BJ bolted from the couch and grabbed her shoulders, effectively halting her pacing. Leaning down, he tried to get in her line of vision but she kept shaking her head. What he could see in her eyes scared him. It was as though she had shut out the room. Shut out him. Trying to shut out the memories.

"Suzy," he ordered gently. "Look at me." Giving her a small shake he pulled her into his chest, wrapping his arms around her shivering body, holding her tightly.

She continued to shake her head, although her movements had slowed. He felt the quivering cease, thinking she was pulling herself together.

Suddenly a sob tore from her body, the animal wailing piercing the quiet of the morning as she went slack, his arms the only thing keeping her from dropping to the floor.

"It's gone. My baby's gone. I lost it. I lost it," she cried over and over, her eyes pressed tightly shut as her head shook back and forth once again.

BJ lowered her to the floor, his arms still around her trying to protect her from the tortures in her mind. *Jesus, baby. Did you go through this all alone?*

"It hurts so bad, Brad. I never wanted to lose it. I

wanted our baby. I wanted us. But I lost it," her anguished sobs continued. "It was my fault," she cried.

Pulling her body into his, he wrapped his legs around her as his arms tightened once more, trying to cocoon her. "Shh," he whispered. "Baby, it just happened. Don't you remember? The doctor told us that it just wasn't the right time. It was nature's way of taking care of it."

Her face contorted in fresh grief as her body jerked with sobs, huge tears sliding down her cheeks onto his shirt. "My baby," she wailed over and over, until her voice choked with hoarseness.

With one hand cradling the back of her head and the other arm wrapped tightly around her middle, he tried to overpower her agony, feeling tears sliding down his cheeks as well. He'd sought counseling at the university, glad that he had and assumed that Suzy had done the same. The realization that she had bottled up all of her grief for four years washed over him, pulling at his conscience. *Jesus, why has she suffered alone?* They had both been close to their high school counselor and he assumed that Ms. Dodd had helped her. *But only if Suzy had let her in,* he realized.

He rocked her back and forth, whispering soothing sounds as he offered his body and soul as comfort.

The sobs began to slow, but her body jerked as her breathing hitched. She burrowed deep into his chest as though unconsciously seeking warmth. Acceptance.

BJ wanted her to talk to him. Get it out. Face it.

Together. Which is what they should have done four years ago, but the inexperience of youth pulled them in different directions. Allowed them to walk away from the love they shared.

Holding her, his mind wandered back to that time.

When she called to tell me that she was afraid she was pregnant, I rushed home, ready to face whatever was coming. On the drive there, I went over the scenarios so that by the time I arrived, I was ready to be what she needed me to be.

My parents owned Smokey's, the nice bar and grill in town, and I worked there in the summers. If I increased my hours and dropped football, I would be able to make enough to support us as long as we could live with my parents. It wouldn't be ideal, but it would work. All I knew was that I would do whatever needed to be done.

Her hand was shaking as she held the stick. Its blue end shining like a beacon proclaiming a new life. I kept assuring her that it would be all right, but I knew she was terrified. Life was getting ready to change, but I wanted her to trust me. I was going to do everything in my power to make us a family.

Her breathing hitched again, jerking him from his memories. He stood, protecting her ribs as he walked back into the bedroom. He sat on the edge of the bed, moved to lean back against the headboard and settled her down alongside him, never once letting her slip from his embrace.

Twisting around, he snagged a couple of tissues from the nightstand before gently wiping her cheeks and nose.

Her eyes fluttered open, red-rimmed but finally seemed to focus. She looked surprised to be in his arms in the bedroom, but did not move. She wanted to be embarrassed but found that she could not even bring that emotion up. There was no other room inside her soul except for grief. So she tightened her grip around his torso and held on.

Her own memories flooded to the forefront of her mind, overtaking her thoughts. Of another time when she was held in his embrace.

The stick was blue. Blue. How the hell did this happen? We used protection. Oh Jesus, our parents are going to kill us. She glanced back down again at the stick shaking in her hand. Nope, it hadn't changed color. It was still blue.

Sucking in a huge breath, she looked up at his face, afraid of what she would see. He was staring down at the stick as well. After a look of shock flitted across his face, his eyes captured hers.

"Baby, it's okay. We'll be okay, trust me."

His words warmed her, filling her with a sliver of hope.

"What about our plans? What about college? What about our parents?"

His arms wrapped around her as he pulled her into his chest. Enveloped. Embraced.

"Suzy, we'll be fine. I'll increase my hours at pop's place and make more money. You graduate from high school in another month. We'll make it."

"What about our parents?"

"Baby, they've been friends forever and were thrilled when we finally got together. This just moves our plans up by a couple of years, but Suzy, you've been it for me for a long time." Kissing the top of her head, he squeezed her tighter. "I'll take care of you, trust me."

Chapter 8

BJ NOTICED THAT she had gone very still. "Baby doll," he said softly. "Had no idea you'd held this inside all this time. I thought for sure that you and Ms. Dodd had talked about things." Knowing how close Suzy was with her parents, he added, "Or your mom."

"Couldn't," came the choked response, her chin quivering as she bit her lips trying to keep the tears at bay. "There was no funeral. Nothing."

His mind raced to process what she was saying.

"There's no funeral for a miscarriage. No closure. Nothing to hold. Nothing to kiss goodbye. Nothing."

"Baby," he whispered.

"No one wanted to talk about it. It's almost as though everyone thought that by not talking about it, I wouldn't think about it." Her head dropped as her tears started anew. "But I never stopped thinking about it. It's with me every day. Every. Day. Right there when I wake up and as I close my eyes at night."

BJ slid his hands to her face gently pulling her away from his chest. "Baby, I want to see your face. I need to see your eyes."

Their eyes searched each other's. One questioning.

One hiding. Both hurting.

"Suzy, you said something last night, when you were out of it, and I want to know what you meant."

She looked at him, confusion along with wariness in her eyes. "What did I say?" she whispered.

"You said that you didn't want to leave me but that you had to. That it was the only way to give me back my life." He searched her face. "What did you mean by that?"

She started to pull away from him, but his arms would not allow it. Looking up sharply, she saw the determined look on his face. Sighing, she stopped her movements and dropped her eyes to his chin. Anywhere but his eyes. Staring into those eyes…she would lose her soul…once again.

"Baby, you have got to talk," he said. "Regardless of anything else that ever goes on with us, we have to talk about this."

"It hurts," came the fevered whisper.

"You think it is easy for me?"

At that, she lifted her eyes to his once again in question.

"Yeah, that's right, baby," he said, more harshly than he intended. Sighing loudly, he continued, "I lost too, you know? I lost my baby too. And then I lost the girl I loved. The girl I wanted to marry. I lost my baby and my future." His voice shook with emotion, tears once again welling in his eyes.

Seeing his tears were her undoing. Her whole body

began to shake once again, this time the sobs coming silently. Eyes closed, tears slid down her cheeks. Moving her head back and forth slowly, she whispered, "I had to let you go. I heard. I heard them."

His hands had slid down to her hips and his fingers flexed tightly at her words. "Heard? Heard what? Heard who?"

"It doesn't matter, Brad. It's done. It's over. We had to be over and I had to make sure it was."

"Baby, you're not going to leave me hanging. You owe me that at least."

This time, the agony in his voice ripped through her, reaching the dark, hidden places. The places in her mind that she never allowed herself to wander.

"I heard...your friends. Before. I...came...and heard them." She winced, the memory bringing new pain.

Shaking his head, he said, "I don't know what you're talking about. What did you hear?"

Sucking in a huge breath Suzy stared over his shoulder, as the words that had been held back for so long began to tumble out.

"It had been a rough week. You were back at school. Trying to get some summer classes in. Remember?"

Her eyes could see his head nod. "It'd been rough. Rob was still pouting and nothing Laurie said would appease him. I felt censure all around. Mom tried to act excited about planning a wedding, but I could tell she was hurt. Dad would always come into the room and kiss the top of my head like always, but I could feel it. Jesus!" she bit out, tears threatening to fall once again. "Everywhere I turned, it was as though I was disappointing someone."

She felt BJ's fingers slide from her hips to her back, gently rubbing. Touching. Comforting. Dropping her head, she said in a small voice, "I just wanted to see you again. Needed to see you again."

Quiet settled over the small room, each in their own thoughts. Memories.

"What happened, baby?" he prodded.

Sucking in her lips, she gave a soft snort. "I drove up to surprise you."

BJ searched his memory but couldn't remember her visit.

"I walked to your dorm. The one where you had the first-floor room. It was hot and you had your windows open. Your room was filled with people. A bunch of guys. Some girls. I heard you. I heard them."

"Baby, I'm coming up blank here. I don't remember what you're referring to. You gotta give me somethin' to go on."

Lifting her eyes to his, she saw sincerity. Nodding, she continued, "They were all talking about how you were throwing your life away. How getting married to your high school sweetheart just because she was pregnant was archaic. Stupid."

She watched as slow dawning crossed his face.

Nodding, she lifted her eyebrows. "Yeah, you remember now, don't you?"

Anger filled her as she said, "I heard the girls, Brad. They chimed in to say that it'd be a waste to keep your body away from the female population just because you got tricked into being a 'baby daddy'."

At those words, he dropped his head to his chest, disbelief filling his being. *Of all the times she would have to drop by, she couldn't have picked a worse time. Oh, Jesus, fuck.*

"I heard the others chiming in too, Brad. I heard them. And all I could think of was that they were right. Tying you down to me was going to change your life. Everything you had ever planned. Wanted. Dreamed for. Hoped for."

Lifting his head while cupping hers with his large hands, he pulled her in close. "Baby, what you heard was fucked. You couldn't have happened on a worse conversation at a worse time. I can only imagine that you took off before I had a chance to answer them back?"

Her confused look was his answer.

"Baby, I told them to shut the fuck up. That you had been my life since I could remember. And you having my baby was just icing on the cake. I said it didn't matter that it pushed our timeline up. All that mattered was you and me and the baby."

Suzanne leaned her head in, resting it on his shoulder, fatigue sweeping over her in waves threatening to take her under.

"I just couldn't stand the idea of ruining your life. So I ran to my car and drove home." Taking another shuddering breath, she said numbly, "It's my fault."

"What happened that night, baby? I never really felt like I understood."

The quietness settled between them. Stretching out. Seeping into corners.

He waited several minutes then with his hand on the back of her neck, gave a little reminder squeeze.

She realized that he was right. She had been so overcome with grief that she had never let him back in. Never told him what was on her mind. What she'd heard. What she was thinking. He deserved to know. At least, he deserved that before they would be able to part ways.

"I...," she began haltingly. "I drove home. Crying. Trying to figure out a way...to make it work. To give you your freedom. I thought that I could...I don't know. Raise the baby. Myself."

She felt his hand flex again and she continued in a rush. "When I got home, I ran to my room. Mom and dad tried to talk to me. They called Rob and Laurie, but I wouldn't talk to any of them. Laurie called Emma. Ms. Dodd. But I told them I needed to be alone."

Sucking in a huge breath then letting it out slowly, she said, "That night I woke and felt something wet. I turned on my lamp and looked down." She began to shudder once more and felt BJ tighten his hold on her. "I began to scream. By the time mom and dad got me to the hospital, I had miscarried. By the time they got a call off to you, it was all over."

A new wave of grief poured over her and the sobs came once again. "Gone. Our baby was gone. And it was my fault." She couldn't bear to look into BJ's face, so she kept hers buried in his neck. Then she felt the wetness of his tears fall onto her shoulder. Not able to resist, she leaned up to peer into his eyes, seeing her own grief mirrored there.

"How was it your fault?" he choked out.

"Don't you see?" she cried. "I was upset! I even thought about what life would have been like if I hadn't gotten pregnant. The baby must have felt it. It must have known what I was thinking!" Seeing the incredulous look on his face, she continued. "I know it sounds stupid, but that's all I can think of. I was upset and then that night miscarried."

She threw her head back, another sob tearing from her throat. "I'm so sorry Brad. I'm so fucking sorry."

"Jesus Christ, baby. It's not your fault. That wasn't what happened! Hell, if everyone's negative thoughts caused miscarriages there'd be no babies born."

"I know, I know," she cried, "But I can't help it. That was the only thought that I had. And then the next day, I heard our parents talking outside the hospital room when they thought I was sleeping. Our dads seem to think it was for the best."

Looking at her sharply, he asked, "What about our moms?"

Sadly she shook her head, her expression lost in memory. "No. The moms didn't agree." Giving a rueful snort, she said, "Mom told dad she'd better not ever hear him say that again." Looking up into his face, she admitted, "I don't think I've ever heard my mom use that tone of voice with him before."

Once again, the silence of their memories moved all around them, coating them in a blanket of grief.

Taking a huge cleansing breath and letting it out, Suzanne wiped her face with a crumpled tissue. She forced herself to look at BJ's face, her eyes roaming over his features. One last time. Committing them to memory. Shaggy, dark-blond hair. The white-blond of youth gone. Full face, strong cheekbones. Square jaw with a morning-after stubble. Thick neck that tapered to wide shoulders. Strong arms, a muscular torso that led to his defined abs. A body that she had loved as a young girl into womanhood. And now, just as she found him again, she knew she needed to let him go once more. *I barely survived the first time. How will I make it this time without shattering into a million pieces?*

Clearing her throat, she stared into his eyes. "That's it, Brad. That's all I have to tell you. That's all there is. I had to walk away four years ago because you deserved your life. One free of commitment and duty. And with the baby gone, there was no way we could go back. Looking at you broke my heart and I knew you would grow to resent me. And now that I've told you everything, you can leave. You can go back to your life."

His eyes flashed anger and his voice shook. "That's it? You've told me why you left four years ago and you think I'm just walking away this time? Fuckin' clueless, baby. You were grieving on your own back then. I get it. But now? Now? That's not happening again!"

Her eyes flashed as well, but before she could say anything, he continued. "You walked away back then and no matter how many times I tried to talk to you, call you, get to you, either you or your family put a halt to it. So I let you go figuring you were moving on. Away from me. Away from us."

"I had to let you go, Brad. I couldn't stand the thought of you being tied to me but not loving me."

"You never gave me a chance to tell you how I felt. Cry with you. Hold you. Hell, grieve with you."

"I couldn't. Don't you see?" she pleaded. "I could barely get though a day. I stopped thinking, feeling, caring. One day I jumped into the car and drove to Richland. I just drove around town, not knowing where I was going or what I was doing. My parents were blowing up my cell phone, but I never answered."

"Fuck, baby. What were you doing?"

"Still running," her quiet voice said. "I couldn't stay in Fairfield. I couldn't take a chance on running into you again. Seeing you. I didn't even want to see your parents." Giving a small shrug, she continued, "I thought I was moving on. I guess it was just running away."

"What happened that day?"

"I saw a beautiful woman with long red hair walking a dog. She was wearing a white lab coat and it caught my attention. I followed her and she went into a small veterinarian clinic." Looking into his face once again. "I know this sounds crazy but I parked and went in. There she was with another worker. He asked if he could help me and I just blurted out that I wanted to work there. That I was moving to Richland in a few weeks and that I needed a job."

BJ stared in surprise, knowing that Suzy had always been a careful planner. Not one to act on a whim.

"I told them that I would do whatever needed to be done." Laughing ruefully, she said,

"They must have thought I was crazy, but Annie hired me. Told me to come back when I was settled."

"What then? How'd you move to Richland?"

"I answered an ad in Craig's List for a roommate and moved into a shared apartment the next week."

"Are you telling me that your dad and brother let you do this? Were they fuckin' nuts?"

"I was eighteen. They didn't have a choice." She thought for a moment, then added, "Plus mom said it was a good idea."

At his surprised look, she said, "Mom knew that I needed space. I couldn't keep living in that same bedroom in that same house. I was going to go crazy in

Fairfield. I don't know how she knew, but she did. I started working for Annie and after a year I discovered that I wanted to become a technician so I started classes."

Giving a little shrug, she said, "You know the rest. I had to get away. Being around you would have broken me."

"Baby, you were already broken." At her gasp, he held tight. "But I was too. Don't you see? We were both broken. But we're the only ones who can put us back together again."

Looking into his face, confusion filled her thoughts. "What are you saying?"

His hands slid once again to the sides of her face, holding her close. He pulled her gently towards him. "Suzy, it's been you since I was fifteen fuckin' years old. Only you. You had me then. You have me now. I let you go because that was the only play I knew. I'm not a kid anymore. And neither are you. We hurt? We do it together. We grieve? We do it together. We fight? We fuckin' do it together. We laugh, we share, we cry, we grow old? We fuckin' do it together. Is this sinking in, baby?"

Her eyes filled with tears once again, threatening to spill over. As one escaped and slid down her cheek, his rough thumb wiped it away. "No more crying alone, baby. You cry, you do it with me."

"I didn't think I could possibly have any more tears." Her face twisted in agony once again. "Brad, I try so hard to not think about the baby. But when I do...it kills me. It still kills me. For the past four years whenever I see a pregnant woman, I grieve. I constantly calculate how old our child would be and think of it when I see a child that age." Turning her tear-filled eyes to his, she choked out, "Will it ever be better?"

Pulling her head into his chest, cradling her once more, he made shushing sounds as he rocked her back and forth. *All this time I thought she had just walked away. Walked toward something better, when she was really just running away. From memories. Our hometown. Our families. Me. Anything that reminded her of our loss.*

His voice rumbled from deep in his chest and she felt it against her cheek. "No more running baby. You belong to me and I'm gonna be here. From now on, no matter what life throws at us, we're doing it together. Trust me."

She closed her eyes, letting his assurances float over her. Filling her. Settling once again into the crevices that that she kept hidden. With that, she allowed exhaustion to take over and she slid peacefully into sleep. Resting on him. In her bed. Where, if she had been honest with herself, is where she always wanted to be.

He let her sleep, his powerful arms around her, embracing her. Then he closed his eyes and allowed the peace to settle on him as well.

Chapter 9

A FEW HOURS later, Suzanne opened her tear swollen eyes, blinking at the harsh mid-day light. Her head was pounding and as she tried to shift in the bed, her ribs screamed in pain. Clutching one hand to her forehead and the other hand to her middle, she tried to roll over but kept running into a large object.

"Baby, what's wrong? Is it your ribs?" BJ's voice interrupted her confusion.

Brad. Memories of the emotional morning flooded back as she gasped for breath. *God, I slept with him again.*

She felt the bed move as he headed toward the bathroom and she could hear water running in the sink. A minute later she felt her hand on her forehead being lifted and replaced by a cold, wet cloth that covered her swollen eyes.

"I don't remember crying so much in a long time," she confessed softly, glad that the cloth kept her from seeing his face.

"You needed it, babe. You'd held things in far too long." He once again lifted her shirt to look at her bruised ribs. "Keep the cloth there while I get a shower going for you." He headed back to the tiny bathroom, looking at the shower. "Wish you had a bathtub, babe. I feel like you need a good soak."

"You and me both," she groused to herself. She loved the cheap apartment that was right over the clinic where she worked, but the bathroom…well that was where she longed for a tub instead of the tiny shower. The water running invaded her thoughts and in just a moment, she felt her side of the bed sink as BJ lowered himself down next to her.

Lifting the cloth from her eyes, he peered into her face. Her eyes were tightly shut as though she were not so much trying to keep out the light, but keep out the present situation as well. He leaned over and kissed each swollen eye. "Come on, baby. Let's get you up."

Assisting her out of bed and into the bathroom, she turned suddenly proclaiming, "I can handle this myself." Quickly closing the door on him, she stripped and stepped into the warm water. Not wanting to look into the mirror to see what he had been seeing, she wanted to wash the dog attack and the hospital smell from her body. Washing her hair, she allowed the warm water to sluice over her body, relaxing her for the first time since yesterday. *Was it just yesterday that I went to visit the clients? It feels as though it was a lifetime ago.*

Drying just as quickly, she carefully saw where a clean pair of panties, her sweat pants and one of his old t-shirts were lying on the toilet seat. *He knows about the t-shirts.* Smiling to herself at his thoughtfulness, she dressed and then pulled her hair back into a wet ponytail.

Walking into the bedroom, she was surprised to see him sitting on the bed. Suddenly self-conscious, she stood awkwardly at the doorway, unsure what to say or what to do. Pulling her lips in, she looked down at her feet.

Hearing him stand, she saw as his feet came into view. Bare feet peering out of his jeans stopped in front of hers. *How can feet look so sexy? They're just feet. But they're his.*

"Suzy. Look at me," he ordered gently. He waited until her eyes lifted before continuing. "Do you understand what's happened? I'm not leaving anything to chance anymore. I'm also not making any assumptions. I wanna know that you know what we are."

"What we are?" she asked in confusion. Licking her lips, she said nervously, "I'm…not sure I uh…understand."

BJ smiled, thinking, *Clueless baby. But utterly adorable.*

"You've been holding that shit in for a long time. By yourself. Baby, I talked to a counselor at the college and went to a couple of grief groups. Just to help. Just to process what happened. Not only with the loss of the baby but the loss of you. I grieved too and know that I always will. No one gets over grief. They move through it, working through the loss with others that can help. You, baby? You've carried that burden by yourself for far too long."

Pulling her lips in again, she said, "Then we kind of had a counseling session? This morning?"

Closing his eyes for a second, he opened them and pinned her with his stare. "Suzy, we re-connected. Yes, I'm gonna be here to help you continue to work that shit out. But baby, you need to clue in. When I said I wasn't gonna let you go again, I meant that I. Wasn't. Going. To. Let. You. Go."

"I don't know what you-"

"I've known you my whole life. I fell in love with you about eight years ago and that never really stopped. I buried it for the past four years. Tried to pretend it was just not meant to be or that it was a teenage thing, but seeing you at the wedding brought all those feelings right back for me. And I know they brought them back for you too."

Narrowing her eyes, she asked, "How do you know I feel that way?"

Smiling, he replied, "Honey, you have a drawer full of my old t-shirts that you still sleep in. And baby, you talk and you talk a lot of sweet when you have pain killers in you."

Suzanne's eyes widened as the blush began at her chest and rose to the top of her head. "Oh my God. What did I say?"

Chuckling, he pulled her into his chest where she found herself wrapping her arms around his waist. "Nothing much. Just that you never got over me."

"You shouldn't listen to people's conversations when they're not in control of themselves," she admonished.

With her head against his broad chest, she felt his laughter this time against her cheek. "You've been hiding from everyone for so long, even your friends who worry about you. That was the only time I think you've been honest about your feelings."

Deciding that staying quiet was the best thing to do, she just kept her face pressed against his heartbeat.

"And more importantly, you take this in and hear it well, girl. You and I are an *us*. As in you are with me and I am with you. We are once again together. I don't know how to say it any more plainly but since you can be adorably clueless, I wanna make sure you are not mistaking what we have."

At this proclamation, she jerked her head back and peered up into his face, confusion once again warring in her eyes. "An *us*?" As in a couple?"

He leaned down until his mouth was a breath away from hers. "Baby, we never stopped loving each other. Life and youthful decisions tore us apart, but those days are behind us. As of last night, we are back together. You and me. Can I make it any clearer?"

"Brad, I don't know about this. I don't know…" she said, panic rising.

"What's flyin' through that brain of yours?" he asked.

"We don't even know each other. I mean…we did.

But not now. I…I don't know you. I-"

"No doubt we've got some catching up to do, but baby, we've got time."

"I don't want to make a mistake. I don't want to assume that a past equals a future. Does that make sense?"

Nodding, he replied, "Yeah, it does. So here's what we're gonna do. We're gonna date. Get to know each other again. But make no mistake, Suzy. You're mine. I'm just gonna have to take this time to prove it to you again."

A slow smile began to spread over her face, the first one in a long time that felt as though it was coming from her heart. Feeling him pull her head back to his chest, she allowed herself to relax…really, truly relax. Tightening her arms around his waist again, she breathed him in. Strong. Masculine. Hers. And right.

BJ INSISTED THAT she rest most of the day while he made some phone calls. First call was to Matt and Lily. He talked to Matt to give him a few more details that she had been able to tell him about the dogs and the attack.

"Is there any way we can have the two older gentlemen questioned?"

"There's no reason, BJ. We've got nothing to question them about. Their dogs weren't involved in her attack and a citizen doesn't have to report something that happened to them."

"Damn. I was afraid of that. What about the creep that she says identified himself as the nephew?"

"Still nothing we can do. If the man wasn't in danger or asking for help, we can't do anything about who he has in his apartment, real nephew or not." Matt paused for a moment before asking, "You still at her place?

"Yeah. I didn't want to leave her alone while she was hurting."

"Uh huh. You sort your shit out yet?"

Silence hung between the two men.

"If that's your way of asking if we are together, then yeah. We are. But don't have Lily go throwing a party. We've got a lot of history and a lot of stuff to sort out and I don't want Suzy's head anywhere but with me right now."

Matt chuckled over the phone. "Gottcha. Lily was planning on coming by today to check on her. I gather that you'd like me to tell her to hold off?"

"That'd be good man. I want some time with just the two of us. You know some of that history is not good and I'd still like some time to help her with that."

"No worries. Give her my best and tell her that Lily will see her this week."

Hanging up, he called Shane next. "Just got off the phone with Matt so he can fill you in on the details I was able to get out of her. But just know that we're together again and tell Annie that she'll see her on

Monday back down in the clinic."

"Done, bro. Glad to hear you and Suzanne are tight again."

"Well, we've got stuff to work out and work on, but yeah it's all good. For right now, I'm staying here to keep an eye on her but I've gotta tell you I'd like to see her out of this apartment and in mine. It's safer by a long shot."

"Yeah, I couldn't wait to get Annie moved out of that apartment."

Saying goodbye as Suzanne walked back into the room, he patted the sofa saying, "Baby come here."

She looked at his face, then moved toward the sofa. As soon as she was within arm's reach, he gently pulled her onto his lap, cradling her once again. It had been so long since she had wanted to snuggle with someone.

"How are you feeling?" he asked.

"Sort of like I was hit by a truck," she joked.

He pulled her head back away from his chest so that he could see her face. Smoothing his thumbs over her cheeks, he leaned in and gently kissed her. Soft. Gentle. Full of promise.

"Who were you on the phone with?" she asked.

"I called Matt and Shane. I needed to let them know what was going on and what the next step might be. I also asked them to let Lily and Annie know that we didn't need them to come over today."

"That was presumptuous," she huffed.

"Suzy girl, I just got you back in my arms after four

years of missing you. Do you honestly think I am ready for a girl-gang invasion into our space?"

Giving a joking snort, she retorted "Girl-gang?" Then sitting up straighter she added, "Our space?"

Holding her face carefully, he reiterated, "Yeah, girl-gang. You know when a bunch of chick friends get together to hash out everyone's problems when the only two people who know what is going on is the actual couple." Leaning over to place a whisper soft kiss on her lips, he continued, "Your friends are great and loyal. They care and I think they'll be thrilled we're together. But we need some time to ourselves."

Feeling the touch of his lips against hers, her kiss-fogged brain moved to the next thought. "Our space?" she asked again.

"Babe, I have no idea what is going on around here and I know that Shane made this place as secure as he possibly could, but this neighborhood is not where I want you alone. So until we get you moved to my place, I'm staying here."

"Your place? I'm not moving in with you!"

"Why the hell not?"

"Brad, we're not ready for that."

"Suzy, we've known each other forever. We dated for several years. We've just had a breakthrough in dealing with the shit that kept us apart for four years. Now that we're together again, I'm not wasting any more fuckin' time."

Looking around at the tiny apartment, she admitted, "But I like my little place. It's the first place that was just mine. And it's above my work." Looking back up to him, she said, "I don't even know where you live."

"I've got a two bedroom apartment over in the Kent side of town. It's not upscale, but it's a nice place. I use one of the bedrooms for a study. It's only about a ten minute drive from here so work's not a problem for you."

She placed her small hand on his cheek, feeling the rough stubble underneath her fingers. "I just need a little time, honey. Give me a couple of days to wrap my mind around everything."

Touching his lips to hers once again, he nodded. "Whatever you need, baby, you got. But as long as you're here, I am too. I want you safe." And he added with a grin, "I want you." Taking the kiss deeper, he slid his tongue along her lips then delved in as she opened for him.

Her taste was intoxicating. Not intending to take the kiss where it was going, he felt unable to stop. His tongue explored her mouth, capturing her moan as she melted into him. His hands slid around her back, pulling her tighter. Hearing her grunt he jerked back.

"Oh shit, babe. I forgot about your ribs." Cursing himself, he gentled his hands along her sides.

"It's okay," she admitted grinning. "I actually forgot about being hurt for a moment."

Knowing if they continued to kiss he would lose all

control, he stood taking her with him until he could place her feet on the floor. "You stay here while I run to the grocery store. If I'm staying here for a couple of days, we need more food."

Suzanne agreed, knowing from his breakfast that a trip to the grocery story was going to be necessary. She walked over to her purse calling over her shoulder, "Let me get you some money."

"Babe."

She turned at the sound of his voice. It sounded pissed. Looking at his face, it looked pissed. Before she could comment, he walked over to her.

Lifting her chin with his fingers, he growled, "You don't pay for me. It may sound chauvinistic, but you're mine. That's mine to care for. Mine to see after. And you don't pay for my groceries."

"I've been on my own for a long time, honey," her soft voice floated over him.

Whispering a breath away from her, he said, "No more, Suzy girl. No more."

Turning, he headed out of the apartment and returned an hour later with bags of groceries. That afternoon, piled up on the sofa watching TV, he kept his arm wrapped protectively around her as she slept once more.

"WHAT THE FUCK went wrong?" Jorge growled to the two men in front of him. Their silence did not appease him. "She was supposed to be chased. Scared. Not attacked." His glare pierced them but they continued their silence, knowing the boss was not wanting to be interrupted with excuses. "Now the police are watching and a fucking guard has moved in with her."

"We whistled. Two of the dog came back. Devil's Spawn didn't. It took several whistles to get him off of her and back into the van."

At this, Jorge's attention re-focused on the dog's blood lust. "Pull him off of the guard fence. We can't take a chance that he'd escape and attack someone." At that the two men turned to quickly leave, relieved to be dismissed. "Oh," Jorge continued, "bring me his trainer."

The men nodded, avoiding looking at each other until out of the room. Jorge walked over to the window overlooking the city. A dog that strong with a blood-lust that powerful… that combination could bring him a lot of money in the fighting arena. He'd come a long way since his upbringing by a junkie, prostitute mother, and his early initiation into the neighborhood gang at the age of eleven. Marcel paid well. But it never hurt to have money on the side. Money just for a time when he might want out. Or when Marcel may need to move aside. A cruel smile slid across his face as he continued to stare out onto the city night-scape.

Chapter 10

THE DAWN PEEKED in through the blinds, sending shafts of soft light across the bed. Suzanne, always a light sleeper, felt the heavy arm across her waist and the firm chest against her back. The weekend had passed quickly and now it was time to face the world again. Trying to slide out of the bed quietly, she felt herself pulled back.

"Um, where are you going?" BJ's sleep gravelly voice asked.

"I need to get ready for work," she giggled as she could feel his cock press against her ass. Turning around in his arms she stared into his beautiful face, sliding her hand around his cheek. "I um…I'm not really ready-"

"Baby, don't worry. I can't help waking up with a raging hard-on just lying in bed next to you. But I know you're not ready for that. It was both a shit-kickin' and a great weekend and we need time to just get used to each other again."

Smiling at his understanding, she glanced at the clock on the nightstand. "You sleep a couple of more minutes and I'll hop into the shower. Then I'll fix breakfast while you shower."

"We gotta get you outta this place and get you in my apartment as soon as we can, babe."

"Why the hurry?"

"Cause I've got a shower big enough for both of us!"

"Somehow I don't think we would take things very slow if we're showering together," she said with another giggle.

"Humph," he growled before a speculative gleam appeared in his eyes. "But I have a huge soaker tub also."

"Oh my god. Now that will get me moving as soon as possible!"

She stiffly maneuvered out of bed and headed to the bathroom. By the time they were on their way out of the door, he almost had her convinced that moving to his apartment this next weekend was the best plan.

Running down the stairs to the clinic below in her fresh parakeet-printed scrubs, she began setting up the office for the day's appointments. Soon Leon and Annie came in, both looking at her speculatively.

Annie rushed over giving her a hug. "I was so upset when Shane said you got hurt this weekend. He told me about the dogs. And about Mr. Marchelli and Mr. Charleston. I just don't understand what's going on."

Leon walked over, hugging both women in his embrace. "Group hug," he exclaimed. Letting them go, he then looked down at Suzanne and said, "Something's different, girl. What's up?"

She looked between Leon and Annie wondering what to say; years of holding tight to her privacy was too embedded to suddenly blurt out her business.

Annie peered at her saying, "Shane mentioned that BJ was taking care of you."

Whirling around, Leon pounced on that tid-bit. "Big, bad BJ? Lily's friend? Ooh, girl. You been holding out on us?"

Blushing, Suzanne just smiled. "I told you we had a history. He came to help me and took me to the hospital Friday night. He stayed the weekend." Seeing their raised eyebrows she quickly added, "But not that way."

"Are you okay?" Annie asked gently.

"It was rough. We had…um…a lot to talk about. Or talk over. Rehash. Oh I don't know." The smile left her face as she struggled with what to say. "We had some things we needed to face and deal with. It was good though." Seeing her friends' concerned faces, she quickly added, "No, really. It was good. I had some things that needed to be talked about and honestly? Brad's the only one who could have understood. So it was good."

Leaning over to kiss the top of her head, Leon said, "That's good honey. You look better right now than I have ever seen you."

Annie continued to peer speculatively. "So where do things stand now? Are you two friends?"

Her flaming face was surely giving her away, Suzanne thought. "Well, we're kind of together. Sort of seeing each other. I guess."

Leon and Annie shared a glance. "Honey, that's the most unsure proclamation of a relationship I've ever heard!"

"I mean, he says we're together. And he spent the weekend, but nothing happened. He wants me to move in with him so it's safer. And he says that I'm his."

Annie smiled as she said, "Suzanne, for men like Shane and BJ, saying that we are theirs is a declaration not to be taken lightly." Walking over to her friend, she put her hands on her shoulders. "Are you ready for that? It's a consuming love but one that will take care of you in all ways."

"When I was sixteen years old, the idea of being Brad's was all I ever wanted. I think deep down, it was still what I wanted. I just assumed I would never have it again."

The bell sounded over the door of the clinic and the three hustled to begin their day greeting the first client.

BJ WAS OUT with Gabe, working on installing a security system in a home built in one of the newer subdivisions of Richland. The multi-million dollar homes were huge by any standards but the one they were currently wiring was larger and more garish than most around. Alvarez Security technicians had already completed the initial wiring of the windows and doors and it was now up to Gabe to coordinate the system and BJ to program it.

Since Lily, Matt's fiancé, had joined the team as a computer programmer that worked in their offices, it allowed BJ to work in the field more, which he loved. It gave him a chance to learn more of the security business and allowed him to get to know the other team members better.

Looking around, he asked, "Who lives in these mansions?"

Gabe, working on the complicated system, never looked up as he replied, "Corporate CEOs, people who made a killing on Wall Street, old money, new money. Hell, you could probably throw some drug dealers in and you'd have the whole mix."

"Drug dealers?" BJ laughed.

"I'm being serious. I'm not talking about the low-level guys. I'm talking about the ones at the top. The ones who rake in all the money and have all the power. They build big in some of these neighborhoods, lording over their castles."

"When you're doing a job, do you know who is who?"

"Nah. Tony'll contract to provide a security system to anyone as long as he isn't aware of any criminal activity. And everyone wants him because he's the best." Gabe thought for a moment. "Now if he finds out that someone is not what they say they are, then he has a problem. There have been times when someone has wanted an escort and he's picky about that. But most of the society's rich underbelly has their own hired thugs to provide their security escorts."

As they finished the system, they went back into the house to talk with the owner to explain how it operated. They were ushered into an opulent study, where they were met with a tall, long-legged blonde.

"Charisse, get these gentlemen a drink," came the order from the man sitting behind the desk.

"Thank you, but we won't be staying," Gabe said, walking over to the desk. "Your system is installed and programmed. The instructions have been downloaded and sent to the private email that was provided to us. If you have any questions, you may call the Agency." He handed the client the packet in his hands.

The man sitting behind the desk looked down at the papers in front of him then lifted his cold eyes back to Gabe before sweeping them over to BJ. Nodding, he barked, "Charisse, see these gentlemen out."

They followed the leggy blonde, dressed more for clubbing than home, and noted her nervousness.

"You okay, miss?" Gabe asked.

BJ noticed her smile did not reach her eyes as she replied, "Yes, I'm fine thank you. I must return now. Marcel doesn't like to be kept waiting." She closed the door behind them and they could hear her heels clicking rapidly on the floor.

Once outside, BJ questioned him. "You made that about as quick as you possibly could. Any reason?"

"Just got a bad vibe. I'll talk to Tony when we get back, but there was just something about that guy that rubbed me the wrong way. Now that I know his name, we'll do some checking."

"Won't Tony already know his name?"

"Some of these guys never use their real names when contracting services. The legitimate ones do, but the ones who aren't exactly making their money legally will use phony names."

"I'll run checks with some new computer programs that Lily and I are developing when we are back in the office."

Gabe nodded appreciatively. "Thanks, man. You just might keep being useful to us after all," he joked.

They drove in silence for a moment before Gabe asked, "So, you done anything about Suzanne?"

BJ was glad for Gabe's concern but found himself protective of his new relationship. "Well, after I got her home and she was feeling better, we had a reconciliation of sorts." He told Gabe more about the dog attack and then just touched on their deciding to see where things went.

Gabe swore at first thinking of Suzanne in danger then said nothing, just listening as he drove. "Girl's been sad as long as I've known her. If you've got what it takes to heal that breach and get the sparkle in those gorgeous blue eyes of hers, then I 'spect you're the right man for her."

Silence filled the cab as they continued back to the office before Gabe spoke again saying, "She's gotta get out of that apartment and neighborhood."

"Working on it, man. I'm working on it."

Gabe nodded with a grin on his face, leaving BJ wondering how he was going to convince her to move in with him.

By Friday, Suzanne and BJ had settled into a routine. She was upstairs in her apartment first and fixed dinner before he came home. After they ate, they watched TV piled on the sofa together before snuggling in bed. No sex. Just snuggling.

He checked her injured ribs each night, glad to see the bruises fade. Each day she seemed stronger, in less pain. And harder to resist. At night, he pulled her into his arms careful to not hurt her but holding her all night.

Saturday morning, the sun was brightly shining through the blinds when Suzanne opened her eyes. The now familiar feel of BJ's heavy arm wrapped around her middle felt comforting. *Can I do this? Can I open myself back up to the possibility that he and I can once again be a couple? What if he expects too much? I'm sure he hasn't been a monk for the past four years. What if I can't…*

"Whatever you're thinking, shut it down right now," came the gentle order against her neck.

"Well, good morning to you too," she said testily. "And how do you know what I was thinking?"

"Babe, we may have been apart for a long time, but I can still tell when your brain has gone into overdrive. You're getting ready to think of all the reasons we shouldn't be together. But right now, I think we've got nothing but good ahead of us."

Before she could think of a retort to that, she felt him press tighter into her. One of his hands slid around her breast while the other pulled her tighter to his crotch. Feeling his cock pressed into her while his fingers expertly rolled her nipple, she couldn't hold in the moan that escaped as she threw her head back. The shock from her nipple went immediately to her core and she began to push back, grinding her ass into his crotch.

"Baby," he growled. "Are you ready to take this to the next step? I don't wanna wait, but if you need more time, I'll give it to you."

"All I need is you," she moaned again, continuing to wiggle against him.

"Thank fuck," he barked as he slid a hand down her panties, immediately finding her wet as he rubbed her clit before plunging his fingers inside.

Turning her toward him, he captured her mouth in a hard, wet kiss. His tongue vying for dominance, tangled with hers and as his fingers mimicked the action deep inside of her pussy. "Goddamn, you're tight," he growled again, this time knowing his dick was ready to explode if he did not hurry.

"I'm sorry," she said, blushing at her inexperience. "It's been a long time."

He wanted to ask how long it had been, but knew that conversation needed to be tabled for another time. And right now…he didn't want to know.

He pulled his fingers out just long enough to slide her panties down her legs. She quickly kicked them off, wanting him to continue the blissful torture. His fingers found their way back to the prize. Moving them around her slick folds, he once again plunged deep while the other hand massaged her breast as he tugged her nipple. Determined to bring her pleasure first, he crooked his finger watching the expressions across her face.

Her orgasm ripped through her, sending her flying apart as the contractions grabbed at his fingers. As she came down he rolled over on top of her.

She slid her hand back between their bodies, finding his cock straining his boxers. Fumbling for a moment, she managed to wrap her hands around him noting that he was much more man than she had remembered. Working her hand up and down his shaft, she fingered the tip spreading out the pre-cum.

"You gotta stop girl, if you don't want this ending before it gets started," he warned. As he quickly pulled her t-shirt over her head. Straddling her, he stilled his hands, perusing her naked form. Perfection. Pure perfection. Just like he remembered. Only better.

Her breasts were fuller, rosy tipped nipples beckoning his mouth. Her hips were curvier but still showcased the tiny waist. Long, black hair spread over the pillow. And those eyes. Irish blue eyes. A blush was appearing on her chest and rose upwards across her face. She began to move her hands to cover her breasts when he stopped her with a command.

"Don't move. Don't ever cover yourself."

Leaning down he captured one nipple in his mouth, pulling it deeply as he sucked. His hand palmed the other breast before his mouth moved to give it equal attention.

The electricity jolted from her nipples to her pussy once again as she felt the warmth spread in her womb. An ache appeared and she began the age-old dance, undulating her hips upwards seeking…

He leaned over and grabbed his jeans lying on the end of the bed. Shoving his hand in his pocket, he grabbed a condom, quickly rolling it on his straining dick.

She watched him, wariness appearing in her eyes for just a second before the sensations of him teasing her clit with the tip of his dick took over. His huge muscular frame towered over her and his gaze was intense. She ran her hands over his rock-hard abs for a moment before sliding them up over his arms, shoulders, and down his back, feeling the ripple of muscle beneath her fingertips.

He looked down at their connection, hesitating for

an instant. *God, what would I give to go in bareback?* As tight as she was, he knew it had truly been a long time since she'd had sex. And while he hadn't been with anyone since seeing her at the wedding, he hadn't been a monk during the past four years. And that was a conversation he did not want to have now.

He hesitated after just barely pushing in a little bit, saying, "Suzy? We do this, you know what it means?"

Her wide eyes just stared back in question, her perfect teeth biting her lip.

"This is no fuck. This is real. This is us. This is you and me joining together in every sense of the word. Do you understand what I am saying?"

His answer came in the form of a smile. A light-up-your-life-forever kind of smile.

Without pushing in further he leaned over her body putting his weight on his hands in the bed beside her, touching his lips to her. "Gotta hear you say it, babe."

"I'm with you Brad. I've always been yours," came the whispered answer.

Plunging his tongue in her mouth, he plunged his dick deep into her pussy.

Gasping at the fullness of him, she reveled in the sensations. Her inner walls grabbed as he moved slowly in and out. "More," she said as her arms tried to greedily pull him closer. "Harder." She thought she had been satisfied a few minutes earlier, but with this fullness she was climbing higher and higher.

He chuckled as he continued his slow movements although it took every ounce of self-control not to pound blindly into her. Savoring every sensation, he could not remember when sex had felt so right. *Yeah, I can remember. It was over four years ago.* "We got a lifetime for harder and more, baby. Now we're gonna do slow."

He grabbed her hands in each of his, pulling them over her head. Leaning down he captured her lips once again, this time the kiss was even deeper. Wetter. Longer.

Lost in the moment, she could tell she was almost there and bent her knees up, giving him fuller access. When he trailed his kisses from her lips to her neck and down to latch onto a nipple, she flew apart. Her fingers, laced with his, tightened as she arched her back.

All of the nights she had lain awake, remembering the feel of him, a touch, the kisses…those memories were nothing compared to the reality of having him buried deep inside of her again.

Just then, BJ threw his head back, roaring her name as he powered through his orgasm. Collapsing on top of her, he quickly rolled to the side taking her with him. Arms wrapped, legs tangled, and bodies pressed tightly together.

As their breathing slowed she kept her head on his chest, listening to the steady beat of his heart. *Is this real? How can this be real?*

"It's real, baby," came his reply.

"Oh…did I say that out loud?" she asked, a new blush spreading across her cheeks.

Using his finger to tip her chin up so he could look into her eyes, he smiled saying, "Yeah. You did say that out loud. And yeah, it's real." Staring into the beautiful face that had haunted him for years, he had to admit that he couldn't believe it himself. "Babe?"

"Hmm?" she responded lazily.

"Do you remember what I said?"

She lifted her eyes back to his, uncertainty showing in their depths. "I…I'm not sure."

"I said that this was us joining in every sense of the word. You gotta know, this is real. This was no fuck for old times sake."

She pushed against his chest, anger now replacing confusion. "I would never do that, Brad."

He pulled her back into him so that they were once again pressed together, chest to chest. "I know that, baby. But I need you to know…I mean really know…deep down inside…that this is us. You and me. A couple."

A look flickered in her eyes replacing the irritation. As he stared at her, his hand cupping her jaw, a single tear slid down her cheek. Her lips pulled in, he saw her chin quivering as she fought to hold back the tears.

"Baby," he whispered.

That was all it took. That simple endearment. She closed her eyes as a few more tears escaped.

"Don't cry."

His gentle order wrapped around her heart. "I used to wonder…" she said.

"Wonder what, baby?" His thumb continued to move across her cheeks, wiping the tears away, wishing he could as easily wipe her pain away.

"My…my mind told me that you were gone. Forever. But my heart always ached. For you. For us. For this," she said haltingly. "But…we're not kids anymore."

"Look at me, Suzy girl." His warm breath washed over her, a whisper away from her face.

She opened her eyes, staring into the blue pools that were so familiar.

"I know we've got things to sort out. New things to learn about each other. You're right…we're not kids. But what we have now is just as real as it ever was."

His lips touched hers in a kiss so light she wasn't sure she felt it.

"Not ever letting you go again, baby," he said.

Pulling her head back against his broad chest, he grabbed the covers with one hand and pulled them up. They fell back asleep for another hour, wrapped up in each other.

A FEW HOURS later, Suzanne found herself entering BJ's apartment for the first time. She was surprised to learn that he lived only ten blocks from where the clinic was located but in a much more up-and-coming area. Here the old warehouses and buildings had been renovated. Modern shops filled the first floor and spacious, loft apartments abounded.

Fingers laced, he ushered her into a huge living area that extended to the dining area and kitchen. The breakfast bar was the only thing separating the entire space. Windows filled one wall of the room and with him living on the fourth floor, the sun streamed in.

His furniture was simple. Bachelor simple. A large sofa facing a large-screen TV. A kitchen table with four chairs. Two stools at the breakfast bar. He looked down at her, watching her eyes take in the space. Suddenly nervous, he said, "You can fix it up, babe. I know it's not much, but…"

"It's perfect," she said truthfully. Turning her head to the windows, she exclaimed, "There's so much light! I love my little apartment, but it's so dark. This is amazing."

He continued to hold her hand as he moved her to the hall next to the breakfast bar. Through the open door, she could see that the small bedroom was used as a study. It held a desk filled with more than one computer, a chair, and a bookcase.

Smiling up at him, she couldn't help but comment, "Your decorating is kind of minimalistic, isn't it?"

Tugging on her hand, he pulled her around until her front was plastered to his. "Yeah, well for eating, sleeping, and working…didn't need much." He leaned down and kissed her, licking the seam of her lips then plunging his tongue in as she opened readily for him. Tongues tangling, she wrapped her arms around his neck, trying to pull him closer.

Leaning back, he said, "Let's see the rest of the place. We might just find somewhere more comfortable to take this further."

Mewling at the loss of his lips, she smiled. "Lead on," she laughed.

Across the hall was a small, but beautifully appointed guest bathroom. The last door led to a spacious bedroom, again minimally furnished with a large, king-sized bed and a dresser. A walk in closet door was open, showing few clothes hanging up. The only color in the room was a dark blue comforter, sloppily pulled up over the sheets.

Leaning around, she peered at the other door in the room.

"Come on, babe," he said smiling as he led her over to the master bathroom.

Entering the large room she stood stunned, looking around. A glass block wall enclosed the shower area definitely roomy enough for two. And to the side, under the small window, was the soaker tub. Letting go of his hand she moved to the tub, fingering the tile as she looked longingly.

He watched her, suddenly hard at the idea of her soaking in the tub, candles lit all around, and her breasts peeking provocatively from underneath a sea of bubbles. *Damn.* The few women he had had in his apartment in the last year had never caused a reaction like this. Just sex. That was all they were. They knew it and he knew it, so he was safe on that score. Admittedly, there was a flight attendant that had regularly called when she was in town after they hooked up the first time. But again…it was just sex. And none of them had used the soaker-tub.

"Hey, where'd you go?" a soft voice broke through.

Startled out of his thoughts, he actually blushed. "Sorry babe. Just thinking of you in that tub had me distracted. That and the knowledge that this is where you belong."

She turned away from the tub and faced him again, reaching up to cup his face. "Kiss me," she said softly.

Smiling, he leaned down capturing her lips. First soft and gentle. Then angling his head for better access, he took over. Wet. Wild. Unrestrained. Picking her up, he headed back into the bedroom, laying her on his bed.

Hours later, as she slept in his arms he knew without a doubt, *This is where she belongs.*

Chapter 11

"SUZANNE? YOU'RE NEEDED in the first exam room," Leon called.

She looked over at Annie saying, "Jeez, the morning is busy."

Annie looked up from the lab table, nodding her head in agreement. "I know. It must be the holidays coming up. Everyone wants to get their animals vaccinated before trips."

Suzanne headed to the room and upon entering found a big black cat sitting on the exam table with a beautiful woman stroking its sleek fur. Long, blonde hair. Big blue eyes. Dressed casually and yet classy. The cat purred under her mistress' attention.

"Hi, I'm Suzanne. I don't think you've been here before."

The woman smiled and extended her hand in greeting. "I'm Sherrie. I just adopted Cleo and wanted to make sure she was up on all of her shots." She handed Suzanne the packet of papers from the city's animal shelter as she noted Suzanne's black-cat scrubs. Laughing gently, she said, "You and Cleo look perfect together."

Smiling as she quickly flipped through them, Suzanne nodded as she said, "It looks like everything is in order. If you like, we can put you on our Wellness Plan."

The two women began to chat as Suzanne did the paperwork after Annie's examination. "Are you new to the area?" Suzanne asked.

Sherrie smiled, her lovely face lighting up. "I moved into the area a few months ago. I'm a cocktail waitress." Looking embarrassed, she added, "It's for a strip club. I don't strip," she said quickly, "But the money's good for the waitresses." Shrugging, she said, "It pays the rent for now while I'm in college until something better comes along."

Suzanne walked her out to the lobby as she was leaving with Cleo and shook her hand. "It was nice to meet you." Leaning down, she peered into the cat carrier saying, "Bye Cleo."

Sherrie turned back toward her when she reached the door and said, "If you ever want to come to the club, it really is nice. In fact, there's a bar area that's in the front away from the stage." Giving a little shrug, she added, "The invitation stands, but I know that may not be your thing."

Suzanne smiled as she responded, "I have to admit that I've never been to a strip club before. Actually, I've rarely been to a bar. Although I've got a few girlfriends that I could invite too."

"The more the merrier. It's the Club Edge, right on

the river." Giving a little wave she left.

Leon walked up to Suzanne. "She seemed nice. I heard her invite you out. You should think about it."

Raising her eyebrow, she replied, "Are you sure you don't just want to go to a strip club?"

"Only if I can take my wife. Shirley would have my balls if I went without her!"

Annie walked in just as Suzanne was throwing her head back in a genuine laugh. Sharing a glance with Leon, she hugged her friend. "It's nice to see you laugh, girl. What's the occasion?"

"We've just been invited to a strip club, supposedly with a nice bar. And what's more...I'm thinking of going."

"Well, count me in," Annie replied. "We can get Lily to go as well."

Leon added, "Well if you ladies think you can get your bad-ass, alpha boyfriends to let you go to a strip club on the river all by yourselves, then you're loco."

"We'll just ask them to go too. What bad-ass alpha guy wouldn't want to go to a strip joint?" Annie quipped.

"The kind who knows that a ton of the men in there will be horny and somewhat drunk and if they can't touch the dancers, they'll certainly be on the prowl for the women at the bar. Which means your bad-ass alpha men won't be staring at the tits on the stage but will be spending their evening keeping other men from starting at their women's tits!"

Annie and Suzanne looked at Leon before the giggles took over. "He's right, you know," Annie said. "Shane would have a fit."

Suzanne had to agree knowing that in the couple of weeks that she and BJ had been back together, he would not be happy.

The bell over the door rang as the next customer walked in. Smiling at each other, it was time to get back to work.

"HOW'D IT GO?" Jorge asked as the leggy blonde climbed into his car after setting the cat carrier in the back seat.

"Fine. I told you it'd be fine," was the curt answer.

"Keep your attitude to yourself bitch. Just remember what's at stake."

Sucking in a breath to keep from losing her mind, Sherrie looked out of the window. "I remember."

"You do what's required and your sister stays in Marcel's good graces. And we know how much Marcel likes his main-girl's pussy."

Biting her tongue to keep from screaming, Sherrie said nothing.

Not even sparing a glance her way Jorge just grinned. "Yeah, his bed is a lot less crowded for her pussy than being back in his stable." He reached his hand over to her legs, sliding his fingers to the inside of her thighs. "Now your pussy... that'd be sweet. Sure you won't give it up? At least now you can still pick who you want to give it to. You keep dickin' Marcel around, he may just decide to take you too."

Shoving his hand away, she bit out, "Not interested. And keep your paws to yourself. I'm not on the table. I'm doing what I'm doing to keep my sister from any more shit than she's already bought. But I'm not Charisse. I'm not for sale."

"Oh, my pretty bitch. Everyone's got a price. When Marcel tires of your sister's pussy, you won't be protected. That day comes, I'll be waiting." With that, he dropped her off at a run-down apartment building. Watching her walk away, cat carrier in hand, he smiled before pulling back out into traffic.

BJ PULLED HIS truck into the alley behind the clinic, parking next to the metal steps leading to Suzanne's apartment. Jogging up the steps, the door was thrown open before he had a chance to knock. A hand reached out, grabbed his shirt, and pulled him inside before slamming the door.

She jumped up in his arms, wrapping her legs around his waist and pulling his face in for a kiss. BJ let her take charge for a moment, loving the feel of her pressed against him before taking over the kiss. One arm around her waist and the other hand supporting her ass, he delved inside her mouth, loving the taste of her.

The kiss was wet, hard and long. As much as he hated to, he ended this kiss but tightened his grip holding her even closer.

"What's wrong, honey?" she asked.

"Nothing babe. Right now, my dick's so hard for you I could pound your headboard through the wall."

"So, what's stopping you," she purred, leaning back in for a kiss.

"Matt and Shane are right behind me."

"Oh." A look of disappointment crossed her face. "Hmmm, so I guess a quickie is out of the question?"

"If I didn't know they were right behind me, I'd have taken you against the door. But as it is, let's get you moved out of here."

Giving a small pout, she looked around and said, "There's not much to take. I feel bad asking our friends to help."

"Baby, your stairs are treacherous and I'll need help getting some of the pieces down them." Giving her a lift up to let her know he was setting her down, he steadied her until she was safely on the floor.

"I'm not an invalid. I can carry furniture too, you know."

"Maybe when you were single, but not now."

"So now that we're dating, I can no longer carry things?"

"You can assist with light things but I'm not risking you falling down the stairs or straining something just to have you move furniture."

Putting her hands on her hips, she looked up incredulously. "That's chauvinistic!"

Just then, Matt and Shane appeared at the top of the stairs interrupting their argument.

"Matt, do you let Lily help carry furniture?"

"Of course not," he quipped.

Shane followed with, "Before you ask me, the answer is there's no fuckin' way I let Annie move furniture if I'm around to do it."

Throwing her hands up in defeat, she turned and stomped into the kitchen. Following her, BJ got right into her space and cornered her in with both arms on either side of her on the counter. "Babe, I've got no idea what's got your panties in a bunch. You can't tell me that your dad and your brother let you lift heavy things when they were around."

At that, she dropped her eyes while biting her lip.

"And I'm telling you right now. Part of being with me is accepting who I am now. Not the boy you fell in love with."

She looked up sharply as he continued to lean forward until his mouth was a breath away from hers.

"And who I am now is a man who will bust his back every day to take care of his woman because he doesn't want to see her hurt. Or stressed. Or anxious. Or in pain. All the beauty that's in her is what he wants to see."

A slow smile curved the ends of her mouth as she leaned in for a kiss. This one slow. Sweet. Soft.

"All the beauty that's in me?" she asked gently.

"Yeah, babe. The woman that smiles at me when I wake up and takes my breath away at night. You're smart, kind, a good friend. You love with all your heart. All that beauty is mine. And I'll move furniture. Hell, I'll move mountains to keep that beauty."

Her smile grew wider.

Kissing her one last time, he whispered, "Now can we end this ridiculous argument so I can get these guys to help us move so that we can have dinner with them and their women, so that I can finally get you naked and in my bed under me?"

Snapping her mouth shut, she smiled sweetly. "Yeah baby." Watching him walk into the bedroom, she smiled to herself as she pulled the beers out of the fridge.

THE GROUP OF friends was sitting around the living room area in BJ's apartment after getting Suzanne moved in.

Pizza boxes were on the breakfast bar, paper plates loaded with pizza on the coffee table. It was one of the contributions she made to his living room. It was big, wide, and easily held their plates, plus the chips and beer.

"I really appreciate all your help today," Suzanne said fondly, looking around the room.

Shane spoke first saying, "Girl, I couldn't wait to

get Annie out of that apartment so it was no problem wantin' to get you out as well."

Annie protested, "I loved that little apartment."

"Sunshine, when I first met you there was a door leading to an alley that had glass in it and no security system. It might as well have had a fuckin' neon sign outside that proclaimed it an easy hit."

Not able to hold in her giggle, Suzanne said, "Well I agree with Annie. It was a cute little apartment, but I have to confess that I liked the security that you added."

Lily looked around at the space and commented, "I really like your apartment BJ. I love my house, but it's a combination of little rooms. I like that, but this is really cool too."

BJ followed their eyes as they took in his space. He was proud of it too, but admitted that decoration was minimal.

"Minimal?" Suzanne exclaimed. "Baby, you had the bare bones of furniture. Of course, our stuff doesn't really match, does it?" she asked, a worried looked marring her beautiful face.

Leaning over to kiss a bit of pizza sauce off the corner of her mouth, he said, "Baby. It's yours, mine and ours. What's not to like?"

Her face lit up with a smile that hit him in the gut. That face that had looked at him in irritation when she was six years old. Looked at him in adoration when she was thirteen years old. And looked at him with love when she was sixteen years old. And every time it hit him the same way. He remembered Shane's words – *"You find somethin' in life so precious that you can't think of breathin' without it, then you do not let that walk away."*

Leaning back from the kiss he caught Shane's smile. Settling back in his seat, looking around, he realized how lucky he was. Good friends…the only woman he ever loved in his arms…and now their first place.

"You guys good?" Shane asked.

Suzanne smiled as she twisted her head up to look at BJ. "Yeah, we're good." A comfortable silence settled over the group. She looked around, thankful for the friends she had; and now with her furniture mixed with BJ's, it felt right.

Speaking softly, she said, "The breakup was on me. It was all me." The others stopped eating and looked up at her. Keeping her hands in her lap, she continued, "It just seemed like I need to say that."

"Babe, don't," BJ said, his voice low and gentle.

"Honey, you don't have to say anything," Lily exclaimed. The others joined in, agreeing with her.

Swallowing deeply, she said, "I need to. I need to say this out loud." Twisting back to look into BJ's eyes again, she continued, "It's like a weight that I've carried around all by myself for so long, as though it was my heartache alone. But I don't want it to always be the unspoken agony that makes others tiptoe around me."

He nodded but shifted her so that she was seated

on his lap with her back to the arm of the sofa, his arms wrapped tightly around her. Supporting her. Caring for her.

Facing their friends, she took a deep breath, feeling cradled and said, "We had been together since I was fifteen years old. When I was almost out of high school, I got pregnant. We were going to go ahead and get married, but…" She felt the familiar sting of tears hit the back of her eyes and she pulled her lips in to stop the quivering.

The silence in the room did not seem heavy…it just seemed still. Taking another deep breath, feeling BJ's arms tighten again, she looked up. "We…I had a miscarriage."

Annie and Lily immediately said, "Oh Suzanne," at the same time.

"Brad was there for me. The breakup wasn't his fault. I…don't know. I just felt like Fairfield was suffocating me. Everyone there knew. I couldn't move in that town without someone patting my hand and telling me that it was for the best."

"Fuck," Gabe said under his breath.

"So I pushed Brad away. I wanted him to have his life. And I wanted to go away. Away from memories. Away from…," she began shaking her head, "any memory of what we lost."

BJ spoke up admitting, "I should've never let you walk away."

"No honey, you can't think that. I needed to grow

up. I needed to find myself outside of Fairfield. But looking back, I wish we could have done that together and that I didn't hurt you in the process."

"But you two are together now. That's what matters," Lily added.

Wiping away the single tear that had escaped, Suzanne agreed. "Now we just have to figure out how to move forward." Taking a cleansing breath then letting it out slowly, she said with a small smile, "And this is a good start. Admitting the past. Facing my grief and not doing it alone.

"You're not alone anymore baby," BJ said gently, kissing her forehead.

"Neither of you are," Matt agreed. With mumurs of agreement all around, the group settled back to the easy camaraderie of good friends.

BJ WALKED QUIETLY into the bathroom, feeling certain that Suzy had fallen asleep in the tub. He wasn't wrong. Sitting on the tiled edge, he looked down. The candles she had lit sent flickering light around the room while the scent of her body wash wafted through the air. Her long, dark hair was piled on top of her head in a messy knot. Her thick eyelashes lay in crescents against her pale cheeks. Her body shape was muted through the water, but he knew it by heart.

The girl he had fallen in love with had matured into a more beautiful woman in the past four years. He could have stared at her all night but knew the water was cooling. Leaning down, he cupped her face placing a gentle kiss on her lips.

"Sleeping Beauty, time to get out so that I can get you dry, warm and in bed."

Her eyes fluttered open and she smiled lazily. "Hey," she said softly. "Have I been here long?"

"Nah. Only about twenty minutes, but I was afraid your water wasn't warm anymore. Here, let me help you," he offered as he reached down to assist her out of the tub.

She stepped out carefully into his arms waiting with a large towel. As he dried her off, she couldn't help but comment, "This towel is huge. And soft."

"What? You think I can't have nice towels?"

"Well, it seems…I don't know. I guess I never thought that guys cared about linens," she giggled as he spent time drying off her legs before moving upwards.

His lips replaced the towel as he ascended from her legs up over her stomach, causing her to giggle more. "I forgot how ticklish you are," he murmured against her skin. His kisses continued their trail up to her breast, giving one nipple attention before moving across to the other.

Suzanne's legs felt weak as the sensation sent a wave of warmth to her core and she could no longer stand still.

He swooped her up in his arms and stalked out of the bathroom and into the bedroom where he lowered her onto the bed. Crawling in with her, he gathered her into his arms.

His lips captured hers while his tongue explored her delicious mouth. The taste of her was intoxicating as the kiss went deeper. Wetter. Hotter. Moving his mouth over, his tongue found the sensitive skin of her neck as he continued to kiss down her body. Giving each breast attention, he elicited moans from her as her hips began to press against his body.

"Patience," he chuckled, his mouth moving lower. Using his hands, he spread her legs wide as he completely exposed her pink pussy to his eyes. With a growl rumbling deep in his chest, he dove in, licking her wetness before sucking her clit in his mouth.

"Aughh," she moaned again, her hips rising. He moved one of his hands up to her stomach and gently pressed her back down.

Plunging his tongue inside, he continued to lap her juices, loving the taste of her. His hand on her stomach rose higher until it palmed her breast, pinching the nipple lightly.

"Brad...I need..." she panted, feeling the coil of tension deep inside her core ready to spring. "I..." was all she managed to say as he gave each nipple a tug as he sucked her clit deeply to his mouth. Her pussy walls clenched and her orgasm raced through her sending all of her nerves tingling outwards. Throwing her head back, she screamed his name once again.

He loved that she still called him Brad, not BJ.

Brad was the name she first screamed in passion years ago and it was the only name he wanted to hear on her lips when she came.

He finished licking her glistening pussy before kissing his way back up her boneless body until he plunged his tongue back into her mouth.

She'd never tasted herself before and it was intoxicating as his tongue dueled with hers. Even sated, she still wanted more. "Please…I need you inside of me," she begged.

"Baby, this was about you. Just you tonight," he responded.

Her eyes imploring sought his as she captured his strong jaw in her hands. "This is what I need. This is what I want," she explained. "I. Need. You. Inside. Of. Me."

BJ held her eyes for just a moment, seeing nothing but truth and trust. Growling he jerked his pants off and rolled on top of her, stilling his cock just at her entrance. Holding her legs apart, he looked down at all her beauty. Dark hair spilling out on the pillow. Pale skin gleaming in the moonlight. Blue eyes looking into his. *Jesus fuck. She's truly mine.* A trusting smile lit her face and he swore his heart stopped as her arms rose up to him.

He plunged to the hilt, his dick reveling in the soft warmth of her body. Leaning over her, his hands on either side of her head, he pounded deeply as though trying to reach the inner most part of her soul. Hanging on to his self-discipline by a thread, he was determined for her to come again.

"Close, baby?" he panted.

"Yes, yes," was her reply as she grabbed his shoulders, holding on for all she was worth. The sparks shot from her womb out through her limbs as her orgasm rocketed. Digging her fingers into his arms, she cried out once again.

He followed her, his neck thrown back as the cords of muscles strained. Continuing to thrust until every last drop was drained from him into her waiting body, he fell to the side taking her with him. Holding her close, he wrapped his arms around her trembling form, pulling her tight into his chest. Legs tangled. Arms wrapped. Breaths mingled. Heartbeats pounding in unison.

Slowly awareness crept in and he looked back into her face, seeing her smiling at him.

"Are you okay, baby?" he asked.

"Perfect," she whispered back.

Kissing her lips softly, he replied, "Yeah, you are."

He cleaned her gently and then pulled the covers over them. Pulling her back tightly to him, he threw his leg over hers as his arm wrapped around her waist. Kissing her softly on her neck, he whispered, "I love you, Suzy. I always have."

She smiled to herself as she allowed the words to slide inside, warming her heart. "I love you too, Brad. I always have."

Nuzzling her one last time before sleep overtook them both, he replied, "I always will. You can trust in that."

Chapter 12

THE ARENA WAS small by comparison to the previous venues. A small warehouse basement...nothing remarkable on the exterior. A steady stream of men, some carrying cages, made their way into the barely-lit interior. The fight manager processed them as they came in and then sent them to a holding area. The head bookie, Taevon, had been busy all day, taking bets over the phone and in person.

Marcel and Charisse made their way out of the back of his chauffeured SUV, meeting up with Jorge on the inside. They walked uninhibited through the crowd as his security shoved people to the side. Ascending stairs at the back of the building, Marcel once again took his stand on a platform overlooking the arena. Charisse stood stoically next to him, seemingly nonchalant, but her awareness heightened to his every whim.

"Take tonight?" Marcel clipped.

"Good night. This expansion could be perfect. Taevon's taking calls from all over the state. So far, money's been tripled."

A smiled crossed Marcel's face as he nodded. "Everything ready? I want no fuck-ups. This time better be fuckin' perfect."

"Camera's been checked out. Internet thread looks good. Got the new IT guy, Charles, here tonight making sure it goes streamed as planned."

Out of the corner of Charisse's eye she could see Marcel's approval of Jorge's report smooth over him. His shoulders relaxed slightly. Her outer stance never changed but inside she heaved a sigh of relief. Marcel was much easier to deal with when he was in a good mood. She'd come a long way from hustling under the high school bleachers for some drug money. Being Marcel's main girl meant she was taken care of. Expensive clothes, jewelry, weekly spa visits, and all for the price of her body. She was fine with that – where else could she live so well? But his temper made life a little less palatable. Sliding up to his side as she noticed his head jerk, she linked fingers with him pressing her breasts up against his arm.

Jorge noticed and began to move down the stairs. Recognizing Marcel's approval of the night's plans, he set about to oversee the fights.

During the next two hours, it became evident their newest endeavor was going to make more money in one night than they previously had in three or four nights. Private internet streaming was allowing higher end clients to bet on the fights and watch them from their home computers. The money rolled in from not only the low-lifes that came or brought their dogs, but the take was tripled with the money coming in from the online gambling.

Jorge checked periodically on the streaming booth. The cameras were focused clearly on the fight ring and the on-line streaming appeared to be working perfectly. He liked the new additions. The screen showed the dogs listed as well as their fight record. The odds were in the corner of the screen, allowing the home-based clients to view as though they were in the building. As one fight began he watched the screen, seeing the dogs as clearly as if he had been ring side. He glanced back at the new additions to Marcel's team. They seemed intent, ready to make some serious money. He smiled; they keep making Marcel money they would find themselves well taken care of. He turned his attention back to the fights. The blood lust of a few of the dogs was going to keep the money rolling in. Satisfied that the evening was going well, he nodded to the men in the room and walked out.

As he walked toward the sawdust-covered ring, his attention was caught by a familiar face. Stalking over he approached the man, grabbed his arm, and whirled him around.

"What the fuck are you doing here?" he bit out angrily.

"What? What's wrong with my being here?"

"Your face is recognizable, asshole. You're in the clinic to keep pressure off of us and you're supposed to keep a low profile. Showing up here is not keeping a low profile. Now get the fuck out," Jorge ordered.

The man stared at Jorge before saying, "Fine, I'll go. But just remember who keeps this shit under wraps. You need me. Don't forget that."

Jorge watched the man turn and stalk away and a slow smile crossed his face. "Oh, I won't forget a fucking thing."

He turned and moved through the crowd, making sure the bookies were with their assigned security. Following them to a small office while the other security details were clearing out the building, he watched as the take was processed. Taevon came over smiling. "Still got monies being processed, but so far it looks like we've hit the mother lode."

Nodding his approval he made his way back to the other small office that Marcel had commandeered. Knocking, he entered to make his nightly report. A quick glance to the side showed Charisse leaning over a table snorting coke before flopping back onto the sofa. Her dress was pulled down around her waist exposing bite marks around her breasts. The skirt was also pushed up and with her legs opened, he could see the glistening fluid between her legs. Marcel had moved away from the couch, tucking his tailored shirt back into his pants.

"Sweet cunt, eh Jorge?" Marcel asked, a smirk on his face.

"Sure boss," came the simple answer, although he knew Marcel was already imagining her sister in that position. Not stoned though. Never high. That wouldn't be Sherrie's style. She definitely got the class of the two sisters. And as much as his boss liked to dress up Charisse…she was a hooker and would always be a hooker.

Back to business, Marcel sat at a small desk looking over the initial reports from earlier. Jorge made his way to him handing him the most recent information from the night. With everything in order and Marcel not needing him further, he went back downstairs to finish the night's job.

BJ SAT AT the Alvarez Security conference table with Matt, Shane, Tony, Gabe and Lily. Tony called the meeting after getting a call from Shane.

"Thanks for settin' this up," Shane began. "Got a situation and there's not enough resources for the PD to do the back-up research needed. Chief wanted us to brief you and see if Lily would be able to work on a retainer with us for a bit."

Lily looked sharply across the table to her fiancé. "Matt, you never mentioned this?" she questioned.

"Baby, I'm not in the habit of worrying you about my cases and especially not when they might involve friends of yours."

Those words quickly grabbed the attention of everyone else in the room.

"I think you'd better fill us in," Tony's voice broke

the silence.

Matt began, "Several days ago we got a tip about a new way to showcase and bet on dog fights in the city. We know they're prevalent. We know the street cops can't keep up with finding them, much less shutting them down. As soon as they break up one, two more pop up. And the money? One fight can bring in tens of thousands of dollars."

"What's the new way you're talking about?" Tony asked.

"Video. Secure live streaming right onto your computer, phone, tablet, wherever."

"How's that work?" BJ asked, his mind already running through the IT necessities for that type of endeavor.

"Don't know and that's why we're here. There's just not enough resources in the department for us to find out the source, how it works, how to locate the fights. Nothing. The only way we found out about it was by accident. One of our officers was at his brother-in-law's house last weekend and saw what the dick was watching on his phone. By the time he realized what was happening, the brother-in-law had shut it down and got off the account. It's not much, but Vice has been able to piece together just a little bit."

Shane looked across the table and said, "BJ, we know Suzanne got attacked last week. We've got no proof, but I've got a bad feelin' that it may not have been random. She's admitted and Annie confirmed that she's been lookin' into some dog attacks in the neighborhood. She may be makin' a target of herself."

"Goddamnit!" BJ interjected.

Lily put her hand on his arm in an attempt to calm him, earning her an approving wink from Matt. Turning to BJ, she said, "BJ, focus on what we can do to work the problem."

She looked back to Matt and Shane asking, "What do you need us to do?"

Matt looked first at Tony before replying, "We were wondering if you could spare Lily and BJ to do some IT investigating for us. Not full time...just enough to see if we can crack where the fight links are coming from. The PD can pay by the hour for some work."

Tony's reply came easily. "Absolutely. Whatever you need, you got." Turning to Lily, he asked, "What's on your plate right now?"

"I'm working on changing our programming for following some of the security feeds we have come into the office. But it's not pressing and can be done at any time," she quickly added.

Nodding his approval, he then looked at BJ, who was already anticipating the question. "I've been going out with Gabe and Vinny as they set up security systems but I can easily move some things around."

Gabe chimed in his acquiescence. "BJ's been a big help, but it's not necessary for him to shadow me at this time. Protecting the clinic and Suzanne while helping the PD is priority."

Tony nodded once again as he turned back to Matt and Shane. "Looks like you've got Alvarez Security in your corner."

They all stood as Shane looked to BJ and stated, "Couldn't ask for anything better."

THE NIGHT FOG was rolling off the river blanketing the couples walking toward Club Edge. The giggling was hard to distinguish over the grumbling.

Annie, Lily, and Suzanne were all dressed for a night on the town. Lily was wearing long, black, silk pants with a cashmere, pink sweater that dipped off of one shoulder. Annie, in a stunning green dress that dipped in the front showing off more cleavage than Shane was comfortable with, paired it with silver, strappy heels. Suzanne's red dress, which was modest in the front and had virtually no back, had BJ's blood pressure rising.

Suzanne looked up at BJ declaring, "You all have to be the only men in town grouchy about going to a strip bar."

Annie and Lily broke out into giggles again, while all three men swore.

"You think we're gonna be looking at tits?" BJ growled.

"We're gonna be doin' nothin' but making sure those horny men in there aren't staring at your racks, baby," Shane added while pulling Annie in tighter.

"Jesus fuck," Matt grumbled. "This is going to be such a mistake."

The three women protested loudly. Suzanne reminded them that they were there just to meet a new client from the clinic who had invited them. "We'll just stay to get a drink and check the place out. You do know that you could have let us come alone."

This statement had BJ pulling her around, plastering her to his front. "Babe, you keep this up and someone's going to find themselves across my knees tonight with that sweet ass bared," he whispered loudly while one hand provocatively patted her ass.

Coming to the club door, they were surprised to see a bouncer in a dark suit standing outside. The exterior of the club was ordinary but after entering, they could see the elegant interior. Dark wood paneling covered the walls with low lighting from sconces. A long, curved bar was situated along the right wall, the red leather bar stools next to the polished wooden bar. Red leather booths lined the left wall and beyond that sitting area was the stage with what looked to be a bar and stools around it as well.

Suzanne noted that Sherrie had been truthful about the strip stage being near the back with plenty of seating up front away from the naked entertainment. Earlier that day she had confessed to her friends that she was nervous about going to a strip club, even knowing it was going to be up-scale. She and BJ still seemed new to her and the idea of him gawking at naked women right in front of her made her nervous. She felt better when Lily admitted the same thing.

Annie had laughed when she agreed. "I know lots of women go, but I have no idea how I will react when women start taking their clothes off in front of Shane. But if he found out I went without him? Well, let's just say he can be a bit caveman when he wants to be!"

"I think Brad has been taking caveman lessons from your men. Thinking back on it, when we were together in high school he was definitely an alpha in the making but now it's…"

"Wonderful and annoying all at the same time?" Lily quipped.

So now the three friends walked in, curiosity mixed with trepidation.

"Suzanne, I'm glad you could come," came a pleasant voice from the bar. Sherrie walked toward the group wearing a modest black blouse paired with a short black pencil skirt. Black hose and pumps completed her outfit.

Suzanne was pleased and surprised to see the waitresses looking so elegant. "Hey Sherrie. I'd like you to meet my friends." She introduced the others in their group before asking where they should sit.

Sherrie led them to a private, curved booth that was angled slightly away from the rear stage. "I think you'll be more comfortable here."

The women shot her a grateful look as the men

quickly maneuvered their women into the booth.

Their drinks followed shortly and the girls began enjoying themselves. Suzanne noticed that the men actually seemed to relax as their fears about the club dissipated. Just then, the entertainment was announced and the raucous clapping from the stage area became louder. The dim lights were darkened even more as the dancers began their pole routines.

Curiosity took over and Suzanne leaned around the corner of the booth to see what was happening. The dancers were pretty but in a very heavily made-up way. Their g-strings were nonexistent and it did not take long for the tops to come off showing large, fake breasts.

BJ shifted her back saying, "Babe, is this what you thought it would be?"

She turned to see Lily and Annie both straining up to watch the show too while Matt and Shane tugged them back into their seats.

"It's kind of…seedy, isn't it?" Suzanne said, her face scrunched in thought. "I mean not the women. They're just dancing and their bodies are great. But…some of the men out there are…"

Lily finished her sentence saying, "Desperate?"

Annie was nodding her agreement as the men looked on in surprise.

Suzanne looked at BJ, trying to explain, "Some men are over there having drinks and enjoying the show. Quietly. And maybe under the table they are…"

"Hard and jerking off," Lily interjected again with a giggle as Matt rolled his eyes.

"Yeah," Suzanne said. "But at least there's a dignity about it. But some of those men…" she paused again as they listened to the loud, rude shouts coming from a bachelor party in the back, "are just jerks."

Sherrie had walked over to hear the last comment. "It's just society, sweetie. Some men think that if a woman dances nude in public then she is a prostitute." Nodding her head toward the stage, "Most of those women are single moms or college students who need the money and they'll never make that much doing anything else."

The noise from the back settled down as a bouncer convinced the bachelor party to quiet or leave. The effects of the drinks began to settle over the six friends and they enjoyed a night out. Suzanne bumped BJ with her shoulder. "I need out, baby," she whispered.

"I'm not letting you go to the ladies' room alone, babe," he said.

Rolling her eyes, they were interrupted when Lily and Annie both started to scoot out of the booth as well.

The men just shared a look, knowing women's penchant for going en masse to the restroom. BJ slid back into the booth, his eyes barely skimming the dancer in the back. *Pretty, but she's got nothing on my Suzy.*

The women exited the ladies' room heading back

over toward their booth. Sherrie came around the corner and greeted them. Annie and Lily walked ahead and Suzanne stopped to talk for a moment.

"I really like where you work," she said genuinely. "I was worried, but it's much nicer than I thought it would be."

Smiling, Sherrie replied, "Yeah I know. I don't like working in a strip joint, but my parents are dead and my sister has made some…poor choices. So I'm trying to make it through community college learning how to be a paralegal and this job pays the bills."

"Are you ever hit on?"

Rolling her eyes, Sherrie admitted, "Not as much as you would expect. The owner wants the waitresses to wear these short skirts, but our blouses cover our boobs. He wants to keep the men's eyes on the dancers. They are the ones who really bring in the drink money from the drunk, horny customers."

Just then, Jorge walked around the corner and saw who Sherrie was talking to. Before he was seen by Suzanne, he quickly turned and ducked into an office. Sherrie saw his reaction and fear flashed across her face.

"Are you all right?" Suzanne asked.

"Yeah, I just need to get back to the floor. I'm glad you could come in."

"No problem, it was a nice night out."

"Maybe we can go out sometime? Meet for coffee or something," Sherrie asked, glancing to the side.

"Sure, just let me know when and where," Suzanne

replied, her eyes darting to where Sherrie had been looking. Seeing nothing, she smiled and walked back to the booth running into BJ.

"Hey babe. I was worried when you didn't come back with the others."

"I was saying goodbye to Sherrie. Are you all ready to leave?"

"Yeah, another bachelor party has arrived and it looks like the back is getting ready to get loud again."

Looking back toward the bar, she saw Sherrie in a deep conversation with a dark haired man. Something seemed familiar about him, but the lighting was too low to get a good look. Whoever he was, he did not look happy. *I hope she didn't get in trouble taking the time to say goodbye to me.*

Glancing at the stage as she walked to the booth, she saw that new dancers had arrived and their pole dancing was much more complicated than the earlier girls. Mentioning that to BJ, he replied that the more seasoned dancers had the later shifts when the crowds were bigger.

"More tips," he explained.

Twisting up to look at him, she lifted her eyebrow. "And you would know this how?"

A slight blush moved across his face as he dipped in low to plant a kiss on her lips. "Haven't been a monk the past couple of years, babe."

Snorting at his response, they joined their friends in leaving, thoughts of Sherrie now out of her mind.

Instead, she found herself wondering, *What has BJ been doing these last four years? And with who?*

"WHAT THE FUCK were you thinking inviting that bitch and her friends here?" Jorge growled, holding tight to Sherrie's arm.

"You said to get acquainted with her and find out if there's anything she knows," she responded, jerking on her arm.

"Did you see who she was with?" he bit out.

"Her boyfriend and some friends of theirs. What's the problem?"

"She's seen me, bitch. I don't want to fuckin' run into her wherever I work. And those men? Gotta be cops or security. They had a look and I don't fuckin' like their looks."

"Fine, I won't bring her back."

"Make sure you don't fuck up again or your pussy's mine and I don't care who your sister's cunt belongs to."

With that, he stormed away leaving her shaking in his wake.

Chapter 13

THE NEXT MORNING Suzanne lay in bed, well sated from the previous night. BJ had barely made it home from the club before he was ordering her to strip off her dress. Feeling adventurous from seeing the dancers she gave him his own private strip and then lap dance. He allowed her to take the lead for a while, enjoying the show much better than the made-up, fake tits on the stage. But he soon took over and showed her just how much more he liked her show than the girls in the club.

Now they both woke lazily, bodies tangled together, as the early morning sun peeked through the blinds on the window.

A sound from the front door had BJ bolting up from the bed. Grabbing his pajama bottoms from the floor he quickly put them on.

"What is it?" Suzanne asked softly, not understanding his actions.

"Sounds like someone's knocking but I don't know who the fuck would come here this early on a Saturday morning. Stay here," he ordered as he headed out of the bedroom.

Not about to stay put, she grabbed his t-shirt and pulled it over her head just as she heard a female's voice coming from the living room.

"BJ! Hey baby, I've missed you," came a voice.

"What are you doing at my apartment Lisa?" she heard him growl.

The female's voice sounded less enthusiastic saying, "I just thought I would drop by since I got an extra flight last night that brought me into town."

"You've always called first, not just shown up."

"I...I'm sorry BJ. I thought it would be a nice surprise."

BJ was ushering the unexpected guest back toward the door when Suzanne came out from the bedroom.

Licking her lips nervously, she looked at the stunning woman in the living room. Tall, big-breasted, wearing a tight pencil skirt, silk blouse, and sky-high heels. Suzanne glanced down at the woman's feet and saw a rolling suitcase next to her.

BJ heard the gasp from behind and knew before he turned around that Suzy was there. *Jesus fuck.* Taking a big breath he turned and walked toward her, the unsure look in her eyes piercing his heart. Reaching her he pulled her stiff body into his arms whispering, "Baby, I love you. This is someone from the past. She has nothing to do with who I am now." Feeling her head nod against his chest, he kissed her forehead before turning back to Lisa.

Stammering her embarrassment, Lisa said, "I'm so

sorry. I seemed to have come at an inopportune time. I should have called first."

BJ, equally embarrassed, agreed. "If you'd fuckin' called, I could have told you that I was involved with someone and we could have avoided this entire scene. You've always called first; just showing up at my apartment is totally uncool, Lisa. We were never that to each other."

Suzanne saw the other woman's embarrassment and suddenly realized that she wasn't as upset as she originally thought she would be. She had walked away from BJ four years ago. She was the one who set him free, therefore she could hardly be angry that he had found other women. *I'm just lucky he didn't find someone he loved more than me.*

Disengaging herself from BJ, she walked toward Lisa with her hand stuck out. "I'm Suzanne," she said.

Something flashed though Lisa's eyes as she took in the dark-haired, natural beauty standing in front of her wearing BJ's t-shirt. "Oh," she said softly. "You're the one aren't you? The one from his past?"

Confusion lit Suzanne's face as she cocked her head. "I…I'm not sure what you mean."

Lisa glanced over at a visibly frustrated BJ and said, "I always knew there was someone special from his past. Someone he loved once. I had hoped that one day it would be me that he cared for, but I think I always knew that it was never going to happen."

Silence greeted the three of them as there seemed to

be nothing else to say. Lisa broke the silence as she leaned down to grab her flight bag. "It was nice to meet you Suzanne. I'm sorry that I made a blunder of things." She walked to the door before looking over her shoulder at BJ. "Goodbye BJ. I hope the two of you find what you're looking for."

He walked up to Suzanne wrapping his arm around her, pulling her front tightly into his side. "We have."

With that she walked out and closed the door behind her.

BJ and Suzanne stood perfectly still for a moment; the only sound in the room was their breathing.

"Baby, I'm so sorry. I had no idea she would just show up. She was never a girlfriend. She was-"

"It's okay. You don't have to explain."

He slid his hand down her arm, linking his fingers with hers, and tugged her toward the sofa. Pulling her down on his lap, he wrapped his arms around her. "No, I need to explain. In fact, this is a conversation that we need to have. And we're going to have it here, not in the bedroom. I want no ghosts in the bedroom."

She looked at him, not sure where the conversation was going and not certain that she wanted to hear what he had to say.

"I lost my mind when you left me, Suzy. When I finally realized that you weren't going to come back to me, I lost myself in the college life for a while. I drank, I partied, and I confess to screwing around. A lot." Seeing her wince, he looked at her blue eyes and confessed, "I'm not saying this to hurt you, just getting it out there baby. If we get it out there, then we deal. And it can't come back and bite us in the ass later."

She pulled her lips in, trying to quiet her racing heart, terrified to hear that he might have given his heart to others while knowing that she had no one to blame but herself.

"Honest to God, they were just fucks. That's all. But I almost flunked out one semester; my dad gave me a good talking to and I cleaned up my act. I focused on school and graduating early and getting a job. In the past couple of years, I've had some hook-ups. Nothing serious." Seeing the doubt in her eyes, he reiterated, "Nothing serious, not even Lisa. We met in a bar about a year ago when she was in town on business. We hooked up and agreed that when she was back in town we could hook up again. She's back in town every other month, so we had an ongoing thing."

Suzanne stared into his beautiful, honest eyes. "Define ongoing thing?" she said softly.

He sighed, hating the knowledge that his words would hurt her. "She'd call and we'd meet up. Dinner. Drinks. But it was always just sex. I liked her as a person but she was never, and I mean never, a contender for my heart. The last time she was in town was just before Shane and Annie's wedding."

He noticed Suzanne's eyes glance over to the hall leading to the bedrooms. He shook his head, "Nope babe. Don't even go there."

He watched her pondering his words, her face unable to mask what she was doing. "You okay with this, baby? I can't change what happened when we weren't together, but I'm furious that she showed up without giving me a chance to let her know about us." Shaking his head, both in anger at himself as much as Lisa, he said, "And I'm pissed at myself as well that it interrupted our morning." Sighing deeply, he added, "This is not how I wanted this morning to go."

She smiled a tremulous smile while lifting her hand to cup his face. "You're right, honey. There is no changing the past. Not before we broke up. Nor the four years since. You had every right to see who you wanted. I'm just lucky. So very lucky."

"Lucky? How, baby?" he asked surprised at her calmness.

"You could have easily fallen in love with someone else. I don't even know how you didn't, but I'm just so lucky that you were still here for me."

All that beauty, sitting right in front of him. Pulling her face toward his, he captured her lips in a gentle kiss. Warm. Wet. Full of meaning. Full of promise.

"Baby, I could have looked a million years, but there was no one in my heart but you."

She smiled at his words, leaning in to kiss him this time.

"I need to ask you something now." He took her silence as her acquiescence. "When we first made love after we got back together, you were really tight and said that it had been a long time."

She said nothing but just held his stare.

"How long, Suzy?" he asked dreading the answer as he thought of other men claiming what he felt was his even though he knew that was a double standard.

Silence greeted him.

His fingers stilled on her hips, pressing into her ass. "How long, baby?"

"What does it matter?" she whispered.

"It doesn't. I just want to know."

"Four years," she whispered again. Seeing the surprise in his eyes, she said, "There's been no one since you."

The kiss came again, this time hard and demanding. His tongue slipped in and tangled with hers for dominance. *A fuckin' neanderthal. I know it, but I don't care.* The realization that she was his and had only ever been his zipped through him.

Standing up with her in his arms, he carried her back to the bedroom.

"Honey, we don't have time. We've got to get ready to go."

Knowing how important this day was to both of them and their relationship, he knew she was right. He also knew that if he couldn't bury himself deep inside of her… "Can you take it hard and fast?" he panted.

Her smile gave him her answer.

Her t-shirt was up and over her head in a flash as her full breasts bounced with the motion. She slid her panties off as he discarded his jeans.

"Over baby. On all fours," he ordered and she quickly complied.

Sliding his fingers over her damp pussy, he was thrilled she was already wet for him. Plunging in from behind he pounded in, her inner walls milking him as his aching cock delved deeper and deeper. Leaning over, he held on to one hip with his fingers digging into her ass and the other hand circling around palming her breasts, tugging on her nipple.

Suzanne threw her head back as the sensations roared through her, straight from her nipple to her womb. In this position it felt as though he were touching a place deep inside of her that longed for his touch. Before she could warn him that she was close the orgasm flared and she screamed out his name.

With only a few more strokes, BJ also came as he poured himself into her. Continuing to thrust until every last drop was out, he gently lowered himself as they both crashed onto the bed. Breaths gasping, legs tangled, they lay exhausted but well sated. Slowly consciousness returned and he rolled over, pulling her with him.

"Brad, we've got to get ready," she said without enthusiasm.

"Sure you don't want to just stay in bed?" he asked, stroking her hip lazily with one hand.

"Umm, actually I do want to stay in bed. But…" she let the response hang between them.

"I know babe. We've got to do this." Patting her ass as he raised to a sitting position, looking down at her beautiful body, he continued lazy strokes along her back, hips, over her ass cheeks and…his fingers encountered a lot of wetness. *Oh Jesus.* "Suzy? Babe, I forgot a condom," he said staring between her legs.

She shot up off of the bed looking down. "Oh my God. How could we have forgotten? Oh my God." Looking stricken as panic began to rise, she said, "BJ, I'm not on the pill. They gave me migraines and well…I wasn't having sex anyway. Oh my God."

He followed her off the bed, grabbing her shoulders. "Baby," he said, but she wasn't calming.

"This is ridiculous, BJ. We of all people should know better. Just too much. Just too much on our minds. With the stress of the trip today and your old fuck-buddy showing up, it's just too much. I can't believe we didn't…"

Giving her shoulders a small shake before pulling her into his chest, he said, "Babe. Stop. It's okay. We've been careful. This was the first time uncovered. We're fine. It's going to be fine." Holding tightly to still her shudders, he asked, "When was your last period? Didn't you just have it?"

Taking a deep breath she looked up saying, "You're right. I just stopped my period so we should be good. Yeah. We should be good." Her mind working overtime, she emphasized, "But no more mistakes. I don't know what to do but I'll call the doctor on

Monday and see what other birth control I can take. Maybe there's something different that won't cause headaches."

Pulling her head back into his chest, he rocked her gently. "It'll be fine, babe. I'll make sure to not lose control again. I'll take care of everything. Trust me," he promised.

THE TRIP WOULD only take about three hours, but half way there Suzanne already felt nauseous. After her third huge sigh in the previous five minutes, BJ looked over saying, "Baby, it's going to be fine."

Shaking her head she admitted, "I want to throw up."

Laughing, he glanced to the side seeing the tension marring her otherwise gorgeous face. Placing his hand on her leg to stop the nervous jiggling he said, "Talk to me. Tell me what you're dreading."

"Honey we talked about this weeks ago when we got back together. Our first trip back to Fairfield to tell the families about us has disaster written all over it."

"Maybe not," he said. "Realistically, it's been four years. Our parents remained friends so there's no reason to think they won't be thrilled."

Suzanne turned in her seat so that she was facing him more directly. "BJ, first of all, your parents remember me as the girl that broke your heart and left you high and dry. They're not going to be thrilled about wondering if I'm going to do that again. Second of all, my parents remember you as the guy that knocked me up and then something happened that had me so upset and I later miscarried. Not to mention my brother punched you when we announced we were pregnant. We've both left home and visited sporadically for four years, much to the sadness of our families. This…" she pierced him with her stare, "is not conducive to a happy reunion where we tell our families that we are back together."

"Well…when you say it like that, I suppose that we'll be walking into a tense situation. But baby, it'll be fine."

"How can you say that?" she asked incredulously. "Haven't you been listening to me?"

"Yes and now you need to listen. Our parents love us. Unconditionally. And they wanted us together since we were children. I think once they get over the shock and work it through, they'll realize that this is our time. And they'll be thrilled." Turning his head to hold her eyes, he said, "We've got us, babe. It'll be fine."

Before she knew it, they were pulling into Smokey's Bar. Recognizing the cars in the parking lot wasn't hard since the bar hadn't opened for the lunch crowd yet. BJ's parents had owned the bar for years and it was known as the local hangout, best bar with the best chicken wings in the area. His dad, Bill, was a bear of a man with a scruffy beard and alert eyes that constantly kept watch over his bar – and his beautiful wife,

Wendy.

Suzanne had called her parents to tell them she was coming and asked them to meet her here. She told them to have Rob come as well. They had been curious but she'd simply said she needed to talk to them and wanted to meet there. Recognizing her brother Rob's truck as well, she sighed.

BJ reached across the seat grabbing her hand and giving it a squeeze once again. "It'll be fine. Trust me, baby?"

Nodding, she tried to give a smile but it felt stuck. Forced. Terrified.

Fortifying herself with a deep breath, she allowed BJ to wrap his arm around her shoulders, pulling her tightly against him as they entered the bar.

BJ's parents, Bill and Wendy, were in front of the bar talking with their longtime friends Mac and Bernie, Suzanne's parents. Mac was a barrel chested man, the fire chief for Fairfield. Irish to the core, he had his arm around his loving wife. All four turned as BJ and Suzanne walked in. The faces registered recognition, surprise, then…questioning.

The silence was deafening. Until Rob turned around. "What the fuck are you doing?" he roared at BJ, taking a step in his direction. His wife, Laurie, immediately stepped in front placing her hands on his chest. "Babe, stop," she ordered gently. At the same time Suzanne had stepped in front of BJ.

Both men instinctively placed their women protectively to the side, but neither man advanced.

"Son," Bill's voice broke through the tension. "Good to see you." Looking down at Suzanne he smiled. "Suzy, good to see you too."

Bernie moved toward her daughter enveloping her in a hug, squeezing her eyes tightly, fighting back the tears. "Baby girl, good to have you home." Opening her eyes, she looked up at BJ. Smiling at him, she whispered, "You too."

"Everyone, there's no sense in beating around the bush," BJ said, tucking Suzanne back into his embrace. "We've gotten back together and wanted to make this trip where we could let everyone know and hopefully have you celebrate with us."

Seeing his mom's nervous look and the unreadable look on Mac's face, he continued, "But I'm not going to stand for anyone upsetting Suzy. So if we can't be civil about this and move forward, then say it now and we'll leave."

Whatever doubts Mac was having must have left at that proclamation because he stepped forward to embrace his daughter, lifting her in the air with his hug. "Baby girl, missed you. It's been months since you came home and we've been chompin' at the bit to see you again."

Tears flowed as she embraced her dad. "I know daddy. I just…we just needed time. To make sure." As he set her down she saw Wendy embracing her son as well. After the parents had their greetings over, Bill invited everyone to sit down after scooting several tables together. Yelling toward the kitchen of the bar, he ordered beer and wings to be brought out for everyone.

As the party was being settled, Suzanne looked over at Rob who was still scowling. Not knowing what to say to make him feel better, she felt a hand on her back moving her toward a chair. Before she could turn, she felt BJ's voice whisper, "Give him time. It'll be fine." Nodding, she sat down then felt him pull her chair closer.

As everyone began to relax, the conversation flowed much easier than Suzanne had expected. She and BJ explained how they met again and keeping the explanations simple, they talked about their relationship.

The parents seemed genuinely pleased as they all warmed to the idea of BJ and Suzy together again. BJ got the feeling that their mothers would have liked to have begun wedding planning and hoped they kept that to themselves. *I don't want them scaring her off now that I have found her again.*

"Heard you were a real player after you went back to college." The statement hung out there, loud and clear. A definite conversation stopper. BJ looked across the table, anger pouring off of him as he stared at Rob.

Laurie turned toward her husband, but before she could say anything Suzanne's voice rang out.

"Coming from the town player himself before

meeting Laurie, I would hardly expect you to throw the first stone."

Rob looked like he wanted to say more, but Laurie's hand on his arm stopped him.

"But thank you Rob, for bringing it up. I suppose now is as good a time as any to get this all out."

BJ leaned over, "Baby, you don't have to do this."

"No, I need to. I'm learning more and more to talk it out. Rob," turning to her brother, "It was always me that stopped the relationship. Looking back I realize that I never allowed myself to grieve properly after the miscarriage. I shut Brad out and I shut everyone out. He tried…but I wouldn't let him back in. So what he did during the past four years is inconsequential. The reality is that we lost a baby and we were too young to know how to handle the emotions. I've started going to a support group for women who have suffered miscarriages." Looking back up at BJ, she smiled. "It's helped a lot, but us being able to talk about what happened has helped the most. What's important is that we've been given a second chance. Another chance at love. Another chance at life. That's what we're choosing."

Looking around the table, she stared into the eyes of family seeing nothing but love staring back. Tears streamed down her mother's cheeks and if she wasn't mistaken, her father was fighting them back himself.

Rob hung his head for a moment before standing and walking over to her. Pulling her from her chair he enveloped her in his embrace. "I'm sorry, sis. I didn't give you what you needed back then."

Tears flowing down her own cheeks, she held tight as she said, "Rob, I didn't know what I needed so you shouldn't be expected to have known either."

After an emotional moment that had everyone at the table in tears, BJ stood and gently took Suzanne from Rob's arms. Tucking her into his side he looked down at her, cupping her face in his hand. Wiping her cheeks with his thumbs, he said, "Told you it'd be all right."

THAT NIGHT WITH Suzanne held tight in his arms, BJ stared at her as she slept. Her tension from earlier had drained her body and she almost passed out as soon as her head touched the pillow. He had slid in behind her but raised up on one arm to stare at the beauty that claimed him. Her face, gentled in sleep, looked angelic. With the moonlight coming through the window, he could see the girl he had first made love to. He had thought her beautiful then, but the woman lying beside him now was even more gorgeous. The youthful adoration was gone, replaced with the knowledge that time and experiences, both good and bad, shaped the woman he loved.

Running his hand lightly over her face, he saw a slight smile curve her lips as she dreamed. Hoping she was dreaming of him, he lay back down pulling her tight. Then sweet dreams overtook him as well.

Chapter 14

CHUCKIE LOOKED UP from the reception desk asking if he could help, startling the next client who walked into the clinic. As Leon came in from the back, he rolled his eyes at Chuckie and took the information from the client before shooing Chuckie and Dwayne from behind the desk.

"Boys, you keep this up and Dr. Annie is going to have to put you on the payroll."

Dwayne looked confused saying, "What's payroll?"

Suzanne answered as she walked from the back with a yowling cat. "That mean's she'd start paying you."

"Cool," the boys said in unison.

"Guys, we just have one more client and then we're closing. Do you need me to take you home?"

"Nah, we're good," Dwayne replied.

"Dwayne," Chuckie whined. "I don't want to have to walk all the way home."

"It's no problem guys. Just hang on about another hour and then I can drive you. Is your dad at home now?"

"Nah, he's gone to work by now. Mom outta be home though."

"Good. I'd like to meet her. Especially if I'm giving you rides," Suzanne replied.

Later, as she pulled in front of their house, Chuckie bounded out of the car to get their mom.

"She might not come out," Dwayne said quietly. "It depends on what kind of mood pa was in when he went to work."

Before Suzanne could respond, a petite woman came out of the front door being pulled by Chuckie. She was wearing neat slacks and a blouse with her sandy-blonde hair demurely cut in a shoulder length bob. Suzanne got out and walked beside Dwayne toward their mom.

Noting the other woman's wary gaze, she stuck her hand out and introduced herself. "I wanted to meet you since I've given your sweet boys a lift twice."

At the compliment to her sons, their mother smiled as she looked down at her boys. "That's very kind of you. My name's Pamela. They told me what you tried to do for their dog. I'm real grateful."

"Well, we were just sorry that we couldn't do more." Watching the two boys run on into the house after saying goodbye, she decided to see what Pamela knew. "It, uh…appeared that their dog had been in a fight."

Pamela's eyes widened as she exclaimed, "A fight? I guess dogs will fight each other. My husband told me that you said the dog had been hit by a car. He must have misunderstood."

Misunderstood, my ass. He knows something, I'm sure of it.

"No, the dog had definitely been in a fight. And it looked like he had been in fights before."

"Sometimes he would disappear for a week or so, then my husband would turn up with him again and say that he found him roaming. I guess he must have been a restless dog."

"Pamela, you haven't heard of any dog fighting around here have you? I mean the kind where dogs are fighting on purpose? For gambling or anything?"

Shaking her head in concern, she answered, "No. I've never been around that. My husband..." she hesitated and Suzanne noted a thoughtful look cross Pamela's face. "No, no...I really don't know anything."

"Well, I was just checking. Anyway, tell the boys goodbye again for me." Turning to walk back to her car, she stopped suddenly. Walking back she placed her hand on Pamela's arm saying, "Be careful. Please." At Pamela's confused look, she continued, "There are some dangerous dogs running around and we're afraid of attacks. Please keep the boys safe."

With that, she got in her car and pulled away from the curb. She glanced back to see the concerned look on Pamela's face. She failed to notice the dark SUV following her. But Pamela noticed the vehicle that did not seem like it belonged to the neighborhood and she hurried back into her home to check on her sons.

BJ AND LILY had been working several hours a day for the past three weeks on an assignment for the Richland Police Department that Tony had agreed to. While they had learned a great deal about illegal dog fighting, they had not been able to isolate where the live-stream video was originating from.

Lily, rubbing her hand over her forehead, said, "BJ, I'm done on this for the day. I've got to finish the new programing that Tony wanted to be set up for some of his clients."

"How's that working?"

"We've got video surveillance outside of some of the clients' homes but some are wanting indoor video surveillance as well. I'm trying to see if we can use the existing wiring and then just install new cameras. I'm trying to make it so that there is as little interference to the clients' home as possible."

"I just can't believe how embedded these codes are for keeping us out of the tracking for the dog fights. We've only heard of this being used once, but I'm sure it's going to start happening more. I can't imagine the money these guys are raking in."

"You know, speaking of money. What would it cost to set something like this up?"

BJ sat thoughtful for a moment before answering. "I don't think the operation itself would cost a lot, but now that we've spent a couple of weeks trying to break this, I would say that a shit-ton of money was spent on the programmer who designed this."

Looking speculatively at Lily, he asked, "Do you know anyone who could do this type of work?"

Giving an unladylike snort, she replied, "Yeah. In college I knew quite a few people who had the intelligence. But…I have to confess that I don't have anyone in mind."

"Well, if you're going to pack it in for today, I'll catch up with Gabe and spend the afternoon working on installations and programming of some more new houses."

Saying their goodbyes, BJ headed out to the field leaving Lily inside the agency, pondering who might be setting up the illegal system. Picking up her phone, she made a call. "Professor Schwartz? Lily Swanson here. I wondered if I could ask you some questions about a project I'm working on? That's great. Can I stop by your office this afternoon? Good, see you then."

THE LATE AFTERNOON appointments were over and Annie, Leon, and Suzanne were cleaning the clinic. Annie, looking nervous, said, "Hey guys, can we talk before you all head home?"

Leon and Suzanne shared a worried look. Annie usually just said whatever was on her mind. The three of them had worked together for so long and so well that the clinic ran smoothly with Annie's laid-back leadership.

"Sure doc. What's on your mind?" Leon queried.

"I don't know how to say this, so I am just going to blurt it out. I'm thinking of selling this clinic and buying a clinic out in the country. It's always been my dream to be able to expand and include boarding animals. I've thought about it so much and tried to weigh the pros and cons until my brain is exploding. But I found one I liked and…"

"What do you need us to do?" Suzanne asked quietly. The idea of not working for Annie terrified her, but she wanted her friend to have her dream.

Annie looked at her two dearest friends and employees. "I…I would…well, only if you want to that is. I…I'd really like you to come with me."

Leon jumped up hugging Annie while shouting, "Thank God girl. You had me worried!"

Annie giggled as Leon lifted her in the air. "Of course I want you with me. I know that you may not want to go…"

"Not want to go?" Suzanne questioned. "Just try to keep us away!"

"So tell us about this clinic," Leon ordered.

"It's on the west side of town, only about ten miles outside the city limits. So it's close for a commute but far enough away that there is some land around it. The clinic isn't too large but has room for expansion. It's being sold by a veterinarian whose husband has gotten transferred. It already has boarding kennels built and has great potential. There are several subdivisions nearby so there is a ready client-base."

Suzanne quickly calculated and said, "That would only be about a twenty minute drive for me which isn't bad." Then laughing added, "Of course, when I lived above this clinic that was the ultimate in convenience!"

"So where are you in the process?" Leon asked.

"Shane and I have talked it over and we think that if I go ahead and start advertising this clinic and can find a buyer, then I'll let the other clinic know that I'm definitely interested."

"Do you know of anyone who would like to buy this clinic?" Suzanne asked.

"Strangely enough, yes. Dr. Ketchum has said he was interested."

"Dr. Ketchum?" Suzanne exclaimed. "Why? He's just right down the street."

"Well, according to him, he hates the hours that he has to work as the ER vet and if he owned his own practice, he could set his schedule and make more money. Plus he says he's really interested in staying in this part of the city."

"Hey, to each his own," Leon quipped.

"We haven't sat down and discussed finances yet, but he says he has the money to buy me out here, so we'll see. Of course, he would like to keep both of you here working for him," Annie added.

"No, not happening," Leon stated firmly.

Shaking her head speculatively, Suzanne added,

"Strange that he wants to stay here. This part of town is kind of run-down. And if he isn't getting much money where he is, how will he buy you out?"

Annie just shrugged as the three of them continued their conversation over the evening clinic clean-up.

THAT NIGHT, BJ held Suzanne after they had made love; first against the shower wall, then he went down on her while she sat on the bathroom counter, then finally ending up in the bed. She, in her post-orgasmic bliss, curled up tightly to him as he held her cheek to his chest.

"Baby?"

"Hmmm?" was the only response he received.

"Are you okay with Annie selling the practice? You seemed distracted when you told me at dinner."

She pulled herself up to a sitting position looking into his concerned face. Smiling, she said, "Yeah, I am. It'll be nice to have a newer, larger space to work in. And I can't imagine working for anyone else but her. It's just…I don't know."

"Don't know what?" he prodded.

She thought for a moment before answering. "I've gotten used to the patients. I recognize them when I see them on the street. It's kind of like belonging. And then there's Chuckie and Dwayne. I feel like I'll be abandoning them."

"How so? There will be another vet there, so all

your former clients will have someone to see. And the kids have parents, honey."

"I know, but with all the crazy dog stuff going on, I'm kind of afraid for them. I didn't mention it, but I'm almost certain that their dad may have known their dog was in fights. I'm pretty sure the mom didn't know though."

At that BJ leaned away from the headboard and twisted his body to face hers. "What are you telling me? Have you been checking up on things?"

"I've been doing some research on dog fights. Brad, it's horrible. They hurt the dogs, starve the dogs, bait the dogs…anything to make them mean. They even breed them to be as mean as possible!"

"Suzy, I know this, but what I want to know is why the hell you are checking into this? I don't want you anywhere near this investigation!"

She eyed him speculatively. "What investigation?"

"Your attack along with other suspicious activity has Vice looking into illegal dogfighting. Matt and Shane have asked Alvarez Security to check into some things." Seeing Suzanne about to speak, he continued, "Hold on, baby. You need to do your job and part of that is letting us know what suspicions you have. Not go fuckin' investigate them yourself."

That bought him a huff, but he wasn't finished. Taking her face in his hands, he said, "You gotta stay safe for me. I need you to promise."

He brought her lips in for a soft kiss, one that

begged her to listen to him. Melting into his embrace, she agreed.

"I love you Suzy girl. I've loved you as long as I can remember."

Her voice caught in her throat as she answered, "I've loved you forever. Absolutely forever."

He deepened the kiss; this time it spoke of a future. Tucking her back into his side, he wrapped his arms around her protectively.

She filled him in on her fears about the kids' dog and her conversations with both parents. BJ promised to talk to Matt and Shane and let her know what they found out.

Sliding back into bed, he leaned over her body to turn out her light before pulling her over to turn out his. Then tucking her tightly into his embrace, they drifted off to sleep.

JORGE GAVE THE nod to the men holding Mr. Johnson between them. Bruised and bloodied, his face battered, he sagged as he tried to plead.

Another punch to the stomach had Chuckie and Dwayne's dad panting on the floor.

"What did you do with your dog?" came the calm question.

"Told you," he replied, spitting out blood. "He ran off."

"Why was he not chained up? You know the security that's needed."

"I had him chained. My kids musta let him off."

"You had a dog trained to fight and let your kids get him loose?"

"I…I…uh –"

Another punch followed.

"Sorry. I'm sorry," he pleaded.

Looking bored, Jorge stared down at the man groveling in front of him. Stepping forward, he put his shoe on the man's neck and said, "You still owe money from your last fight. I suggest you find a way to pay back what you owe or our next visit will not be so…pleasant."

Jerking his head to the side, he and the two associates walked over to their SUV and climbed in, leaving Mr. Johnson laying on the ground wondering how he would ever be able to pay his debt.

His wife was asleep when he crawled into bed that night but was up with the boys when he came out the next morning. The gasps from his family weren't needed to remind him that his face looked as bad as he felt.

Facing her husband, she quietly said, "Do you need some ice?" as she stared at his swollen face.

"Ice ain't gonna fix this, woman. I need money. When's your next paycheck?"

"You know I get paid every other Friday and that'll be this week. Why? You know we need that 'cause rent is due."

"Ain't gonna be able to pay rent this month. I gotta have that money. I get paid on Thursday, so I gotta take it all to pay someone."

Keeping her voice low, Pamela said, "Joe, we need that money. What'll we live off of if you take it all to pay someone for your gambling?"

He took a step toward her, his fist raised, "Don't want any of your lip, woman. I need that money or you'll end up looking like me. You understand? Those stupid kids of ours made a fuck-up of things and now I gotta get some money to make it right."

Dwayne made a move toward his mom, but she put her hand out to stop him.

Her eyes narrowed on her husband. "Our kids? What have you done that involved the boys?"

Turning to Chuckie and Dwayne, he shouted, "Get to school."

Looking scared, they turned to their mother to see what they should do.

"Don't look at her, you little shits. This is all your fault anyway. Get outta here," he growled.

Pamela quickly nodded to them, grabbing their sack lunches off of the counter before hustling them out of the door.

Seeing them walk down the sidewalk, she waved as they turned back to look at her, anxiety written on their faces.

Stepping menacingly closer, his hands balled into fists, he growled, "Don't question me. They took that goddamn dog to the doctor when it died anyway. Got that vet gal stickin' her nose where it don't belong. If that ain't enough trouble, I owe money for that damn dog now."

"Well, you can't have my paycheck. We need that to live on. What'll the boys eat if I can't get to the grocery store?"

"Stupid cow, what'll they eat if I don't come back?"

At this Pamela paled. "What on earth have you gotten yourself into? And what are you dragging this family into?"

"I ain't answering no more questions. You get that money on Friday and you get it in my hands." With that, he turned and headed back to the bedroom.

Pamela stood shaking in the kitchen for several minutes before she noticed the clock. Realizing she was going to be late for work, she headed out of the door quickly, her mind racing.

THAT AFTERNOON, CHUCKIE and Dwayne bounded into the clinic looking for Suzanne. She walked out of an exam room and saw them in the reception area.

"Hey guys, how was school?"

The two boys shared a glance and then looked back at her.

She moved to stand in front of them. "What's up? Did something happen at school?"

Chuckie looked at Dwayne then burst out, "Dad

got beat up and he's gonna take all mom's money."

"Shut up Chuckie," Dwayne said, looking uncomfortable.

Another client came in and Suzanne checked them in then called for Leon. When he came from the back, she asked quietly if he could see the cat because she needed to talk to the boys. Leon readily agreed and she told the boys to follow her.

Passing Annie, she motioned for the boys to go into the small office. Giving Annie a quick explanation, she followed them in and shut the door. Setting them in the chairs, she leaned against the desk and said, "Okay, guys. Tell me what is going on."

Chuckie was quiet now, looking to Dwayne for instructions. Dwayne sighed and finally said, "Pa's gotten into some kind of trouble." He told Suzanne what had happened that morning.

Her anger began to rise as she realized that their dog had probably been in fights and that their dad must have been the one who was doing that. Determined to keep from scaring them, she asked just a few questions and then told them that they could hang out in the clinic until their mom got home. "I'll drive you all home today to make sure you're safe and that way I can also chat with your mom. Just to make sure everything is okay," she added.

A few hours later, she pulled up to their house. Pamela was getting out of her car and when she saw the boys she smiled, welcoming them with hugs. Suzanne walked over to greet her then said, "Hey boys, why don't you run inside and let me talk to your mom."

They boys looked warily around, then obeyed.

"Pamela, I won't beat around the bush. The boys came to tell me what was going on and I wanted to make sure that they and you're all right."

Sighing, Pamela looked down at her hands. "I'm sorry they drug you into this. We're going to be fine, I'm sure. He's just gotten into a little money trouble and he wasn't in a good mood this morning."

Placing her hand on Pamela's arm, Suzanne said, "I know he was beaten up. I don't want to embarrass you or make things worse. I'm just concerned about the boys…and about you."

Drawing herself up, Pamela said, "Thank you. Really. You are making me realize that I can't take a chance with my boys. Whatever trouble Joe's gotten into, he's going to have to get out of it himself. I have to protect the boys."

Smiling her encouragement, Suzanne shared her cell phone number with Pamela. "The boys have my number, but I want you to have it too. If you need me for anything – anything at all – just call. Day or night. Please."

Looking down at the number written on the back of a clinic business card, Pamela smiled. "I will."

Suzanne waved at the boys still standing at the door and turned to get back into her car.

"Ms. McDonald?"

Turning back, she replied, "Please, call me Suzanne."

"Thank you for caring about my boys, Suzanne," their mom said with tears in her eyes.

Smiling, Suzanne just nodded before getting into her car and driving away.

THREE NIGHTS LATER Suzanne's cell phone rang, jarring her out of sleep. BJ reached for it first, looking at the number which had come up as **Unknown**. Suzanne was sitting up trying to focus her eyes when she saw BJ answer the phone. Glaring, she held out her hand.

"Who is this?" he answered.

"I...I...uh...I'm trying to reach Miss Suzanne," came the small boy's voice.

BJ turned his questioning gaze to her and he gentled his voice as he questioned. "She's here but I need to know who's calling."

"Can you tell her it's Dwayne?"

BJ said, "Dwayne, I'm going to put you on speaker so that Miss Suzanne can hear you, but I can hear as well."

She quickly asked, "Dwayne, where are you? Are you all right? Is Chuckie with you? Where's your mom?"

"Baby, let him talk," BJ whispered.

"We're not at home. Mom and Chuckie's with me.

We're at some place called Safe Haven."

Suzanne's eyes quickly looked to BJ's in confusion. He whispered again, "That's a shelter for women and their children who need to get away from a volatile situation at home."

Nodding her understanding she continued, "Dwayne, what do you need me to do?"

"I told momma to call you but she didn't want to bother you in the middle of the night. She and Chuckie are asleep, but I wanted to let you know where we were. Didn't want you going by the house and us not be there."

"Oh honey, thank you so much. Can you tell me what happened?"

"Pa's been upset for a couple of days. Think he owes money to someone. Yelled at momma to give him her pay and she said we'd have no money for rent or food. He said he didn't care and last night he hit her. I tried to stop him, but he hit her again then hit me before he left. Said when he got back, she'd better have the money."

She looked at BJ with tears in her eyes, not trusting her voice to speak. BJ took over asking, "What happened after that Dwayne?"

"Momma packed up some stuff and we left. Got on a couple of buses so I don't have any idea where we are. She said she'd already found a place for us to go if he got mean."

"Sweetie, I'm so glad you called," Suzanne said.

"Dwayne? This is BJ, Suzanne's boyfriend. You did real good, man, trying to take care of your mom. Right now, you need to get some sleep. In the morning tell your mom that you called Miss Suzanne and tell her that we'll come visit you tomorrow to see what we can do to help. We may even bring some friends with us. Okay, buddy?"

"Yeah. Thanks. Suzanne?"

"I'm here, honey," she answered.

"Well…thanks. I'm glad we met you. You're sweet."

"Oh honey," her voice choked. "Hug your brother for me."

BJ hung up the phone, replacing it on his side of the bed. Seeing her questioning gaze, he said, "Baby, anyone who calls in the middle of the night is never gonna have good news unless it's a birth and we've got no friends expecting now. On top of that, it was Unknown. I'm not having you deal with anything like that alone. I take care of you so you can take care of others."

A lone tear escaped down her cheek. "Thank you," she said softly, his words flowing over her.

"Why are you crying, baby?"

"Because I've got a man who wants to take care of me. Pamela doesn't have that."

Sucking in a deep breath, BJ nodded. "We'll go see her tomorrow, Suzy, and see what we can do to help. I'll call Matt and Shane in the morning and they may go with us."

"But they're Vice. They don't deal with domestic violence."

BJ cupped her face with his hand. "You told me that you have a bad feeling that he may be involved with dog fighting or at least had his dog in fighting. This makes it a Vice problem."

She leaned her head into his hand, feeling the warmth seeping into her. They slid back down in the bed, pulling the covers up. He wrapped his arms around her and threw one leg over her thigh, enveloping her in his warmth and protection.

"Love you, baby. We'll take care of the boys tomorrow. Trust me."

Pressing her face into his chest, she nodded. "Love you too, BJ." Then she allowed sleep to overtake her once again.

Chapter 15

THE NEXT DAY, Matt and Shane met them at the Safe Haven House. Suzanne filled them in on what she knew about the dog that the boys had brought into the clinic. They promised to check to see what happened to the report that Annie had made to Animal Control. She took the boys to the den area while BJ, Matt, and Shane talked to Pamela.

After being satisfied that she was pressing charges against her husband and with the information that she gave them, Matt and Shane left. They were opening up an investigation on Joe and his possible involvement in dog fighting. BJ walked into the living area with Pamela.

"Dwayne, let's go outside and talk for a bit," he said.

Suzanne nodded to Dwayne and smiled at Pamela. After the two had left the room, Suzanne turned to her and said, "Don't worry. I think Dwayne just needs some man time. And there's no one better to give it to him than Brad."

Blushing, Pamela looked at Chuckie for a moment but his attention was riveted to the TV. She nodded as she spoke softly, "Joe started out that way. He was a good husband. A good father. But lately…he's gotten so messed up in something. Then he got grouchy, then mean, then needing our food money." Looking back down at Chuckie, she said, "I can take a lot. But I'm not taking a man hitting on me or hitting on the boys."

"What will you do?" Suzanne asked, leaning over to place her hand on Pamela's arm. "What can I do to help?"

Sighing, Pamela's reply came hesitantly. "Well, they've got real good help here at Safe Haven. We can stay here for a month if needed, but I've got my money and a bit saved that Joe didn't know about. They'll help me find an apartment. I've still got my job, which pays decently. I just need to make sure the kids are in school and safe after school."

Suzanne quickly said, "The boys can keep coming over to the clinic after school and I'll bring them here when you're off of work."

"That's sweet, but the Haven has an agreement with the local Boys Club for after school care. I'll have them do that."

"Well, if you ever need me, just call. You know, Brad and I are visiting our parents in Fairfield for Thanksgiving next week. My parents throw a huge meal for anyone and everyone. How about if we pick you all up and take you? The boys'll love it."

Smiling the first smile of the day, Pamela agreed. "I think I'll take you up on that. It'd be real good for the boys to be around good people then."

Coming back in from the front porch, BJ's arm slung loosely around Dwayne's shoulder as he and Suzanne exchanged looks, both assuring each other that everything was fine. She kissed the boys goodbye and hugged Pamela.

BJ pulled her in close to his body as they walked back out to his SUV.

"Honey, I invited them to our family's Thanksgiving next week," she said.

Leaning his tall frame over to kiss the top of her head as he pulled her tighter and he said, "Baby, you're the best."

"I CAN'T BELIEVE what a terrible story that is," Sherrie said, her face filled with concern. She and Suzanne had met for coffee several days after Pamela and the boys had escaped.

"It is horrible, isn't' it? Suzanne agreed. "We're taking them to our family for Thanksgiving so at least the boys will have a good feast."

Sherrie, not able to look Suzanne in the eyes, played with her pastry and barely sipped her coffee.

"Are you all right?" Suzanne asked. "You look…well, I guess our topic of conversation wasn't very uplifting was it?"

"I just…well, it's just eye-opening to think of all of the lives affected by gambling. Or fighting. Or any illegal things that go on. I guess I didn't really think about all of that until you told me about those kids."

"It just makes me so mad. My boyfriend was explaining how those fights work. Dogs are tortured, starved, and forced to fight. Small town gamblers make and lose money, but the big-wheels of the business make tons of money. It's just awful. And if I could find anyone involved in that mess I would…I would…well, I don't know what I'd do. But I'd sure as hell try to stop them!" she said emphatically.

"Suzanne, you just need to stay out of it and let the police do their jobs," Sherrie implored. "It sounds like these are people that you don't need to be snooping around."

Laughing, Suzanne said, "I'm not snooping. Honestly, BJ would have a fit if I were. But…," she said, "if I come across anything, I'm going to do something about it. I mean anyone who knows about this stuff and doesn't do anything, is just as guilty in my eyes!"

Sherrie sat still, her hands playing with her coffee cup. "I hadn't thought about it like that. I guess you're right."

The two women parted company outside the coffee shop, Suzanne heading back to work and Sherrie pulling out her cell phone. "Charisse? We need to talk."

THE FOG ROLLED off the river that night, creating a thick blanket of secrecy. The dogs coming into the old warehouse were muzzled, keeping the noise to a minimum. The cameras were in place over and around the pit.

Marcel and Charisse walked in the back door and seeing his head jerk, she moved to the upper platform. Her tight, short dress left nothing to the imagination as she ascended above the crowd.

Jorge approached Marcel, noticing Charisse's bare pussy was visible from the platform. He knew that was a sign that Marcel was losing interest in her. When Marcel was infatuated, he protected his main pussy. In Charisse's case that even extended to her request that none of his men harass her sister. If Charisse was falling out of favor, that would leave Sherrie vulnerable.

Keeping his face void of emotion, he moved to Marcel to see if there were any specific instructions.

"Anything new?" Marcel questioned, his sharp eyes glancing around.

"Everything's on schedule. Got a larger crowd than the previous streamed fight. The girls were brought back," indicating that Marcel's stable of prostitutes would be working the crowd.

"Keep them out of the sight of the cameras," he ordered. "The johns pay upfront and then they take the girls. Not having a gangbang videoed.

Nodding his agreement, he replied, "I'll talk to the IT guy. Make sure Charles keeps the cameras on the dogs."

Marcel turned briskly, walking up the steps past

Charisse without a word and she quickly followed him. Entering the small office, he turned to her.

"You high?" he asked, unbuckling his belt. The scent of blood from the dogs always fueled his lust. He remembered the days before he took over the business, when he joined in the gangbangs. Looking at Charisse, he chose her for her class. But now, her need for coke was overpowering her class. And a man in his position didn't need a cokehead for an escort. But her sister…she was unsullied by drugs. Jerking Charisse's skirt up over her hips, he pushed her over the desk taking her roughly from behind. Pounding into her, he pulled her top down freeing her breasts. Giving them a squeeze he quickly came.

Pushing her forward on the desk as he pulled out, she lay still. A soft snore came from her lips. Marcel straightened his clothes, brushed off his immaculate jacket and walked out of the room. Seeing the two guards outside, he jerked his head toward her. "Boys, take a few minutes and enjoy yourself."

The two large men glanced inside the door, seeing Charisse's naked form passed out on the desk. With a grin, they entered the room closing the door behind them.

Jorge watched some of the fighting that night, checking to see which dogs were the most vicious. The money he was earning on the side was feeding his off-shore, secure bank account. "Things are falling into place," he said to himself as he walked out of the building and disappeared into the fog.

SHERRIE, HER BLONDE hair pulled back with a simple clip and dressed elegantly in winter-cream pants with a sky-blue sweater, waited at the restaurant for fifteen minutes before pulling out her cell phone to call her sister. Just then Charisse walked in. Sky high heels. An expensive dress. Her hair and makeup immaculate. And sunglasses that she did not take off.

Sherrie stood up to hug her sister before they settled down to eat. "Are you okay? Aren't you going to take off your glasses?"

Charisse's hand shook as she cautiously slid the glasses off of her face. Sherrie gasped as she saw the small bruise next to her sister's eye.

"What happened? Did Marcel hit you?"

"No. He'd never do that," Charisse protested. "I-"

"Don't lie to me," Sherrie quickly interjected.

Charisse sighed. "I don't know how I got it. I…um…was with Marcel and…"

Sherrie just looked at her in concern. Reaching across the table, she put her hand over Charisse's hand giving it a squeeze.

"I must have taken a nap and when I woke up, I had this. I know it wasn't him, but…um…don't know exactly what happened."

The women were quiet a moment, each in their own thoughts. They ordered food and spent a few minutes making small talk while waiting for their meals.

"So what did you want to talk to me about?" Charisse asked.

Sherrie haltingly began to tell her about Suzanne and the boys that had gotten caught up in the aftermath of the dog fights. "Charisse, it's been you and me for a long time looking out for each other. I took a job at the Club Edge and I've done some work for Jorge that wasn't illegal but I knew it wasn't on the up and up. I did it because he told me that it would make things better for you. I know you've made your choices for your life and while they aren't the decisions I would have wanted you to make, I've done what I could to make things better for you. I know you've done the same for me."

Nodding, Charisse looked into her sister's eyes. "You were the smart one." Seeing Sherrie start to protest, she put up her hand. "No, I know. You were always the smart one. The one going to college. I never had anything going for me except my looks. I learned a long time ago how to use it to my advantage."

Before Sherrie could reply, Charisse continued, "I like my life. I get to live in a mansion now. I get clothes and spa treatments and live a life I never could before."

"But at what cost? I know you're still using drugs. I worked to get you off after high school, but once you got in with Marcel, you've been high almost every time I see you. And you didn't start off in a mansion.

Remember? You started off in his stable with a different john every night."

Pursing her lips, Charisse hissed, "I know. And I'm not going back to that life. I've got it good and I'm gonna keep it good. I've been protecting you, you know. I begged Marcel to extend his protection over you. And he has. He had his eye on you from the first time he saw your virginal ass. You owe me, Sherrie. You can't screw this up for me."

"Do you hear yourself? I've just told you of kids who are getting hurt by this. I've stayed quiet because Jorge told me that my assistance in keeping track of some things in the neighborhood would keep things easier on you."

Charisse looked down at her plate, tight lines around her mouth. Sherrie perused her sister, seeing her in a different light for the first time. Her eyes were slightly glassy. She could see that Charisse's complexion underneath her makeup was pale and pasty. The evidence of drugs in her system was still visible.

"I'm quitting Club Edge. I'm handing in my notice tonight. And sis? I'm not doing any more snooping for Jorge. I love you, but I can't keep this life trying to protect you. I finish my paralegal degree next month and have been afraid to look for jobs because of you, Jorge, Marcel…all this shit that has spilled from your life to mine. But having a friend sticking her neck out to help some kids…I can't turn my back on that."

"But you can turn your back on me?" Charisse bit

out. Huffing, she said, "Sis, I have no choice. This is how I earn my living. But if you snitch on any of this, I could lose. I'd be out on the street." She looked pathetic as she beseeched, "You can't do that to me."

Sherrie's hand shook as she pushed her plate back. "You have to make the decision to get clean. I can't do that for you. You have to make the decision to face the consequences of a lifestyle of selling your body to the highest bidder. I can't do that either." Softening her quivering voice, she said, "I'll always love you. But I can't be a part of your life. Not even on the edges like I have been."

She stood, walked over to her sister and kissed the top of her head. Then she turned and walked out of the building, taking a deep breath of the cool fall air.

Charisse left the table and walked over to the bar. Signaling to the bartender, she ordered a martini. The first of several for the day.

JORGE DROVE DOWN the long, narrow, dirt road toward the run-down barn. Ever alert, he scanned the area but heard nothing. Pulling his car next to the barn, he stiffened as a man came out of a small house nearby with a shotgun in his hand. Eyeing him angrily, he got out of the car.

"Oh sorry, Mr. Fernandez. I wasn't sure it was you." The man lowered his gun and laughed nervously. "Can't be too sure, you know?"

Not saying a word, Jorge stalked toward the man, watching him step backward. Stopping within a few feet of him, he said in a low, calm voice, "Pull a gun on me again and it will be the last thing you remember."

"Yes sir, Mr. Fernandez. I'm sorry, sir." Trying to divert the attention away from himself, he pointed toward the barn. "You want to see 'em? Got my boy working on 'em right now."

Without another word, Jorge turned and walked toward the barn followed by the quick steps of the other man who hustled around to open the door ahead of Jorge. The sounds of snarling and growling came from the interior, as well as the stench of blood and feces.

The exterior of the old barn was unassuming, camouflaging the activities on the inside. As Jorge looked around in approval, his anger toward the old man lessened. Several treadmills were in the corner, one with a running dog chained to it while a cage sat in front with two bait animals inside. The dog's sides were heaving as its tongue lolled out to the side. His ribs were showing, indicating near starvation.

There were a couple of carcasses in the middle of a ring with several dogs chained to the edges of the pit, straining toward the food. A younger man near the pit area, a long pole with a stun gun taped to the end, was keeping his eyes on the dogs. Two other men let the dogs go at the same time and they both ran to the middle, snarling and snapping trying to get to the meat.

As the destruction continued, Jorge moved his practiced eye around to the other dogs chained to the perimeter. His gaze landed on the dog that he had sent here to be trained. Nodding toward that dog, he lifted his eyebrow in question to the old man.

"Oh yeah, Mr. Fernandez. He's a good 'un. We're workin' with him and he's got the instincts. You got a good eye, Mr. Fernandez. Yes sir. You know a good 'un when you see 'em." The man continued to babble, but Jorge had already stopped listening. He could see it in the dog's eyes. Hunger. Anger. The dog, with the right training and steroids, would become a contender.

Nodding his approval, he turned and walked out of the barn, his footsteps followed quickly by the old man. Approaching his car, he turned and handed the trainer an envelope. "No. One. Knows," he stated, holding the man's eyes.

His Adam's apple bobbing as he swallowed nervously, the old man agreed quickly. "Oh, yes sir. No one knows it's your dog. Just me. Not my son. No one."

"Let me know when he's ready." As the old man was still bobbing his head, Jorge climbed back into his car and drove away.

LATER THAT AFTERNOON, Jorge entered Marcel's office, passing the accountant as he was leaving. Quickly assessing Marcel's mood, he could tell that his boss was in good spirits. Closing the door behind him, he approached the desk.

Marcel smiled and pointed to a chair. "Good news, Jorge. Our accountant has been showing me our profits from the last two streamed fights." Handing some papers to Jorge, he continued, "We are making more with the streaming than with any other fights combined."

Jorge looked over the figures, quickly calculating what his profits would be. Nodding, he said, "And the security?"

"Still having Charles check into it. So far, they are able to mix up the signals so that it is untraceable." Marcel eyed Jorge carefully. "You are doing very well for me. If you notice the second page, that is your bonus."

Jorge flipped the papers over, surprised at the figure. He looked back up at Marcel saying, "You are very generous."

Marcel's smirk crept across his face. "Money can buy anything, Jorge. Even loyalty."

Keeping his face void of emotion, he held his boss' stare. "You doubt my loyalty?"

Throwing his head back in laughter, Marcel admitted, "No. Not you, Jorge. You are the only person I trust." His laughter slowed and he added, "But I believe in rewarding that loyalty."

Nodding, Jorge handed the spreadsheets back to Marcel. "Was there anything else you wanted today?"

Marcel turned his chair so that it faced the window

and for a moment sat in silence. Jorge sat quietly, knowing his boss would speak when he was ready. Turning back toward him, Marcel said, "I think Charisse has outlived her usefulness to me."

Saying nothing, Jorge continued to sit quietly. Marcel was known to have gone through many women, most staying for a very short time in the esteemed position of being his main escort. Charisse had lasted longer than most and Jorge had begun to assume that Marcel had feelings for the girl.

"Let's just say that her exquisite pussy is no longer holding my attention. She's now become a sloppy drunk and is so high most evenings that even if her legs are spread, I'd just as soon fuck a corpse."

"Do you want me to find a replacement?" Jorge asked.

"It will need to be handled with some delicacy," Marcel responded. At this, Jorge just raised his eyebrows. "Charisse will not take the demotion well, which I don't care about. But I'm not interested in someone from my stable. That pussy's getting used as well."

"So, do you have someone in mind?"

"Charisse's sister is a beautiful woman."

The statement hung out there between the two men. Jorge maintained his silence.

"I'm looking for something fresh. I've seen her at Club Edge, but know her pussy's not for sale."

"I'm not sure that Sherrie is looking for what you're

offering, boss."

Smirking, Marcel looked at his right-hand man. "Remember what I said? Everyone has a price. What I want you to do is find her price."

Thinking of the dark-haired Suzanne, Jorge smiled. "I'll look into it boss. I just might have some leverage."

Walking out, he found himself thinking, *we both may get the pussy we want.*

Chapter 16

THANKSGIVING AT SUZANNE'S parents' house in Fairfield had gone without a hitch. Even her brother Rob behaved himself around BJ. Her parents had moved into the country and had a large barn attached to their property. They had transformed the old building into a massive family room years before and hosted a Thanksgiving meal for friends and family every year.

Suzanne looked around the tables laden with food and couldn't help but think of the many changes over the years. Her parents were older and grayer, but bustled around just as enthusiastically, welcoming guests and arranging the meal. BJ's parents always brought the wine and beer and BJ was off helping Bill get it out of the truck. Wendy was in the kitchen with Bernie, trying to finish the platters. Rob and his best friends, Jake Campbell and Tom Rivers, were moving the tables around while their wives, Laurie, Emma, and Carol completed the decorations.

The past four years had been difficult. The first year after she and BJ broke up, her parents begged her to come home for the holidays but afraid to run into him, she spent them alone. The next two years were spent with Annie. It was only last year, assured that BJ wouldn't be in town, that she allow herself to come back. But it wasn't the same. There was an empty space at the table and in her heart where he should have been.

Hearing the squeal of children's laughter, she looked over to see Dwayne and Chuckie playing with her niece, nephews, and the Campbell and River's children. Her eyes found Pamela's and she saw both joy and sadness there. Walking over, she gave her a hug.

"How are you doing," she asked her.

Pamela smiled as she replied, "I'm fine. The kids are happy and your parents' place is wonderful. It's like something out of a magazine!"

"Yeah, it was great celebrating Thanksgiving here every year growing up. I was just thinking about how time has flown. It seems like yesterday that BJ and I were running around the yard." Glancing back at the children, she asked, "But how are you really doing?"

Sighing, Pamela replied, "I don't miss the Joe of recent times, but this holiday is reminding me that years ago, me and Joe used to have Thanksgiving with our families too and had a good time. I always thought it would be like that." She turned back to Suzanne and smiled. "But thank you so much for this. If we hadn't come here, we'd be at the safe house, which would have been good but wouldn't have given the boys a chance to feel normal like this."

Just then, Mac announced that the meal was ready

and for everyone to have a seat. The adults corralled the children to their tables and helped them with their plates. BJ walked over, claiming Suzanne with a quick kiss and scooted her closer to him.

Once seated, Mac stood at the head of the table, peering down at his family, friends, and the return of his daughter and her only love back into the fold. Bowing their heads, he gave the blessing, this year its meaning running deeper than ever for everyone.

The next week found Suzanne and Annie meeting at Lily's house to help her with Christmas decorations, deciding to do it themselves instead of waiting on the men to get back. The men had been dispatched to find Christmas trees, using Shane's truck. Lily, with her left leg amputated below the knee, had a prosthesis and climbing her ladder was something that Matt would never agree to.

The women stood outside of Lily's one-story house, looking at the roof while unrolling a long strand of icicle lights.

"Who hung these for you last year?" Suzanne asked.

"I have a neighbor who came over, but Matt said he'd take care of it this year. It's just that he's been so busy with work, we kept putting it off."

Annie looked up dubiously. "I'd do it, but I'm afraid of heights. Even just your one story house scares me."

"Well, I'm not afraid of heights and don't mind ladders. If one of you will hold it steady, I'll start," replied Suzanne.

The three friends began hanging the lights while sharing about their holidays. Lily and Matt had gone to his parents' house and Annie and Shane went to both parents' houses.

"Oh my God – I ate so much," exclaimed Annie. My parents always eat at noon and Shane's family eats at about six in the evening. So we had two full Thanksgiving meals that day. We barely made it home before crashing into a turkey coma and didn't wake up until much later the next day," she laughed.

"No wonder we had the clinic closed on Black Friday," Suzanne shouted from the roof. "Hey Lily? Do you want some lights around the chimney?"

"Oooh, I forgot that I have a nice lighted wreath that can go there." She ran in and in a few minutes returned with the wreath. She climbed a couple of steps up the ladder to hand it to Suzanne with Annie holding the ladder steady, then Suzanne disappeared behind the chimney to tie it in place.

Just then, Shane's truck pulled into the driveway. Lily glanced over her shoulder nervously as Annie said, "Uh oh."

"What the fuck?" Matt roared, jumping out of the truck before it came to a stop. "Lily?" he shouted.

She quickly descended the two steps, carefully landing back on the ground as he stalked toward her, anger written on her face.

Shane and BJ chuckled as they got out, knowing

that Matt was having a coronary seeing her up on the ladder at all, even if it was just the second rung from the ground.

"I'm glad Annie's afraid of heights," Shane commented. "It keeps me from having to worry about her falling." The two men walked up to the front of the house, hearing Lily try to explain her way back into Matt's good graces. Shane leaned over and kissed Annie as she still nervously stood at the base of the ladder. "You can let go of the ladder now, baby," he teased.

"Umm," Annie stammered, looking up at her husband nervously.

"I was just two rungs up, Matt. It wasn't like I was in danger of falling," Lily was protesting as he pulled her petite body into his strong arms, his eyes raking over her to make sure she was fine.

BJ looked around wondering if Suzanne was still inside the house. Before he could ask Lily where she was, a voice came from above.

"Hey girls, does it look straight on the chimney?"

The stunned men's eyes flew upward, seeing Suzanne scrambling from behind the chimney with the lighted wreath proudly displayed against the red brick. Her eyes grew wide as she realized the men were staring up and the anger was pouring off of them. Especially BJ. He seemed to have swelled as his body flexed with tightened muscles.

"Suzy! What the fuck are you doing?" BJ roared, moving to the ladder as Shane grabbed it from Annie's hands to steady it for his friend.

Matt held Lily by her shoulders, peering down into her face. "Baby, what the hell were you thinking, allowing her to get on the roof?"

"She volunteered, Matt. It's not like we're incapable of hanging decorations!" Lily retorted.

Annie wisely kept quiet as Shane's eyes pierced hers. Having been with a loving, alpha man longer than her friends, she knew when to push for something and when to let them take charge. And right now, she knew their protectiveness was overflowing.

BJ, at the top of the ladder, held out his hand. "Move slowly, Suzy girl. Take my hand."

"Jeez Brad. I got up here by myself and can certainly handle getting down by myself," she huffed, moving toward the ladder.

"Baby, you do not want to make me madder than I am right now. This little stunt has earned you a warm ass when we get home, if I can even make it that far. I'm tempted to take you in Lily's house and tan your butt as soon as we get down."

"Bradley James Evans, you do not threaten me," she cried, halting her descent.

Taking a deep breath to both quell his fear for her and his anger, he said, "Babe. This is non-negotiable. I want you here taking my hand now. And I'm not threatening you. What I am doing is promising you a punishment for this. But I'll take care of you always, even after."

Suzanne looked into his intense gaze and found herself strangely turned on by his comments. *He threatens to spank me in front of our friends and I felt it right down to my...*

BJ's eyes quickly picked up on her change in breathing and knew she was turned on. "Come on, baby," he said gently. Taking her hand, he assisted her onto the ladder and they descended together. His breath washed over her ear as he leaned in and said, "I'll never hurt you, you know. But I'm not having you put yourself in danger. I'll wait till we get home, but baby you can expect to have your ass bared to me."

She pushed her ass back slightly, feeling it nestle against his cock which had definitely stood to attention.

"Careful, baby or we'll be leaving immediately."

She couldn't help but giggle as they descended to the ground. He pulled her into his embrace, his hands resting on her ass giving her a reminding pat.

The rest of the afternoon went without a hitch as the men unloaded Lily's tree and they got it in place in her living room. After hot chocolate for the women and beers for the men, BJ moved his tree over to his truck and he and Suzanne left for their apartment.

Hauling the tree up through the elevator took some effort, but finally it was installed in their living room. Not having had decorations of her own, Suzanne had taken great pleasure in purchasing ornaments for their first tree.

BJ's good mood had returned and they spent the

evening decorating. He watched her as she carefully choose where each ornament would be placed, patiently answering when she asked his opinion. Her sleek, glossy, black hair was freely hanging down her back and her porcelain complexion was illuminated by the glow from the tree lights. His eyes were diverted to her luscious ass cupped in tight yoga pants that was displayed to perfection every time she raised her arms to place an ornament high on the tree.

Glancing over at him sitting on the sofa, she asked, "Aren't you going to get up and help?"

"Nope," he answered, a smirk on his face.

Turning to him, she set the box of decorations on the coffee table, placing her hands on her hips. "And why not, may I ask?" she huffed.

"Cause I'm watching your ass as you're taking care of the tree."

"That's it? That's the reason I'm doing all the work, so you can oggle my ass?"

"Yep." Seeing that she was getting ready to protest, he continued, "Babe. You're not hurting yourself. You're having a fuckin' good time, humming Christmas carols and decorating the tree. You're safe, warm, and happy. So yeah, I'm sitting here, admiring all of you, and that includes your gorgeous ass."

She couldn't help but smile as she turned back to the tree. "Fine. You can check out my ass then. At least you've gotten over your earlier fuss."

"Who says I've forgotten one thing that was promised?"

Glancing over her shoulder, she looked at his face. *He looks serious. He can't be serious! He'd really spank me?* Once again, she wanted to be incredulous but found her pussy clench in anticipation.

He looked up, seeing her eyes dilate and couldn't stop the grin from spreading across his face. *Oh yeah, she wants it.* Standing, he stalked over to her placing her hands on her shoulders. "You ready, babe, for your punishment?"

Licking her lips, she nervously answered, "Um, I'm not really sure about this."

"Oh Suzy girl, the punishment is non-negotiable. You earned it and you're going to get that ass reddening I promised." Sliding his hands down her back, one rested on her ass and the other linked through her fingers. "But I promise, babe. I'll make it so you may decide to be bad all the time."

Leading her to the bedroom, his fingers still linked with hers, he stopped when they were next to the bed. "Strip," he ordered gently. Seeing her hesitate, he said, "The longer you wait, the longer the spanking."

Her eyes wide, she knew he would never hurt her, but the unknown of this new activity had butterflies flying around her stomach while her core clenched.

"By the time I'm finished with your punishment, baby, your pussy's gonna be crying for my dick," he promised. "Now. Strip bare."

She pulled her sweater up over her head tossing it

down onto the floor. Her bra quickly followed. She saw his eyes now dilating and she couldn't help but smile. *Looks like I still have some of the power.* Hooking her thumbs in the waistband of her pants, she slid them slowly down her legs, stepping out of them once they reached her feet. Standing in only her red-lace, Christmas panties she stood very still.

He lifted an eyebrow and she slid the panties off as well. Now completely naked, she suddenly felt vulnerable in front of him. *But I trust him. Always.*

"Turn and face the bed," he ordered gently. "Bend over and place your hands on the mattress."

She did has he commanded, both turned on and uncertain at the same time. She hadn't been spanked by her parents since she was very little and certainly not on a bare ass. She pulled her lips in, awaiting what he would do next. She did not have long to wait.

Smack. His large hand landed hard on her ass and she jumped from the sting.

"Ow, Brad. That hurts!" she exclaimed as she stood to turn around.

He placed his hand gently on her back, holding her in place. "Was that so bad you couldn't stand it?"

"No," she admitted.

Smack. Again his hand landed on her ass, but in a different place this time. He rubbed his hand over the reddened area, smoothing the sting.

"Do you know how dangerous it was for you to be on the roof without someone else around?"

"But, I had Lily and Annie –," she began.

Smack. Smooth.

"But-"

Smack. Smooth.

This time she wisely kept quiet, allowing the rubbing to soothe the sting. Strangely, she could feel the wetness between her legs increase and she began clenching her thighs together to ease the ache.

Chuckling, he continued to smooth his hand over the red globes, loving the feel of her warm, firm ass under his fingers. "Have you learned your lesson yet, baby?"

"Yes," she replied as she moved her hips back and forth seeking her release.

"No more dangerous activity. You wait and let me handle things that might hurt you?"

She wanted to protest once again, but the sting of her ass and the overwhelming desire to have him inside of her, won over.

"I can't stand the thought of anything happening to you, Suzy girl." He leaned over her back, sliding his fingers over the wet slit of her pussy, before plunging his fingers deep inside.

She screamed out as he finger-fucked her with one hand and pulled her nipples with the other hand. Her orgasm rolled through her and she pushed her hips back against his jean-clad dick, happy to feel it swollen and straining against his zipper.

"I need you. Inside. Now," she panted.

"You got it, babe." He quickly pulled out of his clothes leaning his tall, muscular frame over her and slammed inside her drenched pussy. Her hands were still on the bed as he leaned over and filled her to the hilt. Gasping for breath on the heels of her orgasm, she could feel the incredible friction of his engorged dick reaching a place deep inside that made her body once again tighten up like a coil.

BJ looked down at the beauty bent over in front of him and realized that her arms must be tired. Pulling out quickly, he chuckled as he heard her mewl from the loss of his cock. "Come on, babe," he called as he gently pushed her onto the bed. Pulling some pillows up under her stomach for support, he immediately slid his aching dick back inside, as deep as he could go. His balls slapping against her, he continued his pounding. He reached around to palm her breasts before tweaking her nipples.

Higher and higher Suzanne climbed, aiming for the peak that was just beyond her reach. "I'm close," she cried.

Barely holding on, he ordered, "Finger yourself."

She slid one hand down and rolled her swollen clit in her fingers, giving it a pull. At the same time, he squeezed her nipples and she screamed out his name once again as her second orgasm rippled from her core outward.

Feeling her pussy walls clench his cock, he leaned his neck back, muscles straining as his orgasm tore through him. Pouring his hot semen deep into her, he continued to flex his hips as he pumped until he was utterly drained.

Falling forward onto her back, he quickly rolled taking her with him. Tucking her quivering body close to his, he held her close to his heart. They lay for a while, sweat mingling, hearts beating in unison, as the force of their coupling washed over them. Slowly awareness took over and he slid one hand down to her ass, gently rubbing the smooth skin of her perfect derriere. She stretched and snuggled closer.

"Are you okay, baby?" he asked.

"Um hm," was the lazy reply.

"I don't mean about the sex, darlin'. I'm talking about the punishment."

She raised up and peered down into his eyes, warm with love and concern. "It was kind of scary," she admitted. "But the results were…"

"I'll always take care of you."

"I can do things on my own, you know."

"Let me ask you something. What would your dad or Rob have done if you were on a roof by yourself?"

She immediately dropped her eyes, knowing that they would have had a fit also.

"That's what I thought. Babe, look at me," he ordered softly.

She lifted her eyes back to his.

"You're strong. Independent. Capable. But in this relationship, I won't have you take chances. The man I am is the same man you knew years ago only older and wiser. The same kind of man your father and brother are. The same kind of man Shane, Matt, and Gabe are. Old fashioned? Hell yeah. Dominating? Only when it counts. In control? You better believe it. But babe, I will take care of you in all ways. You jack up, then take your punishment. And I will always make it good for you afterwards."

Pulling her lips in as she thought over his words, realizing that they didn't upset her in the least. "You think Shane and the other men do this too?" she wondered out loud.

Chuckling, he replied, "Oh baby. We don't talk much, but I can tell you that both Lily and Annie have had their asses spanked on occasion. And your brother? Hell yeah."

Glaring, she asked, "You're going to talk to the others about this?"

"Won't have to."

"What does that mean?"

"Baby, they knew the minute I saw you on the roof that your ass was going to be burning tonight."

Blushing, she tried to push up off of his chest but he wasn't having it.

"Oh no, babe. You stay right here. No running out of bed in a huff. You put yourself in danger and I just made sure that you won't do that again."

She stopped pushing but continued to glare.

"And can you tell me honestly, Suzy girl, that you

didn't just have the hardest orgasm you've ever had?"

Continuing to blush, she retorted, "That's not fair. You know I did."

"So then? What's the problem?"

Put that way, she couldn't come up with a good reason to stay huffy as the warmth of the lovemaking continued to spread over her. Her body relaxed against his again. "Have you had a lot of practice with that?" she queried softly, both wanting the answer and hating what his response might be. Knowing that each experience was new to her but that with his sexual escapades in the four years since they had been together, she disliked the possible comparison.

"Never done that before."

At that response, she raised back up and peered down to see the honesty in his eyes. "Never?" she asked disbelieving.

"Baby, I've never cared about anyone but you. So the answer is no. I've never spanked and then taken care of someone before." Seeing the surprise in her eyes, he continued. "I've only ever loved you. Just you. So I vow to take care of you in all ways, both when you're good and when you're not."

A slow, beautiful smile spread across her face causing his chest to squeeze.

"I love you too, Brad." She hesitated for a moment and then said shyly, "I might have to occasionally be bad."

Laughing deeply, he held her tightly to his chest.

"Girl, you can be bad all you want and I'll give you exactly what we just had."

She lay her head on his still-rumbling chest and found herself finally giving in to exhaustion.

BJ lay there listening to her soft snores and then turned her gently to lay her in a more sleep-comfortable position. He slid out of bed to turn out the lights and secure the apartment for the night. He walked back in and looked at her sleeping, her form illuminated by the lights outside. Long, midnight hair spread on his pillow. The lights and shadows making her alabaster skin seem as though she were carved from perfect marble. Ample breasts rising and falling with her breathing. Feeling his cock beginning to stir once again, he willed it to behave.

Sliding back in bed behind her, he pulled her once again to his chest with his arms protectively around her. Jerking the bedcovers over their bodies, he settled in as well. Sleep eluded him for a while as he thought about the miracle of her entering his life once again. *I thought I'd lost her. And for four years I lost myself.* Nameless fucks floated through his mind momentarily as he realized that what he had told her was absolutely true. No one had ever held his heart. *Only her. Only Suzy.* And with that he joined her in a peaceful slumber.

Chapter 17

Early the next morning BJ was jarred awake by the sound of retching coming from the bathroom. Bolting out of the bed, he found Suzanne on her knees with her head hanging over the toilet. He grabbed her hair and pulled it out of her way. Leaning over to the counter, he snagged a hair clip and awkwardly managed to get most of her hair on top of her head.

"Baby, what's wrong?" he asked, wetting a bath cloth and holding it to her pale forehead.

Keeping her head on her arm, she plopped down onto her bottom as she looked wearily at him. Tears slid down her cheeks as she stared into his slate-blue eyes. Images of years ago flashed through her mind. Her voice shaky, she whispered, "I'm late."

Concerned with her health, it took him a moment for her words to sink in. "Late? As in *late?*"

Afraid to speak, she just nodded.

BJ's face broke out into a huge grin. "Late?" he asked again. Throwing his arms around her, he exclaimed, "Oh baby, that's wonderful."

"Wonderful? Brad, what a mess! We just got together. What will everyone say? Jesus, haven't we learned from past mistakes? We haven't even talked about anything. What if it happens again? What if I can't carry a baby? What if –."

"Shhh," he said, placing his fingers over her lips. He sat on the bathroom floor, pulling her into his lap. Wrapping her body into his embrace, he held her tightly. "You're getting all upset and we don't even know what's going on yet."

Warm in his arms, she looked at him with his fingers still pressed on her mouth. A single tear slid down her cheek.

Cupping the back of her head, he pulled her into his chest. "Baby, we'll take it one thing at a time. We'll get you cleaned up. Get a pregnancy test. If it's positive, then it's fine. Suzy girl, we're in love. Have been for years. We already live together and we're planning on getting married anyway."

She quickly pulled her face from his chest, looking up to search his eyes. "Married? You never mentioned marriage."

Throwing his head back in laughter, he pulled her to a standing position. "Baby, you and me? Back together? Do you really think I don't want to spend the rest of my life with you? Girl, that's all I've wanted since I was sixteen years old."

Standing in the bathroom they faced each other. His eyes latched onto hers and his laughter stilled. "You and me. Always. In sickness and in health," he promised. "No more running, babe. Whatever life throws at us, we deal. And we deal together."

Tears streaming down her face, she could only nod.

"How late are you?" he asked.

"About a week. I've been worried but with so much going on, I thought it might be stress."

His body stilled against hers. Tight. Angry.

She felt the change and peered back up at him, a questioning look on her face.

"You've thought for a week that you might be pregnant and you got on Lily's roof yesterday?" he growled.

She stood quietly, not wanting to poke the bear.

"I ought to turn you back over my knee and redden your bare ass again for that."

She instinctively took a step back and her hands automatically slid behind her to cover her butt.

He noticed her movement and forced himself to calm. *She doesn't need this now.*

Taking a deep breath, he gently pulled her back to his chest. "No baby, no more, I promise. But you'd better promise that you'll take no more chances and no more risks." He felt her nod against his chest. "Do you think you can eat something? Let's at least get a little breakfast down you and then I'll head to the drug store."

"Now? Today?" she asked.

"No sense in waiting."

Nodding once again, she allowed him to lead her out of the bathroom toward the kitchen. A small breakfast of toast and green tea settled her stomach.

One hour later they stood back in the bathroom, just like four years ago. Looking at the blue stick once again. Looking in each other's eyes once again. Her fear was palpable and he reassured her once again.

And he kissed her once again. This time lightly. A simple touching of lips promising forever.

BJ LOOKED OVER at Suzanne the next day in the kitchen as he was piled up on the sofa watching football. Matt and Shane had originally planned on coming over, but he begged off saying that she had a stomach bug. She had become very quiet since realizing that she was pregnant. He wanted to shout it from the rooftops, but she was afraid of letting anyone know.

"Please don't tell anyone," she had begged. "The first three months are the miscarriage time and I just don't want to tell anyone yet."

He had agreed, knowing it was best, but was concerned. She was making chili and the delicious smell was wafting through the apartment. Every once in a while, he would see her just standing looking out of the windows. Not moving. Her face lost in thought.

Finally, he could take it no more. He stalked over and wrapped his arms around her. "Baby, what's goin' on in that mind of yours? I can feel it racing from over there."

Shaking her head, she looked and just said, "I don't

know. Lot's of things I guess." Sighing, she lay her head back on his thick chest, comforted by the steady sound of his heartbeat and the feel of his powerful arms around her.

He bent and scooped her up, then walked to the sofa and sat gently with her in his lap. With one hand, he grabbed the remote and clicked the football game off.

"Okay, let's break it all down. What all is bothering you?"

She gave an unladylike snort. "You want a list? I'm pregnant again. Again, Brad. I didn't do a great job the first time and I'm no more prepared now than I was four years ago. And my job. I just got my vet tech degree and now have to consider my job hours. We're not even married or engaged. I can't plan anything…there's not enough time. My parents. Oh my God, Rob. My brother will have a fit…I can just hear him now. And we just got back together. You say you've loved me since you were sixteen, but we've been apart for four years. Brad, do I need to remind you that it was just a few weeks ago that one of your fuckbuddies showed up at your door!" She burst into tears again as she covered her face with her hands.

BJ looked stunned and for the first time felt unsure of himself. *Is this pregnancy moods or is she this worried about everything?*

Holding her head tucked up under his chin, he rocked her for a few moments letting her cry. As her sobs slowed to just sniffles, he leaned forward and snagged some tissues from the end table. *I may need to restock on tissues.*

Giving her a minute to wipe her tears and blow her nose, he then tilted her head up with his fingers under her chin. "Baby, you're overthinking too much too soon. You're letting everything overwhelm you, but we have time to work on each of those concerns one at a time."

Her eyes latched onto his as though his words were going to make or break her. Trying to keep her chin from quivering under his fingertips, she just stared, not trusting her voice.

"You need to make a doctor's appointment tomorrow. Let me know when it is and I want to be there as well. We can ask about your job at that time. If you want to keep working and are safe, then there should be no problem with it. Babe, I think your parents and mine are going to be thrilled. We're not teens anymore. We're independent adults who are planning on spending the rest of our lives together. Our parents want nothing more than to become grandparents."

He stopped for a moment, checking to see her reaction as he took her emotional pulse. She seemed calmer, so he continued. "Rob? He'll be fine and Laurie will bring him around if not. He'll love being an uncle and his kids will have cousins to play with."

That got a smile out of her and he breathed a sigh of relief. *Okay, she's getting this. Now for the sticky part.*

"Suzy girl, we've already had the conversation about Lisa. You know that I haven't loved anyone since you. And whatever I did was in the past. You never have to worry about me being faithful, I hope you know that. I haven't been with another woman since we saw each other at Shane and Annie's wedding several months ago."

"But she was so beautiful. And what happens when another one from your past shows up, all tall, thin, and big breasts that don't sag and you turn and look at me waddling around with a huge stomach and boobs that hang down?"

His eyebrow quirked in question. "Seriously? You're seriously asking what would happen?"

She tried to stifle a giggle, but it slipped out anyway.

"Maybe I should turn you over my knee," he said jokingly. Brushing her hair away from her face with his hand, he cupped her cheek, feeling her lean into his palm. "Baby, do you know what I was thinking when I was looking at you earlier standing by the window?"

She held his eyes as she shook her head.

"I was thinking that you're the most beautiful woman I have ever seen. And that you would trust your heart with me again? Amazing, baby. Fuckin' amazing. And here is something else I want you to take down and take it down deep. The idea of you growing large with my son or daughter…there is nothing that would compare. No other will ever hold my interest. Only you. It's always been, only you."

"It's only ever been you for me, too," she whispered.

"So does that take care of everything that's clogging up that gorgeous head of yours, baby?"

"What if –"

"Nope. We're not going there. We can't help what nature allows, but we're not going to waste our time worrying about what we can't control. So you make that call to the doctor on Monday and we'll see where to go from here. Okay?"

Taking a deep breath, she slowly let it out. "Okay, honey. I'll try."

"Good girl. Now is that chili about ready 'cause the smell is driving my stomach insane."

SHE CALLED THE obstetrician's office on Monday but was unable to get an appointment until later in the week. Her group session for women who had had miscarriages was meeting that night and she wondered if she should go. *Will it depress me? Will it make me feel guilty?* She went back and forth all day trying to decide what to do. At the last minute, she decided to go when BJ called to say that he was working a little late on a surveillance program.

Entering the basement of the church, she smiled at the familiar faces. Grabbing a cookie and a water bottle, she sat in the circle just as they were ready to start. The group always started with a round-robin where everyone had a chance to say how they are doing. She listened as she heard the others, all in different places in their lives. And it struck her for the first time, how they are all different. Until now, she only focused on the fact that every woman there had suffered a miscarriage. That was what brought them there. That was what bonded the group of individuals together. She had listened with close attention as they described their miscarriages. At home. At the ER. Some early in the pregnancy. Some late. Some carrying full term and having their babies be stillborn. Always the same common thread. They were pregnant. And now they weren't, but there was no baby to hold.

But this time she noticed their uniqueness. One woman had a miscarriage years ago but had two normal, healthy children now. The group leader had suffered three miscarriages before having a healthy child. Other women had recently lost but were anxiously trying again. Some were afraid to try. And a couple of women were now single, their relationships not strong enough to carry the couple through their grief.

There is no pattern. There is no sameness here except that we all had a similar experience. Her hand slid down to her stomach, fingers splaying out across her flat belly. Glancing to her right, she noticed the expanding stomach of one of the women who was now pregnant. Suddenly she was filled with the realization that she wanted that. She wanted this baby more than anything. Feeling her fingers pressing inward, she found a sob catch in her throat. *One miscarriage doesn't mean another miscarriage. I can do this. I don't want to spend the next eight and a half months in dread. I can't control the future, but I can control now.*

The meeting finished and she hurried out of the building. The wind was cold and she pulled her coat around her protectively. Hustling to her car, she started it and headed to their apartment desperately wanting to see him, breathing easy for the first time in days.

He was just getting home when she ran through the door straight into his arms. Concerned, he held her tightly and as he lifted her feet off the ground, she wrapped them around his waist as though desperate to be connected to him in all ways.

"Baby, what's wrong? What happened?" he asked, holding her trembling body.

Not receiving an answer, he carried her over to the sofa and sat down, settling her across his lap. Pulling her head gently from his neck, he peered into her tear-filled eyes. "Baby, you have to talk to me. What happened? Are you hurt?"

She shook her head as she tried to find the words to tell him what she was feeling. "I…I want…us. I…want the…baby. I want the…baby." Her voice broke as sobs hiccupped through her.

Still not knowing what had happened, he pulled her in closely again giving her time to gain composure.

He rocked her gently as he smoothed his hand over her back, willing his strength to give her ease. Her tears lessened and she finally pulled back to look at him.

"I'm sorry, Brad. I didn't mean to scare you. I just…I don't know," she said, suddenly weary.

"Shhh, it's okay." He brushed her tear-stained cheeks with his thumbs.

She took a few halting breaths, each one easier than the last. Grabbing another tissue, she wiped her eyes and then peered back into the slate-blue eyes that had first captured her all those years ago. The ones that taunted her and played with her as a child. The ones that first looked upon her as a woman of interest and not just as a pesky kid. The ones that held hers as she gave him her virginity. And the same eyes that told her to trust him when he said he would always take care of her. *They're the same eyes. The same ones that I trusted but then forgot to when things got rough. But no more.*

"I trust you," she said simply.

He sat quiet, not knowing what she was referring to but knowing that an important breakthrough had occurred.

"You always told me to trust you and I did. But four years ago, I forgot that. I didn't trust that you would stay with me. Or keep loving me. Or needed me. I didn't trust that I even knew what I was doing. I don't want to do that ever again."

"What happened, baby?"

"I went to my Finding Daily Strength Miscarriage

group this evening." She looked up to see that he was listening intently. "I've always seen our common thread – that we're just a group of women who are grieving together because we had miscarriages. But tonight, I saw us as complete individuals. Some are pregnant again, some have had children now. Some are single. But we're all different. Don't you see, honey? I finally realized that one miscarriage does not have to define me. It's possible to get pregnant again. And carry the baby. And want the baby."

She had shifted around so that she was straddling his lap, holding on to his shoulders. His fingers were on her hips and she could feel them flexing.

Lifting her hand to his cheek, she continued, "I was so afraid that I would never love again. Or get pregnant. Or have a child. And I know life is unpredictable. Something could happen again. But this time, I want to trust that you'll be there. And we'll stay together to face whatever happens."

"Oh, Suzy girl, I'm not going anywhere. We're in this together. I'm getting what I've always wanted: you, us, and now another chance at a baby. There's nothing else in life I want but you." Leaning in he placed a soft kiss on her lips. Gentle. Light. Pulling back he looked deeply into her sky-blue eyes, remembering the teenager who stood in her mother's bakery when he came back from football camp that summer and knew once again that she was the only one in his heart. Kissing her gently once more, he whispered, "You can trust in that."

Chapter 18

SUZANNE HAD EVERY intention of not telling anyone about the pregnancy until she made it to the three-month mark, but the first surgery day in the vet clinic had her running to the bathroom to throw up. Annie and Leon stood outside of the door, worry written on their faces.

"Suzanne, are you all right?" Leon asked.

Annie rolled her eyes at him saying, "She's throwing up. What makes you think she might be all right?"

"Oh. Dumb question, wasn't it? Do you think she has the flu? Should we reschedule some appointments?"

"I don't know. Do you think it could be something else?"

Annie and Leon shared a look as he raised his eyes widened in surprise.

A weak voice came from the other side of the door. "I can hear you, you know."

"Can we get you something?" Annie asked.

They heard the sound of a toilet flushing and water from the sink running. Leon grabbed a water bottle out of their small refrigerator. The door opened and a pale Suzanne emerged, dressed in dog-print scrubs, her fingers pressed to her lips.

She dropped her eyes, not willing for them to peer too deeply inside and mumbled an apology.

Annie grabbed her pulling her into a hug. "Oh honey, you don't have to apologize. Are you okay?"

"Must be something I ate," she offered.

"Are you sure? Could you be pregnant?" Annie prodded.

"Lord girl, just look at you! I'd say you were definitely carrying," Leon effused.

Suzanne lifted her eyes, her face unable to hide her secret. A slow smile spread over her face. Leon whooped as he grabbed her swinging her around in the lab. Giggling, she hugged him back. He settled her carefully down on the floor.

Annie walked over, placing her hands on Suzanne's shoulders. "Are you okay with this? Are you happy?"

Familiar tears hit the back of Suzanne's eyes as she stared at her dearest friend. Nodding, she admitted, "Yeah. I am. Really happy."

Annie pulled her in for a heartfelt hug. One that, while Leon witnessed, would never be able to quite understand. The hug of two women. Women who knew love. Loss. Emotions that come from the deep center of a woman's soul. Suzanne felt them to her very core.

Stepping back, she continued, "I admit it was a shock. Certainly unplanned. I must be the most fertile woman to get pregnant with one unprotected time!"

She blushed looking at Leon, who just laughed.

Looking back at Annie, she said, "But Annie I promise it won't interfere with work. Well…" she glanced behind her at the bathroom. "I suppose until I get my sea-legs back, it will affect me a bit."

Annie laughed and said, "No worries, honey. You can work the front and I'll let Leon help me with the surgeries."

Annie hesitated, staring at her two co-workers and friends, suddenly looking slightly nervous. Pushing her long, copper hair away from her neck, she bit her lip as though wondering what to say. Suzanne and Leon then shared a glance and turned back to her.

"I know that look, doc. What's going on?" Leon asked, pretending to glare.

"Well, I've got three things that are happening that I needed to talk to you all about and was going to wait until later today, but now is as good a time as any, I suppose, since we are sharing secrets."

Leon mumbled, "Ya'll are sharing secrets. I don't have any."

The women rolled their eyes and Annie continued. "First of all, Suzanne's not the only one having a baby."

The statement hung out there in the air for a moment before her words sunk in.

"Oh my God!" Suzanne shouted, jumping forward to hug Annie once again.

"Group hug," Leon laughed, grabbing both women in his embrace. "I must be crazy working around all these female hormones. My Shirley will wonder what's happening to me."

The three shared their moment of joy, then quickly found out the details. Annie told them that she was three months along and Suzanne admitted that she had wanted to wait since she was only about a month along.

Leon stared down at Annie, saying, "Okay, spill the rest of the beans, doc. You said there were three things happening. Being preggers is one. What're the others?"

"Okay, you all know I was trying to sell this practice. Well, I have. The initial papers are signed and the final closing will be in a month. And I have been able to arrange the buying of the practice in the county." Looking at them nervously she continued, "You both said you would go with me and I can't imagine having a clinic without you. But I will totally understand if you want to stay here."

"No way!" Leon declared. "I've already talked to Shirley and she's on board. It only changes my commute by about fifteen minutes each way and I'd be heading out of the city, so it'd be a nice ride."

Smiling, Suzanne looked at Annie. "You know I'm staying with you." Looking around at the small lab room, she admitted, "Although it will be weird not being here every day."

Annie agreed. "Yeah, I'll miss this place, but the new facility has so much more room. And a client base ready to expand."

Leon interjected once more. "Okay, so that's the

second thing you needed to tell us. What's the third?"

"Well, we're going to get some help in here for the next month. With me being pregnant," Annie stopped and looked at Suzanne, "and you being pregnant, it will be nice to have an extra pair of hands. The new owner of this clinic wants to go ahead and start working part time here to get used to our clients and have them get used to him."

"And that would be...?" Leon prodded.

"Dr. Ketchum. Phil. From the ER clinic."

Suzanne's eyes quickly looked to Annie's, not masking her concerns.

Annie saw her look and continued quickly, "I know you're concerned about his lack of reporting some things to Animal Control, but he and I have talked and he has assured me that all protocols were followed. He has even showed me copies of reports that he sent. He still maintains that the ER clinic fulfills the highest standards. Its owner, Dr. Marker, certainly demands that of his employees."

Suzanne nodded, understanding Annie's desire to get the clinic sold and, while she promised her support, she still could not quiet the nagging feeling that he wasn't to be trusted.

Annie continued her news, "So, tomorrow Phil will be starting with us part time. He's turned in his notice to Dr. Marker at the ER clinic and will be working there only part time and then with us." Looking at Suzanne, she said, "He agreed to do surgeries two mornings a week and then spend another two mornings helping with the appointments.

"Are you guys good with all of this?" Annie implored after giving them a minute to process the new information.

Leon and Suzanne immediately gave her their approval. Suzanne replied, "It's a lot to happen in the next month, but with us three together, we can accomplish anything!"

One last hug amongst the three friends and they separated as the bell over the front door rang, signaling a new day starting.

THAT AFTERNOON, SUZANNE received a text from Pamela asking her to meet her at their house. *Not the shelter? I wonder what's up with that. Please don't let her be back with Joe. I don't trust that man.*

Annie let her go early and she hopped into her car, heading to see what was going on. Knowing BJ would want to know where she was, she texted him. She was surprised when she got an immediate text back. **Mtg you there.**

She drove to Pamela's house, now more curious than ever about what was going on. As she pulled up, she saw several police cars parked out front. A policewoman was standing with Pamela in the front yard, but Suzanne did not see Dwayne or Chuckie anywhere. She then saw Matt and Shane coming from the inside of the house.

Hopping out of her car, she ran up the front walk toward Pamela, who turned toward her, eyes wide in shock.

"What's going on?" she asked breathlessly. "Where are the boys? Are they all right?"

"Yeah," Pamela said with a shaky voice. "They're still back at the shelter with one of the other ladies." She took a quivering breath and continued, "It's Joe. He's dead. The police found his body and he was murdered."

"Oh Pamela, I'm so sorry," Suzanne exclaimed. While she did not like the man, she felt for Pamela's loss. "What happened?"

"He was in the back shed," she said as she jerked her head toward the back of the house. "He'd been shot. The place is messed up like someone was looking for something."

Just then, Shane and Matt stalked over. "Called BJ. He's on his way," Matt said.

"How'd you know I was coming?" she asked.

Shane just raised one eyebrow in response before replying, "Seriously? We knew she'd call you and you'd drop everything to get right here in the middle of this fuckin' mess."

She was in the middle of an eye-roll when BJ's SUV came around the corner. Peering inside, she could see Gabe as well. *Great. The whole macho patrol is going to be here and probably scare Pamela to death.* Glancing at her friend, she could see her shock-filled eyes take in the wall of testosterone that surrounded them quickly.

BJ's eyes only sought out Suzanne's and she gave him a small nod to let him know she was fine. He quietly wrapped his arms around her shoulders, offering her warmth from the chill and emotional comfort as well. Gabe gave her a look that she interpreted as him knowing about the pregnancy. She gave him a small smile in return.

"Mrs. Johnson. I don't know if you remember, but I'm Detective Dixon and this is my partner Detective Douglas."

Pamela nodded at the men and Matt continued. "We need you to go to the shed with us to see what may be missing or what your husband may have been involved in."

"Can I go too?" Suzanne asked, then noticed that both Matt and Shane gave BJ a look first. Huffing, she turned up to BJ saying, "Honey, she needs me."

He nodded but added, "Only if I can go too." Matt agreed and the four of them walked to the back of the house while Shane and Gabe talked to the policemen inside.

Entering the small shed, Suzanne could see that it was wrecked, but then not knowing the state it was in before Joe was murdered, she turned to see Pamela's reaction. It was strangely blank.

Then Pamela's eyes landed on the blood splatter stain on the back wall and her knees buckled. Matt quickly grabbed her while assisting her to a stool. BJ pulled Suzanne back in protectively against his hard body.

"Detective, this may surprise you but my husband kept this old shed locked. I don't know what he had in here or what's missing."

Nodding, Matt asked, "What can you tell me about his habits with the shed. When did he come out here? What did he carry? Was it at night or daytime?"

Her brow crinkled in thought as she answered, "In the old days, he just kept tools and the lawn mower. But they eventually got moved outside and he just said he needed a place to get away from me and the noise of the kids. Sometimes, he would bring the dog out here."

Matt was quiet letting her remember details that would slowly come. His patience paid off.

"He'd meet people out here. They'd come to the house and he'd say he was taking them to his office. I just thought it was a dumb name for an old shed. Kind of like he was trying to play at being a big man."

"A big man?" Matt prodded, looking around the shed.

Sighing, Pamela continued. "My husband was a proud man. A good man when we were first together. But his job didn't pay much. It rankled him when I would get a raise and he became angry. He kept saying that he was going to find a way to make more. To begin with, he'd say that it was for me and the boys. But then, it just seemed like he got all puffed up with importance when others would come to him."

Suzanne walked over and placed her hand on Pamela's shoulders for support and received a small smile in return.

"Detective Dixon, I don't know what he was involved in. I'm embarrassed about that. He got meaner and began drinking. And between my job, trying to raise the boys right, and just keeping the house together...I just didn't ask too many questions. Joe bounced between having money that he'd wave around like he was a big earner and then other times he'd hound me for the housekeeping money, taking food away from our boys to do God knows what with it.

"Looking back, I should have realized that he must have been gambling. Winning big sometimes and losing bigger other times." Shaking her head, she confessed, "I feel so stupid. I should have done something earlier. Or left him earlier. I don't know."

Suzanne rushed to her defense saying, "You did the best you could. Joe made his own choices. His. Not yours. If he was gambling, then he was addicted and there was nothing you could have done."

Matt asked, "So if he was using this as a bookie joint, you haven't been out here to know what may be missing?"

Pamela shook her head. "No. Once, he caught the boys out here, trying to snoop in a window. They used to play here before he took it over and I know they missed their play area. But he caught them. I wasn't home and he whipped them something fierce." With tears sliding down her cheeks, she admitted, "That was when I first knew I might have to leave him some day. I told him if he ever touched the boys like that we'd all take off. He just told me to keep them away. And I did."

"Ma'am, we'd like to talk to the boys. We don't need your permission, but you need to be present. Can we do that now? Do they know?"

Her eyes grew wide in fear, but she agreed. "They don't know he's dead. They just know something bad happened when the police came to bring me here. I need to talk to them first. And I want to be there when you talk to them."

She looked up at Suzanne. "The boys really trust you. Do you think you can be there too?"

Before she could answer, BJ squeezed her shoulders. "Babe," he whispered. "Don't want you getting upset."

She twisted her neck to look up into his concerned face. Warmth spread all through her. Here was a man who would lay down his life for her. Care for her. Comfort her. Protect her. *And he'll be the same with our children. Not like Joe. Never like Joe.* Smiling, she whispered back, "I love you."

"Love you too, Suzy, but that doesn't answer my concerns."

"I'll be fine. In fact, why don't you go with us? You can keep an eye on all of us."

Another shoulder squeeze was all the answer she

needed. Turning back to Pamela and Matt, she said, "Let's go."

No one noticed the binoculars trained on the group moving out of the shed, following them with interest. Nor did they notice a signal to someone else to follow the group. Not the police. Just Suzanne. Just to follow her.

SEVERAL HOURS LATER BJ drove Suzanne home, both quiet in their own thoughts. He kept looking over at her face, pale with dark circles under her closed, red-rimmed eyes. She barely stirred when they arrived and didn't protest when he carried her to their apartment. He quickly pulled off her scrubs, leaving her in just her panties. She sat on the edge of the bed, weariness pouring off of her. He grabbed one of his large t-shirts and pulled it over her head.

She looked up at him, recognizing his concern. "Honey, I'm okay. Really."

Pulling her up into his embrace as he pressed her tightly against his chest, he replied, "Babe, what you are not, is okay. You're strong and kind. You're trying to be there for your friend and the boys, but you gotta take care of you." He took her by the shoulders and gently pushed her back so that he could capture her eyes. "Warning you right now, babe. You don't take care of yourself, I'll shut this shit down quicker than you can blink."

Wanting to be irritated at his show of caveman skills, she couldn't help but love his concern. Nodding, she agreed.

"Good. Now let's get some food in you and then tucked in."

She couldn't argue with that plan, so she linked her fingers with his and headed toward the kitchen. After a simple meal of eggs and toast with a large glass of milk, she fell into bed and was sound asleep in no time.

BJ tucked her in then went into the living room to make some calls. First up was Shane and Annie.

"How's she doing?" Shane asked.

BJ could hear Annie in the background, wanting to know as well. "She's resting. Annie tell you that she's pregnant?"

"Yeah, congratulations man."

"I hear congratulations are in order for you too."

"Thanks. We're excited," Shane answered. Then softer he said, "Baby, Suzanne's fine. Go on in the other room and let me talk to BJ. I promise to tell you if there's something you need to know about."

BJ laughed as Shane got back on the phone with him. "Hard to separate the women from the job, isn't it?"

"You know it. Letting you know that we're going to relocate Mrs. Johnson and the boys. When we got back and talked to chief, we felt that considering what the boys told us they could be at risk and the Safe Haven House just isn't safe enough. They're not officially in protective custody, but your boss has some extra apartments stashed around the city for various reasons and we called him.

"Tony? He's a good man. Runs a tight security business and has a big heart. Especially when it comes to kids."

"They're moving tonight. Gabe and Vinny are takin' care of things for them. We gave 'em clearance to go into the house to grab some more of the clothes and personal items for Pamela and the boys. They're gettin' things set up right now. Just didn't want Suzanne to try to visit them at the Haven tomorrow and be upset when she couldn't find them 'cause no one knows where they went except us."

"You think they'll be safe there?"

"Kids are out for Christmas break and so they've got two weeks off of school. Tony's got a woman that'll watch the kids when Pamela needs to work, but her boss likes her and has given her time off to take care of the funeral arrangements."

"Still gonna be hard to keep her out of the view of anyone wanting to find them."

"Tony says he's got it."

BJ laughed, saying, "Then it's done. Never seen anything like him. He'll keep her off the grid."

Hanging up, he then called Matt and Lily. Before he could say hello, Lily was asking about Suzanne. Knowing she'd shared with her friends, he assured her that she was fine and resting.

Satisfied, Lily handed the phone over to Matt.

"Just went through the same routine with Annie," he joked.

"Yeah, they're tight, those three. But Annie and Lily went through hell dealing with shit that Shane and I were investigating. Make sure that Suzanne stays out of this mess."

"Don't worry. She's staying out. I'm making sure of that," BJ offered.

The men talked a few minutes, reiterating what Shane had said. BJ then asked to speak to Lily again.

"What's up?" she asked.

"You've been working on the reverse signals from some of the houses we've wired recently. Wanted to know how that was going."

"It's working well, but you know there's nothing legal about any of this," she stated. "We can monitor for safety, but for the clients that did not want that service, if we monitor anyway nothing would be admissible in court."

"I know, but Shane and Matt are convinced that Marcel Washington is involved in gambling, prostitution and who knows what else. But the man is slippery and they've got nothing on him. I know that was his house that Gabe and I wired."

"I'm still trying to write code to let me get in. Should have it later this week, if it'll work."

"Gottcha. Okay, Lily have a good night."

Making one last call, he wanted to talk to Tony.

"Hey man. Sorry to bother you. Just wanted to thank you for helping with the Johnsons."

"No problem. Glad to do it," Tony answered. "Gabe and Vinny got them settled in, made sure they weren't followed. In fact, Gabe is spending the night just to make sure they're okay. How's Suzanne?"

"Resting, thanks. That's the reason I'm calling. She's gonna want to talk to Pamela and the boys. How safe are they? What should I tell her?"

"The boys saw their dad go in the shed a lot and even admitted to peeking in the windows. Their mom 'bout had a shit-fit when they admitted that, but the boys were good. Told everything they saw. Said their dad had a strong box and when he opened it there was a bunch of money in it. They even peeked a couple of times when someone else was in there with the dad. They didn't know what was going on but said that the men would give their dad money and then sometimes their dad would give money to whoever was in there." He laughed ruefully, "They said their dad was always in a bad mood when the money left and in a good mood when taking it."

"Police figure gambling? Tied up in these dog fights?"

"Yeah. Had a talk with Matt and Shane this evening. Seems he's probably been on the fringes of the fighting activity, going so far as to having a dog in the fighting. The one that the boys took to Suzanne and Annie. Joe was winning some and losing some but then lost big when his dog was killed. He probably had no back up money to pay what he owed."

"Is that enough to get him killed?"

"Shane's got a theory that he was getting desperate. And desperate men do stupid things. Like maybe keep tabs on the ringleaders. Or really stupid things like threaten the leader and think that they'll buckle and bring him into the fold. Dumb fuck," Tony cursed.

"You know Lily's working on the feeds from Marcel Washington's house? What makes you think he's gonna let his business pour into his personal home knowing a security system's in place?"

"The man's smart. But sooner or later they all fuck up. And when they do, we want to be ready."

"How'd he get on your radar?"

Tony laughed. "He paid cash for my most expensive security system. Legitimate businessmen want it as a tax write-off. He's not paying taxes on whatever is earning him that money. I figured he was worth keeping an eye on."

"How do I keep Suzanne safe with all that's going on with the kids?"

"She needs to stay away from them for now. Anyone after them might assume she knows something."

"Thanks man. I owe you," BJ said.

"No way, BJ. No debts between friends."

Ringing off, he went back to the bedroom to check on Suzanne. Her face, still pale in the moonlight, now had the peaceful quality of slumber. *Sleeping beauty. Absolutely fuckin' sleeping beauty. And the mother of my child. Gonna keep you safe baby. Trust in that.*

Chapter 19

SUZANNE WAS PROFESSIONAL and friendly when Dr. Ketchum showed for work the next morning. He was excited to be in the clinic and followed Annie around taking careful notes of the clinic's procedures.

"Of course, I know you'll be looking at things to change once the ownership is transferred, but to keep down confusion for now, we want to keep things the same," she offered.

"Absolutely," he agreed. "Your system is perfect just as it is." As Annie moved to the other room, he turned to Suzanne as she walked into the back lab area. He grinned as he asked, "Sure I can't tempt you to stay on as my assistant?"

Forcing herself to smile, she simply shook her head. "Sorry. I'd follow Annie to any clinic."

His eyes moved over her as he said, "Such loyalty. And here I thought that everyone had their price."

She turned and left him standing there. *Jerk.* The thought struck her that with him out of the ER office, she could go over there and talk to Ralphie herself. Asking Annie if she could take an early lunch, she felt guilty when Annie quickly acquiesced assuming that

Suzanne needed food.

She hustled to the ER clinic and was pleased to see the waiting area empty and a young man at the reception desk talking to an older gentleman.

The man she assumed was Ralphie looked up and smiled as she walked in. The older gentleman turned and smiled at her also.

"May I help you ma'am?" the receptionist asked.

Glancing between the two of them, she quickly said, "Please finish with this gentleman. I'll wait."

The older man replied, "Oh we were finished, my dear. I'm Dr. Marker, the owner of the Animal Emergency Clinic. Retired now of course, but still like to come in and check on things."

At that information, she looked at him in interest. Tall, thin, dapper. His gray hair was neatly trimmed and he had a distinguished air about him. *He looks like what I imagine a British gentleman would look like.* She almost giggled then quickly recovered to maintain her professionalism.

Stepping forward, she stuck out her hand saying, "Hello. I'm Suzanne McDonald from Donavan's Veterinary Clinic down the street."

Dr. Marker immediately took her hand in his but, instead of shaking it, he bent over and brushed his lips over her hand in greeting. "Delighted to meet you, my dear. In my day, all of our associates were men, but I must say that the fairer gender makes for a much more positive atmosphere."

This time she was unable to contain her giggle. "Well, thank you. I'm not a veterinarian though. I am just the vet tech," she corrected.

"Ah, Ms. McDonald. In this business, there is no such thing as just a vet tech. Your work is invaluable to the veterinarian, as well as the animal and its owner."

Smiling up at the elder veterinarian, she said genuinely, "Do you no longer practice?"

Holding up his hands, bent with arthritis, he ruefully admitted, "No, my dear. These hands are no longer able to provide the care that I would demand of myself. But, through the emergency clinic here I can give back to the community that served me so well over the years. But I must be off and will let you attend to your business here. I wish you a good day and a happy holiday, Ms. McDonald."

With that, he nodded to the receptionist before he left. She found herself staring after him as he walked through the door until her thoughts were interrupted by the sound of a throat clearing.

Whirling around, red-faced, she apologized. "I'm sorry. It's just that…well…"

The young man standing behind the desk laughed. "It's okay. Uncle Edward does that to everyone. Quite a personality, wouldn't you agree?"

"Absolutely." Looking at the man she said, "Uncle?"

"Yes. Ralph Ritchner. I'm known as Ralphie around here. Dr. Marker is my uncle." Smiling, he lifted his shoulders in self-deprecation. "I admit it. Nepotism landed this job for me."

Ralph wasn't anything like she had expected. Somehow Dr. Ketchum had painted a picture of a slovenly boy who couldn't learn the simple job of being a receptionist in a vet clinic. In front of her stood a man about her age, also tall and thin with boyishly handsome looks.

"Well, I landed my job just by going in and introducing myself to the veterinarian and begging her to hire me," she laughed.

"My brother was the smart one. He went to college and has a degree. I just really wanted to work while deciding what I wanted to be when I grew up." He added with a laugh, "Here's to getting jobs however we needed to."

She couldn't help but smile at his humor.

"So, Ms. McDonald, what can I do for you?"

Suddenly unsure of what to say she found herself blurting out, "I wondered what you thought of Dr. Ketchum and how some things were handled when he was here."

Ralphie's genteel demeanor changed as his face took on a sour look. "Oh yes. The big Dr. Ketchum." His eyes gleamed with recognition. "You're from the clinic that he's buying, aren't you? Wondering what it will be like to work for 'the great Phil'?"

Taken aback by his change in temper, she rushed to explain, "No. I'm not going to be staying and working for him."

Ralphie raised his eyebrow in question. "Then what are you looking for?"

"Answers," she said simply. Sighing, she said, "Look, I've been trying for several months to get a straight answer from him about some dog attacks in the neighborhood. He kept deflecting and then —"

"Blaming me, right?" he interrupted.

"Um…well, yeah."

"Let me guess. I had the clinic closed when I went to lunch. I didn't file reports with the city. I turned people away when they came in. Especially if there was anything to do with dog attacks."

Suzanne stood stunned, her heart pounding. *Have I had this all wrong? Phil's been making it look like he's blameless in all of this.*

Ralphie took a deep breath and then reached in a file behind him and pulled out a form. "Look," he said. "I fill out the form and then it has to be signed by a doctor. Not me. The doctor. That was Phil."

"But you didn't see that they were sent in?"

"I just followed protocol. I leave about five p.m. each night and then the night receptionist comes in. Phil was almost always here when I left. I had a folder of things for him to sign and the next day the folder would be empty and on my desk. I assumed that after he had signed them then he faxed them over or had the night receptionist do it. I'm also allowed a lunch break. I usually leave because I like to get things done or just get some fresh air. I didn't put a closed sign on the door because either he or one of the vet techs was here."

Suzanne stood for a moment, pondering this new information. Biting her lip in concentration, she asked, "How did you know what my concerns were?"

"Your boss, Dr. Donavan, called several times to talk to Phil. I overheard her concerns and heard him place them squarely on me. Pissed me off, I can tell you."

"You didn't talk to your uncle about it?"

"Ms. McDonald. You're a vet tech, right? That's not a veterinarian."

She looked at him in confusion. "I know. What's that got to do with anything?"

"Dr. Edward may be my uncle, but he's old school. He was educated as a veterinarian and has a great deal of respect for others in his...life station, shall we say."

"He'd believe Dr. Ketchum over you?" she asked incredulously.

"The key word here, Ms. McDonald, is *Doctor*. So yes, he would believe another veterinarian over me."

"Oh, I see," she said softly, her mind whirling with the questions about Dr. Ketchum and why he would want to cover up dog attacks.

At her acquiescence, Ralphie gentled his tone. "Look, you obviously have a great working relationship with Dr. Donavan and that's wonderful. I haven't had that here. So I apologize for coming off as a prick earlier."

Smiling at him, she answered, "No, it's fine. I'm sure it's been horrible working for someone who blames you for things that aren't your fault." Looking down at her watch, she quickly added, "My lunch break is over and I need to get back. Thank you for your time."

Shaking his hand, she hurried out into the cold winter air. Walking quickly down the street for the blocks that it would take to get back to her clinic, she hoped that Phil would already be gone by the time she arrived. *I need to talk to Brad about all of this. None of it is making any sense.*

Pulling her scarf up around her nose, she walked briskly down the street, her eyes downcast to make sure of her footing on the uneven sidewalks.

The ever present eyes on her, hidden behind the dark, tinted windows of a black SUV followed discreetly behind her. The man inside, losing the battle of self-control, rubbed his swollen dick as he kept his eyes on her. "You'll be mine soon, my dark-haired beauty," Jorge said to himself.

THE NEXT WEEKEND found Jorge at his usual place near Marcel's temporary office above the fight ring. Glancing to the side, he saw a visibly shaken Charisse standing near the small window. She had taken extra care with her appearance tonight, wearing a tight dress that showed more skin than Marcel would have wanted his main escort to show – but he knew it was wasted on

Marcel. Marcel was into class. Or at least the illusion of class. And Charisse had none. She'd been great at pretending for longer than most, but her time was up and if her desperate look was any indication, she knew it.

Marcel jerked his head toward the door and she immediately moved to it and went into the hall. Looking at Jorge, he got to the point. "Haven't fucked that cunt in a week. She's getting desperate, but instead of trying to get back in my good graces she's been high and dressing like one of the girls downstairs most of the week. I want her sister."

"Working on it boss. She's different. She quit Club Edge and just landed a job with a legal firm."

"Legal firm? Fuck." Marcel twisted his face in disgust.

"But we may still be able to use her. I've got some…leverage."

Marcel turned to look at Jorge, "Well for tonight, get me one of the girls. One I would like. And have someone collect Charisse's things from the mansion. She's out tonight. I won't send her back to the stable. At least not now. She can stay at one of the apartments. She'll make a good escort for some of my guests who are looking for easy pussy while in town."

Nodding, Jorge headed out of the room to do Marcel's bidding. The sound of snarls and snapping jaws was in the background. Immune, he walked by the pit looking for a suitable fuck for Marcel. Seeing one of the younger, less used girls he walked over, whispered in her ear, and saw the gleam of hope light up her eyes. Motioning to one of Marcel's bodyguards to escort her upstairs, he continued around the pit. Hearing the name Devil's Spawn he stopped short. Turning back to the pit, he watched as the dog mauled and quickly killed the other dog in record time. Holding back a grin, he mentally added up his night's winnings. Looking over at Charisse, he saw her see the other woman being escorted up. Her face flushed with shock, then anger before she stormed off. Nodding to another man, he gave silent instructions for her to be stopped so that she could continue to do Marcel's bidding. Having sorted his boss' cock problems, he turned his attention back to the fights. Yes, Devil's Spawn was going to make him a lot of money. It was time to get back to the farm to make sure his investment was being properly taken care of.

LYING IN BED after BJ had worshiped her body into oblivion, Suzanne draped herself half over him, feeling boneless. Sleep was overtaking her and she did not even have the energy to move. She had talked to BJ over dinner about her conversations at the ER clinic, with both Dr. Marker and Ralph Ritchner.

He rested one hand on her ass and the other rubbed the smooth skin of her back. Smiling to himself, he shifted her so that she would be more comfortable. So far, the pregnancy hormones had her moods swinging from tearful to sex starved. He particularly liked the latter. Tucking her naked body in close to his, he wrapped his arm around her waist, splaying his fingers over her stomach. *Can you feel me, little one? Do you know how much you are wanted and loved already?*

His mind wandered back to the counseling he sought at the college after Suzy's miscarriage and subsequent leaving. He knew there was no rhyme or reason to the loss of their other child, but he had to admit that he felt the same desperate hope that this child would make it full term. *No matter what, I have to be strong for her. But I really want to hold you, little one.*

Pulling her in tight, he allowed himself to join her in sleep.

Hours later, he awoke suddenly. Listening intently, he heard no sounds except for the soft snoring coming from her. His mind raced back to what thoughts had woken him up, remember the conversation that they had had in the evening. Something was in the back of his mind, just out of reach. *Something she said?* He went back over what Ralphie had said about Phil Ketchum. He'd never like the good doctor and disliked him even more now. He'd first pursued Annie and then Suzanne, not even realizing that if one of the women had liked him it would be awkward since they worked together. But being a prick didn't make him a criminal. *Unless, he's the one who was destroying the reports to Animal Control.*

Determined to get Shane and Matt to get their hands on the Animal Control records, he felt that was key. But as he drifted back to sleep he couldn't help but feel that there was a piece of the puzzle that was just out of reach.

SEVERAL DAYS LATER, Suzanne accompanied BJ to his work. Gabe was bringing the boys into the security agency for a few hours while their mother took care of more business. Their father had been buried with little ceremony, but she wanted to be there for the boys. She had managed to avoid Phil on the two other mornings that week that he had come in. He and Annie had gone over records, lab equipment, needs of the clinic and the clientele while she had managed to stay up front taking care of the appointments.

Each morning found her hanging over the toilet for a few minutes, but every time BJ held her hair back and wiped her face with a cool washcloth. *He truly seems okay with this.* Her hand found her stomach and she couldn't hold back a smile. *We've got to tell our parents soon.* Rolling her eyes, she couldn't help but wonder how that would go.

"You're quiet this morning, baby. Are you sure you feel up to this?" BJ asked.

"Yeah, I can't wait to see the boys. Just a little tired." Sneaking a look over at his profile, smiling as she perused his square jaw with its Saturday morning stubble. "Of course, if you hadn't kept me up so late, I wouldn't be so tired."

"Me?" he joked. "If I recall correctly, it was you that was insatiable."

"Hmmm, must be the pregnancy hormones kicking in."

"Well let me just say they can kick in any time they want!"

Pulling into the underground parking garage, they saw Gabe driving in with the boys in tow at the same time. Getting out of their vehicles, they greeted each other enthusiastically.

Once BJ had Suzanne and the boys settled in one of the safe rooms, he went in search of Lily and the briefing they had with Tony.

Suzanne sat down on the sofa in the room and noticed that the boys ignored the large TV, but focused on her instead, as though they needed her connection. "How are you doing, guys?" she asked softly.

Dwayne, always stoic, looked at his brother. His hair was freshly washed and combed, his clothes neat and clean, but his face carried a worried look upon it. Chuckie piped up, "We were asked questions by the police about what we saw."

"That's not what she meant, Chuckie. She wants to know about dad," Dwayne said.

"It's okay, Chuckie. I want to know about every-thing. What you're feeling. How you're doing. If you want to talk about the funeral, that's fine. If you want to talk about the police that's fine too. Or if you just want to watch football, we can do that also."

Dwayne's eyes cut over to the TV that was larger than any he had probably seen. Finding the remote, she turned it on, finding a game for them to watch. Chuckie settled in quickly on the floor, his head propped up on his hands and his face glued to the screen. Dwayne made his way over to the sofa sitting near Suzanne. After a few minutes, he said quietly, "Dad was messed up wasn't he?"

Trying to word her thoughts carefully, she began, "Well, I think that he may have gotten himself in some difficulty –"

"You don't have to make it sound better than it is. Just say it. He was messed up and then got killed for it."

Sighing, she agreed. "Dwayne, in talking to your mom, it sounds like your dad was a good man once. He loved her and he loved you boys. But yes, he got messed up in something and made some bad choices. But that doesn't mean he didn't love you."

"The police think he was gambling and I heard mom talk about dog fighting." He turned his face up to hers. "I looked that up on the internet at school."

Seeing his tortured face, she pulled him in for a hug not caring if it embarrassed him or not. "Oh, honey. You shouldn't have."

She felt wetness against her neck and hugged him tighter.

"Do you think that was what he did to our dog? The pictures on the computer were awful."

Just then, Gabe stuck his head in the door. He looked over at the scene in front of him and mouthed, "Are you all right?" to her. She nodded and he slipped back out. She knew Gabe was going to tell BJ, but she desperately wanted a few more minutes alone with the boys. *They've been questioned so much. I just want to give them a few minutes of comfort.*

Lifting his head away from her so that she could see into his eyes, she said, "Dwayne, listen to me." Glancing over she saw that Chuckie had stopped watching the TV and had moved toward her feet. She leaned down to gather him up on the sofa as well. With her arms around both boys, she said, "Yes, there are people who do bad things to each other and to animals as well. I know Pepper looked bad when you brought him in to see Doc Annie, but your dog knew a lot of love from you boys. Most dogs in fights don't get that and you gave that love to him."

She saw their tear-filled eyes meet hers and she continued, "As badly as he was hurt that morning, he came home to you two. He wanted your love and felt safe with you."

Chuckie's eyes spilled over with tears, but Dwayne dashed his away, saying, "Yeah, but dad had him doin' stuff that hurt him."

"It couldn't have been that bad, Dwayne. Not for your dog to come back to you. That means that your love was stronger than anything else Pepper knew and he was coming back. Back to where he felt safe and where he felt love."

Squeezing them tight, she said it again, "He just wanted to come to where he felt love. And that boys, is a gift that not everyone can give. But you did. You gave it to him. And you've got all that love inside of you to give again."

IN THE BRIEFING room, the employees of Tony's security team were assembled, along with Matt and Shane, around a large wooden table, all listening to the conversation happening in the safe room. Lily wept unashamedly.

Tony looked across the table and said, "That's quite a woman you've got there, BJ. But then, we all knew that."

BJ simply nodded, not trusting his voice.

Gabe spoke up, "I think those boys'll be all right. Their mom seems like good people and with support like Suzanne...I think they'll make it through and maybe not turn out like their dad."

The group got down to business, discussing the latest on the dog fights and gambling. Tony looked over to Matt and Shane. "What've you got?"

Shane spoke first, saying, "Vice has been looking at Marcel Washington. So far, he's kept the business clean. Lives in one of those big houses over in the Bel

Grande Estates. But his right-hand man is Jorge Hernandez. Came up from the ranks of the Richland underbelly. Gangs, fights, gambling, drugs, prostitution. Came from a shit home and joined a gang when he was only eleven.

Matt continued, "Smart though. Not just street smart. Worked his way up the chain and it appears that he is now an associate of Marcel. The goddamn dog fights have been a thorn in the side of the street cops, gang detectives, and Vice for years now. They find and shut down the small ones, but new ones crop up continually. What we're looking at now is a big operation. Big stakes. Big money."

Vinny looked over. "What about the peons who handle the dogs and have petty bets? Won't they roll over on the others?"

Lifting an eyebrow Shane answered, "And end up like Joe Johnson?" He looked around the table, "The fuckers have the backing of one of the most notorious, organized gangs around. Fear, drugs, money, and threats keep 'em in line."

Gabe shared a look with Tony, receiving a slight nod. Gabe turned back to the group saying, "We set up the security wiring in a home recently. Owner was Marcel Washington."

"Are they wired into your security system?" Matt asked with renewed interest.

Tony shook his head. "They only wanted internal visual. So he could use his own security people to watch the feeds."

BJ wondered out loud, "Could we get back in? Say that they needed maintenance?"

Tony shook his head. "Normally, I'd say yes. But not this guy. If he's as big as you say he is then he's smart too. He'd never fall for that."

"But, it is possible to reprogram," a soft voice came from the end of the table.

The mountain of testosterone that sat around the table focused their attention on Lily, sitting quietly at the end.

"I've been working on the programming that BJ set up and while the original programming and feeds were for internal monitoring, it's possible to tap into what they're seeing." Looking over at Matt and Shane, she quickly added, "But nothing would be admissible in a court. Wiretapping, you know?" she said with a little shrug.

Tony nodded his approval. "Keep working on that angle."

"I'm also talking to one of my old professors to see if he knows who would have the skills to streamfeed the dogfights with a secure line that we can't tap into. I met with him last week and he gave me some ideas. I'm checking into a couple of them to see if they are still in the area and if so, who they're working for."

"Damn, girl," Gabe said. "You're putting the rest of us to shame."

She blushed as Matt winked at her. BJ filled them

in on the information that Suzanne had received from Ralph and her suspicions about Dr. Ketchum.

Shane growled, knowing that Phil was working in the clinic for another couple of weeks with Annie and Suzanne. "Gonna check that bastard out. If he has his own clinic then he is free to do what he wants."

BJ sat silently for a moment, frustrated as the feeling that a tiny piece of the puzzle was hovering just out of his reach. "Tony, how about you reassign me to working with Lily again. With the two of us working on the programming, we should be able to figure out something." Looking over at Shane he added, "Know you can't use it, but just in case we need it, we'll be able to tap into Marcel's place."

The meeting quickly came to a close and BJ headed down the hall to find Suzanne. Stepping into the room, he was greeted by the sounds of laughter as she and the boys were watching TV. Dwayne was sitting next to her, his head on her shoulder, while Chuckie was on the floor between her legs with his head against her knees. Looking up, she smiled at him and his heart pounded in his chest. *Beautiful. So goddamn beautiful. She looks like a mother there.* He found it hard to breathe for a moment as he took her in. *Strong, caring, and loving. She'll be perfect. The perfect mother. Please God,* he prayed, *let this child live. Let her hold this one in her arms. And I'll do everything I can every day to be worthy of them.*

His eyes moved back to hers and saw questions

there. Smiling, he just shook his head. "You 'bout ready to go, babe? Gabe'll be coming for the boys in just a few minutes."

Nodding, she said goodbye to the boys, lingering a moment in their embraces. Chuckie quickly kissed her and turned back to his movie. Dwayne moved in for a real hug then pulled back, embarrassed as he looked up at BJ.

BJ kissed the top of her head and motioned for her to go on ahead of him. Nodding her understanding, she left with a glance back over her shoulder as she reached the door. BJ had leaned down to Dwayne's level with his hand on the back of Dwayne's neck, looking him in the eye and was saying, "You're not too young to understand that you want to be a different kind of man than your dad was. You find a woman, you take care of her. Always. But you're also not too old to accept the hugs from a good woman who wants to help you. So don't ever be embarrassed."

Dwayne looked at BJ in awe, nodding as he smiled over at Suzanne when she turned and left the room. Her mind wandered and took her to a place that touched deep inside of her. *I can see him talking to our child like that. Please God let me give him this child.*

Looking up, she saw Gabe coming. Stopping in front of her, he stood silently. Hands on his hips. Towering over her. Waiting.

"Hey Gabe," she said reaching out to lay her hand on his arm. He'd been like a brother to her for the past year.

"That's all you got to say to me? Hey?"

"Um…Merry Christmas?" she said, uncertainty filling her mind. "Oh!" she said suddenly. "You know?"

"And just what am I supposed to know, darlin'? Since you haven't told me shit, just what am I supposed to know?"

"That I'm…um…pregnant?" she said hesitantly, looking up into his dark brown eyes.

His face broke out in a huge grin as he grabbed her up and swung her around in circles. "It's 'bout time you told me yourself. Got tired of waitin' when I heard it from everyone else."

"Put her down you big dickhead," BJ warned as he came out into the hall. Pulling her out of Gabe's arms, he looked her over. "You don't twirl an expecting woman around in circles."

"Honey, I'm fine," she giggled as BJ tucked her into his side.

Gabe looked at her with affection. "You look real good sweetheart." Looking over at BJ, he said, "Congratulations, BJ. You both deserve all the happiness you can get."

With a wink he headed into the safe room to collect the boys as BJ and she headed home.

Chapter 20

SEVERAL DAYS LATER, Suzanne knocked on Mr. Charleston's door once again. He answered with a smile on his face, but still had a wary look in his eyes.

"Hi Petunia," she effused as Mr. Charleston opened the door for her to enter. Standing, she looked at him saying, "Dr. Donavan, Leon, and myself are making the rounds to some of our favorite clients just to let you know about the changes that are going to be happening." *At least that is not a lie*, she said to herself, not letting him know that she had chosen him especially to visit.

"Dr. Donavan is selling the practice and another veterinarian will be taking over."

Her words were met with shock and dismay as he immediately grabbed her hand. "You're leaving? But you know Petunia so well. You've always looked after her."

"I know, Mr. Charleston. But it'll be fine, I promise." *Now that may be a lie.* "Dr. Phil Ketchum will be taking over the practice and he's very excited to be there."

Mr. Charleston's sharp eyes held hers. "Dr. Ketchum…where have I heard that name before?"

"Well, he currently works in the ER clinic that is a few blocks over. He seems to be a very capable veterinarian."

"Bah! I've been there. Not impressed with that clinic."

"Well, it won't be the ER clinic. It'll be his own clinic like Dr. Donavan's."

Not convinced, they continued to chat for a couple of minutes while she reassured him that Petunia would receive the finest care.

As she walked to the door, she turned as he called out to her, his voice shaky. "It's good you are leaving. I will miss you. But…you are not…safe. It's good that you…well, it is good."

Confused, she asked, "What do you mean? I'm not safe?"

He hurried to the door and hustled her out. "I'm sorry Ms. Suzanne. I've said too much. Ignore this old man's ramblings. You go and know that you will be missed."

With nothing else to say, she turned and started down the stairs from his apartment. The sound of his voice whispered so softly that she wasn't sure she heard. "Stay safe, Miss Suzanne. Stay safe."

After a few more stops she was heading to Mr. Marchelli's place. On her way, she called BJ. "Hey sweetie, I'm just letting you know that I'm almost finished with our house visits. I'm going to see Chaucer and Mr. Marchelli."

"Suzy, isn't that the apartment where you said the creepy nephew was visiting?"

"Yes, but I'll –"

"Stop right there. You do not go in by yourself. Can't Leon go too?"

"He's got his own list of clients that he's seeing. Besides, it's broad daylight. Nothing's going to happen in the middle of the day. There are lots of people around."

"Suzy girl, don't you move. Is there a shop nearby?"

Looking around she replied, "Yeah, a coffee shop is a few doors up the street. Kofie's Koffee."

"Go there and stay. I'll be there in about fifteen minutes. I do not want you going to that apartment by yourself."

Agreeing, she had just ordered her cup of herbal tea when BJ walked in. She saw him first and couldn't help but notice how his eyes searched around until they landed on her. No one else but her. A flashback to her seeing him walk in her mother's bakery washed over her, filling her senses with the smells of home and him.

Several minutes later they knocked on Mr. Marcelli's door. His expression at seeing Suzanne was similar to Mr. Charleston's, but his eyes grew wide at the presence of BJ filling the doorway behind her. As she quickly explained the change in the clinic's ownership, he also was sad to see them move away.

She introduced BJ as her boyfriend who just wanted her safe in the neighborhood, which seemed to fill Mr. Marcelli with relief.

"I am glad you're with her. The neighborhood is usually safe, but…" his voice trailed off.

"Has your nephew been back to see you lately?" Suzanne asked.

Mr. Marcelli's eyes glanced at hers and then over to BJ's tight face. "He…I…uh, no. What I mean to say is…no." The silence in the room was only broken by the panting of Chaucer. Mr. Marcelli hung his head, shaking it slightly. Heaving a huge sigh, he looked up at Suzanne with tears in his eyes. "You must forgive an old man. I am so ashamed."

She walked over and placed her hand on his arm in reassurance. "What's wrong, Mr. Marcelli? You can tell us. We can help."

He hesitated then bent over to rub Chaucer's ears and looked up at the couple standing before him. "I don't have a nephew. I don't know that man's name but I do know he's dangerous."

"What was he doing here?" she probed gently.

He stood and clasped his gnarled hands in front of him. "He came to warn me that someone from Dr. Donavan's clinic might be trying to snoop about the attack on my poor Chaucer. He had just said that he would hate for my words to cause any harm to come to one of you."

Her sudden intake of breath was matched by the anger she could feel at her back. Mr. Marcelli's eyes darted between hers and BJ's angry visage.

"It was pure coincidence that he was here when you stopped by." Mr. Marcelli's voice shook, "I was so scared, Ms. Suzanne. And after you left, he threatened me to stay quiet."

"What was his threat?" BJ's question rumbled from deep in his chest, his fists clenched at his sides.

"He said he would go after you Ms. Suzanne, and I believed him. The man is evil. I've never seen such evil."

A string of cursing erupted from BJ and she turned to try to calm him. He had pulled his phone out and quickly made a call. "Lily? Get some pictures of Marcel Washington's known associates. Anyone you can pull up. Send them to my phone. Yeah, thanks."

Suzanne and Mr. Marcelli stood quietly as BJ placed another call. "Matt? With Suzanne. Got a problem. Meet us at the clinic. We may finally have a lead on Marcel. Make it look like a visit to see Annie."

Just then BJ's phone chirped indicating a message was coming in. Looking down to see that they were coming from Lily, he said, "Damn, she's good."

Turning the phone around, he began showing Mr. Marcelli several pictures. On the third one, he gasped. "That's him. That's the one."

As BJ turned the phone around to Suzanne, she carefully looked at the picture before nodding. She lifted her eyes to BJ's saying, "Yeah. That's the man who was here."

Turning to Mr. Marcelli, BJ said, "Okay. Here's how this is going to go. If anyone asks why we were here, you just tell them the truth, and that is that Ms. Suzanne was here to tell you about a new vet taking over the practice. She's been doing this for the past couple of days, so it's believable. If anyone asks why I was here with her, you can say that we told you it was because she wasn't feeling well and wanted her boyfriend nearby. That's it. You don't know anything else. We're getting ready to leave and as we open the door, make it sound good. Okay?"

Mr. Marcelli nodded his agreement as he walked them to the door. "It was so nice of you to come see me Ms. Suzanne. Chaucer and I will miss you at the clinic when we visit."

"I will miss you too, Mr. Marcelli. Thank you for letting me come say goodbye," she said, her voice shaking, as BJ reached down to hold her hand.

As the door closed behind her, BJ led them down the stairs and out into the street. A discreet scan revealed a black SUV parked on the corner. "Kiss me and then smile," he said, as he pulled her around for a kiss.

"What?" Suzanne asked, too stunned to think quickly. His kiss took over and she melted against his body.

He pulled back ever so slightly to whisper, "I think we're being watched. Smile as we head over to the car."

Gifting him with a glorious smile, that only he

could see did not reach her eyes, they walked hand in hand back to his vehicle. Driving to the clinic, he saw the SUV pull away from the curb but noticed it did not follow them.

At the clinic, they greeted Matt and Shane as though the meeting was nothing more than old friends getting together. As they moved to the back of the clinic, Suzanne took Annie and Leon aside to explain the situation. Matt and Shane went into the small office with BJ for his report.

Shane looked down at the picture. "Jesus fuck. Jorge fuckin' Hernadez."

"You know him?" BJ asked.

"When I was undercover, we knew of him. He worked his way up in a rival gang's organization. Word was he was ruthless. Something's totally wired screwy in him. He'd just as soon kill someone as look at 'em."

The men were quiet for a moment, then BJ asked, "What do you have on him? Anything that can stick? This fucker has seen Suzanne. Talked to her. Jesus, he's threatened her!"

"Stay with her. In fact, stay here until Annie closes and see her home. The clinic is closed for the next three days anyway for the holidays. We're heading back to meet with the chief. But BJ? We want him and we want him officially tied to Marcel. And we want to shut them down."

Before BJ could explode, Matt jumped in. "We get it, man. We're not going to put Suzanne at risk, so you gotta stay with her. But give us a chance to bring them all down. Arresting Jorge because he threatened an old man isn't going to even put him in jail for one night. We gotta play this smart."

BJ clenched his fists, dropping his head. He knew they were right. They had to take these fuckers down. *But I gotta keep her safe. Her and the baby.*

Lifting his head, he nodded. "Okay. As soon as Annie closes up I'll see her home, and then I'm heading to Tony's with Suzanne. I want to report to him and let them know what is happening."

With that agreement, the men left the office and proceeded to their destinations. Matt and Shane held a meeting at the police station, focusing the investigation squarely on Marcel's organization now that positive identification of Jorge had been made. Shane called Tony to arrange a conference call so the police could hear while Tony was talking to Suzanne.

Once Annie was in her home safely, BJ drove Suzanne to the security agency. This time, Tony had Suzanne sit in on the meeting. BJ described the dark SUV, adding, "I know they saw me make them. They didn't follow, but they left quickly. And I never got close enough to see the goddamn plates."

"Don't beat yourself up," Tony said. "They've already ditched that vehicle or just changed plates on it. In fact, they probably rotate plates regularly, so the police would never find them." He turned his attention to Suzanne, who had been sitting quietly. "Honey," he said gently. "Have you ever noticed anyone following you?"

Looking around at the faces of Tony's crew, all filled with concern, she answered, "Not really. I…it's just that…I don't know." Realizing that she was not being clear, she began again. "I try to be careful when I'm out. Follow all the normal rules for a female, like running during the daytime, having my keys out when I am getting ready to get to my door, things like that. But I don't stare around me at all times to see if someone is out there. My brain just doesn't work that way."

The group was quiet as they could see she was deep in thought. BJ started to say something, but the shake of Tony's head held him silent. Glancing down at her sitting next to him, he could see that she was working the problem.

Looking back up, she continued, "I remember the night of the dog attack. There was a whistle that called the dogs back and as I looked to the end of the alley, there was a dark SUV that the last dog jumped into. I also remember seeing a dark SUV near the Johnson's house. It stood out because it was so new looking and most of the cars in that neighborhood were older. It never occurred to me that it could be following me. I…I mean lots of people have dark SUVs." Twisting to look up into BJ's face, she asked, "Why would someone want to follow me?"

BJ threw his arm around her protectively and

pulled her close. "Baby, we don't have all the answers, but you're not leaving my sight. You got that?"

Gabe, Vinny, Jobe, and Lily looked at the couple with concern, before turning their attention back to Tony.

"It may be because you simply fell into the dog fighting situation. With the animals that came to the clinic. With the boys. With you befriending the Johnsons afterward. With you calling the ER clinic."

Suzanne's eyes grew wide. "But I was never trying to investigate. I just wanted to do my job. Well, at first. Then I met the boys and just wanted to help them."

"We know that, sweetheart," Matt assured her, listening into the conference. "But that's put you on their radar."

Shane spoke up next. "We just met with our task force here and the chief. We can now focus on Marcel's organization and places of business. Both legal and where we think his illegal activities are. BJ, stay with Suzanne as we try to tighten the noose around their necks."

The conference went on for several more minutes, but Suzanne was no longer paying attention. Her mind was racing, thoughts swirling around faster than she could process. *The clients who had been threatened. The clinic being watched. Dwayne and Chuckie. The look in Jorge's eyes when he spoke to her.*

"Baby? Baby?" a voice sounded in her ear. Startled, she jumped as she saw that the meeting was breaking up.

"I want to get you home. We're taking the next three days and not leaving our apartment except to visit Fairfield," BJ promised. Seeing that she was still shaken, he assisted her up from her chair and led her out of the room. Hugs from their friends along with Merry Christmas wishes filled the air.

She just wished her heart felt as light as the holiday season, but a sense of impending doom settled around her.

Chapter 21

THE NEXT DAY, the apartment was filled with the sounds of Christmas music as she and BJ settled in to enjoy the day. They were driving to Fairfield on Christmas day to see their families and let them know about the baby. The gloom of the previous day seemed far away, as though it had been a bad dream that was now chased away by the sunshine.

That evening, as they sat under the tree, she excitedly lay several brightly wrapped packages in front of BJ. "It was hard to know what to get you," she said apologetically. "So, I got a couple of things that I hoped you would like."

He looked at the woman sitting cross-legged in front of him. Long, silky black hair pulled back with a dark green headband, showcasing her blue eyes peering at him anxiously. Flawless skin, with just a hint of blush on her cheeks. Black yoga pants paired with an emerald green top – which he tried to not focus on because the thought of her luscious ass and perfect breasts would make all other gifts pale in comparison.

Leaning in to kiss her lips, he admitted, "All I want is sitting right in front of me." Gifted with her brilliant smile once again, he couldn't believe his good fortune. "All I've ever wanted is you."

Dropping her head, a blush spreading across her face, she felt the tears spring to her eyes. "Go on. Open them," she encouraged gently.

He proceeded to open his gifts, enjoying each one. A few items of clothing. A new watch. And a wallet. Smiling, she encouraged him to open it. Inside were five tickets to the Richland professional basketball game. He looked up in surprise.

Laughing, she said, "Grab some friends next month and have a good time."

Leaning over, he kissed her lips enthusiastically. Licking the seam, he plunged in as her mouth opened to his. She tasted of apple cider and cinnamon. *Earthy. Heady. Delicious.* Sliding his arms around her body, he gently pulled her closer until she was straddling his lap, her breasts pressed against his chest. Pulling back, he gave her a quick kiss before twisting his body around to look under the tree.

"Now where can your present be? I'm sure I had it here," he said, pretending to look around puzzled.

Giggling, she pushed against his chest. "Well, if you can't find it, I'll just go clean up the kitchen and pout by myself."

Before she could move, he growled, "Oh no you don't, baby girl," stilling her movements with his hands. Then lifting his eyes upward to a tree branch just above their heads, he exclaimed, "What's this?"

Her eyes sought where his hand went, noticing a pretty angel ornament on the tree. "I don't remember that being there."

The angel was delicate china, with soft feathers for its wings. Above its head sat a halo. Or rather two halos. As he brought the ornament closer, she could see that one halo belonged to the angel. The other halo was actually a…

Plucking the second halo from the angel's head, BJ held a diamond ring in his hand. A white gold band held a large center diamond, encircled with numerous diamonds.

Staring into the eyes that had enraptured him for as long as he could remember, he held the diamond out to her. "Suzanne McDonald. Will you do me the greatest honor in the world and become my wife?"

Tears streamed down her face. Her hand shook as she held it out for him to slip the ring on. Time was repeating itself only this time it was better. Stronger. Ready to face life, whatever uncertainties may come. Staring down at the perfect ring on her finger, she couldn't stop the tears that flowed unchecked down her cheeks.

"Well?" he prodded.

"Yes, yes, a thousand times yes," she cried, throwing her arms around his neck and pulling him down for a kiss.

They fell backwards on the rug. Clothing was soon tossed aside, as were all inhibitions. Making love under the Christmas tree with the twinkling lights reflecting off of their bodies, their passion exploded and hours later found them fast asleep in their bed.

THE EARLY MORNING drive to Fairfield on Christmas Day was much different than the trip they had made earlier in the fall. A light sprinkling of snow blanketed the horizon and Suzanne leaned back in her seat watching the beautiful countryside go by. Glancing down at her left hand, she couldn't help but admire the sparkling diamond that now rested there. The sunlight caught the facets and colorful prisms danced all around her hand.

BJ looked to the side seeing her staring at her new ring. Pride filled his chest as he once again thought of how lucky he was to have a second chance at love with this woman. He then saw her right hand slide over and rest on her stomach. *And a baby. Jesus, I'm a lucky fuck.* His mind flashed to the warnings from Tony and the situation surrounding Suzanne back in Richland – *No. Not today. Today is Christmas, family, good news, and good times.*

"Are you nervous?" her voice broke into his musings. Glancing into her sparkling eyes, he smiled. "Nah. It's gonna be all good. You okay with everything?"

Taking a deep breath, she nodded. "Yeah, it's going to be fun."

"So where are we starting? My parents or yours?"

"Mom said yesterday to head to their house. They were going to host a Christmas morning brunch and invite your parents and grandparents over. They're also having Laurie's dad and stepmom come over as well, since Rob and Laurie will be there with the kids. They put a big tree out in the barn and said we could all have presents there."

"Hmmm, wonder what Santa's gonna bring you since you've been such a good little girl this year," he joked.

Holding her hand up with the diamond catching the light, she laughed saying, "All I want is you and this baby. So, Santa's already been to see me."

BJ reached out and grabbed her hand, pulling it to his lips. Placing a soft kiss on each fingertip, he then kissed the ring. "Together always, baby. Trust me."

They pulled into her parents' driveway and drove around to the back where they parked in a row next to several other vehicles. Bernie was already pushing a small cart, carrying out what looked like some steaming platters. They waved as BJ assisted her from the SUV and hustled into the barn out of the cold.

It didn't take long for her ring to catch someone's eye and the congratulations flowed. Everyone crowded around to admire the beautiful setting on her hand. BJ caught a look between the mothers and he knew that Wendy and Bernie had gone instantly into wedding planning. The women had maneuvered Suzanne over to one side, so he took the opportunity to walk over to

Mac, giving his dad a quick nod first.

"Mac, I didn't get a chance to ask you for your daughter's hand, but I'm doing it now. I've loved your daughter for as long as I can remember and I want you to know that's never changed. We're older now and ready to face whatever happens in life together."

"I appreciate that, Brad. I was ready to welcome you into the family four years ago and that still stands." Reaching out to shake the younger man's hand, he held it tightly as he leaned in. "I liked you as a child and a young man. I never minded my daughter dating you when ya'll were younger. I hated that you had to get engaged when she got pregnant, but I was never upset that it was you that she was going to marry." Mac stopped for just a moment, thinking on his words. "She's my only baby girl, Brad. When you two broke up, it felt like I'd lost my daughter for a long time. She didn't come home as much and when we would see her, the sadness in her was…well, it 'bought broke this old man's heart. But I look at her now," he said looking to the side at Suzanne surrounded by friends as she beamed, "and I see happiness. So son, welcome to the family."

With that, Mac pulled BJ into a bear hug, slapping him on the back heartily. BJ looked over at his father who gave him a wink. He then walked over to his dad who embraced him as well.

"Proud of you son," Bill said. "Real proud."

Helen, BJ's grandmother, came over to hug him as

well, standing on her toes to wrap her arms around his neck. "You and that little girl over there have been destined for each other since you were born. Glad to see that the stars have once again aligned and you found happiness."

"She sees things you know?" came the wizened voice of his grandfather, Roger, who was smiling behind his wife. "She knew you two would get together. Never lost faith."

BJ laughed as he shook his grandfather's hand, knowing his grandmother's gift for *seeing*. Helen placed her hand on his arm and whispered so no one else could hear, "There will be difficult days, but this child will come."

He sucked in a breath, looking into the gray eyes of his grandmother who just patted his arm, smiling as she walked away. *She knows? How can she know?* For the first time he believed what his grandfather always said about his grandmother. *Maybe she can see things?* Then realizing what she had told him, he sucked in another deep breath as he looked over at Suzanne, radiant in her pregnancy. *Please God, let her be right.*

He walked over, straight through the throng of women and wrapped his arms around Suzanne, pulling her back against his tall frame. One arm around her chest and one around her middle, he completely embraced her, kissing the top of her head. Bernie approached him from one side and he accepted her hug and kiss of congratulations before releasing one arm to hug his mother on the other side.

"Good folks, let's eat!" Mac boomed and the gathering quickly found a seat around the table. Breakfast casseroles and pastries, along with juice and coffee, soon had everyone stuffing themselves. Rob and Laurie were seated across from them and BJ was glad that Rob had come around. He shook BJ's hand and kissed his sister, genuinely congratulating them as well.

After brunch everyone settled on hay bales that Mac and Bill had arranged in a semi-circle around the large, decorated tree. Bobby and Caroline, Rob's children, jumped into the gifts immediately and soon the adults followed, until all of the gifts were opened. Knitted scarves, new boots, clothes, electronics, tins of homemade goodies, and toys soon appeared with torn wrapping paper littering the area.

The group continued to sit, making small talk and enjoying the children playing. BJ and Suzanne shared a look. He leaned down and whispered, "Suzy girl, you ready for this?" Seeing her nervous nod, he stood up pulling her gently along with him. Moving toward the tree, they turned so that they faced the gathering.

"If I can have ya'lls attention," BJ said loudly, capturing the eyes of everyone. "We have one more gift to give to everyone," he said as he held Suzanne in front of him, this time with both arms around her middle and his hands resting on her stomach.

"You know we're engaged, but just to let you know, we want to keep it simple and get married right here.

We just want family and friends. And we're going to get married in about six weeks, near Valentine's day."

At this, the mom's began to speak, but he interrupted. "Wait, that's not all." Everyone quieted again, listening.

Suzanne twisted her head around and up to look into his face, smiling her encouragement.

"Our biggest gift of all this Christmas, is that in about seven months, we'll be having a baby."

At this news, the group jumped to their feet and a new round of tears and congratulations began again. Only this time, BJ refused to let go of Suzanne. They accepted the well wishes and excited hugs with her wrapped into his embrace. *Not letting you go, girl. Never letting you go again.*

Suzanne snuggled back into his arms, loving the feeling of them enveloping her. Safe. Secure. Protected. Loved.

THAT NIGHT, BACK in their apartment, they lay together after making love. Arms wrapped around each other, hearts beating as one, they talked as lovers do, planning and hoping. Suddenly, she leaned back so that she could peer into his eyes.

"I know you want me safe and to stay here, but I bought some presents for the boys. Do you think that I could visit them tomorrow? We could go together. I also thought I could try to meet Sherrie for coffee."

BJ thought for a moment, wanting nothing more than to keep her in their apartment for the next day or so. *Preferably naked and under me.* His cock stirred at the thought and she felt it nudge against her leg.

"So soon? We just made love," she giggled.

"With you, it appears that it has a mind of its own," he growled as she pushed him onto his back.

"Well, let's see if we can do something about that," she purred, kissing a trail from his lips downwards until she circled his swollen cock with her lips.

He sucked in a breath as she slid his length in her warm mouth. He was too large for her to take all of him in so she fisted the base with her hand. Working her hand and mouth in rhythm she continued, noticing with pleasure as his balls tightened.

BJ held her hair in his hands, fighting the urge to move her up and down even faster. "Baby, I'm close," he panted. "Come here."

Shaking her head while not breaking rhythm, she continued to suck until the hot semen hit the back of her mouth. Sucking until the last drop came into her mouth, she slid off looking satisfied.

BJ lay back, unable to move, not remembering ever having felt this way from being sucked off. *I never think of any other,* he realized. He had never spent much time thinking of any of his past fucks, but at this moment he was aware that all others in the past four years had completely moved out of his mind. *It's only Suzy. It's always just been her.*

Continuing to lay as sleep was almost upon them, she asked again about her visits. Ready to grant her anything, he said, "We can go see the boys tomorrow so you can take them the gifts, but we'll stay together. As far as your other friend, you can meet for coffee somewhere but I'll be there as well." Seeing that she was about to protest his intrusion into her girl-time, he placed his finger on her lips. "Hear me well, girl. You may meet your friends and I will give you privacy, but I will not let you out of my sight."

Nodding with his finger still against her lips, she kissed his finger. Laying her head on his chest, smiling to herself, she drifted off to sleep taking comfort in the knowledge that she and their child would always be protected.

Chapter 22

THE NEXT MORNING found Suzanne and BJ sitting on the sofa of Pamela's temporary home. A small, decorated tree sat in the living room and the boys were ripping off the paper of the gifts she had brought. A couple of electronic toys immediately had their attention and once the hugs and thanks were said, they ran off to play.

After a few minutes of comfortable silence where Pamela poured cups of hot tea, Suzanne asked, "How are you? I mean, really…how are you doing?"

Pamela seemed lost in thought as she pondered her answer. Looking up into her friend's eyes, she said, "You know, I should be crazy right now. My husband is gone…I still have a hard time saying that he's dead." Tears sprang to her eyes, but she stoically dashed them away. "A part of me still can't believe it, much less say it." She sighed deeply. "I want to remember the good times and I want the boys to remember those times too. Dwayne will, I think. Chuckie? I'm not so sure he remembers Joe before he got so involved in things that made him angry all the time."

BJ silently moved his arm to the back of Suzanne,

giving her shoulder a little reassuring squeeze knowing that any talk of grief brought on her own. She lay her hand on his leg, acknowledging his comfort.

"Is there anything that we can do?" she asked Pamela.

"Oh goodness, no. Mr. Alvarez has loaned us this apartment for as long as we need it. I still have my job and our health insurance was through my job, not Joe's. The only thing I hate is that we have to stay sort of hidden for a while, so I feel so badly when one of Mr. Alvarez' men has to drive us somewhere."

BJ spoke up, "Don't worry about that. His security business is the best around and he wants you and the boys safe. I know the noose is tightening around the higher-ups; the ones who went after your husband. It shouldn't be long now before enough information is gathered to take them down."

"And then you can feel like you're getting some of your life back," Suzanne added.

Just then the boys ran back in, wanting to show the adults what they were playing with and they settled in for a friendly visit.

A couple of hours later, they sat in a coffee shop awaiting Sherrie's arrival. As soon as she appeared, BJ discreetly moved over to the counter where he could keep an eye on the door.

The two women talked excitedly as Sherrie noticed Suzanne's engagement ring. The conversation then moved to Sherrie's new job.

"Well, being a paralegal doesn't make nearly as good a paycheck as waitressing at the Club Edge, but it pays the bills and is a helluva lot more respectable," she laughed.

"I never wanted to pry, but how did you end up at that strip club?" Suzanne asked.

"It's kind of a long, involved story but let's just say that my sister, who has always managed to get herself in situations that I have had to jump in and help with, once again got in with a dangerous crowd. I was…sort of…encouraged to take the job and was promised that my sister would be looked after. It seemed harmless enough. I just waitressed, not stripped. But then I was asked to do more and more things that I was uncomfortable with and finally quit. I told my sister that I couldn't protect her anymore; she'd have to live with the consequences of her decisions."

"I'm so sorry about your sister, but so glad you got a better job."

"The law firm I work for is small, but they're so nice and seem to like the job that I'm doing. Plus putting my degree to work is such an amazing feeling," she added.

The women continued to talk and laugh for a while, enjoying each other's company and their newfound friendship.

BJ looked up as a woman entered the coffee shop. Tall. Blond. Large, dark sunglasses. Tight shirt showing off her rack and jeans with sky-high heeled boots. She looked around as though trying to find someone when her gaze stopped on the back of the café. Staring for a moment she turned and walked out.

BJ looked in the direction she had been staring, noting that all of the booths and tables were filled with customers. Assuming she didn't find who she was looking for, he didn't give her another thought.

Charisse stormed out of the coffee shop. Seeing Sherrie laughing and talking with a friend the way they used to created an anger-storm inside. *My sister. Marcel wants my sister instead of me. My perfect, never-makes-a-mistake sister. Well, he wants her, he can have her.* Pulling her cell phone out of her large, designer bag, she made a call.

"Jorge? You still interested in getting my sister? Well, just let me know how to help and I'll do it. Yeah, I'm serious. I've got a proposition for you. Fine, I'll meet you there."

MARCEL PACED ANGRILY in his office. Jorge watched the boss as he moved from his desk to the window, over to the liquor cabinet, and back to his desk.

"You are supposed to be taking care of everything," Marcel shouted. "I want to know what the fuck is going on. Nothing you are telling me is adding to my confidence that you can handle your job."

Jorge knew to ride out the storm. When angry, Marcel lashed out at everyone in his path. "Boss, we've got another streamed fight lined up. I'm suggesting that we change locations and make it streamed only – cut out the foot traffic coming in from the streets and that way the police wont' find it."

"The goddamn, fuckin' cops shouldn't even know that my name is wrapped up in this. I work hard to have those under me protect my name. So can you tell me why I get a call from my lawyer, who I pay a fuckin' load to keep my name out of this shit, telling me this morning that the word from the cops is that they are now scouring the city for fight locations trying to pin them on me?"

Walking over to his desk, he pressed the intercom. "Get me…whoever that bitch is up in my bed. Now."

Jorge narrowed his eyes. Marcel was getting careless. Pushing Charisse out of his bed and back to earning her keep with different men, might not have been the smartest move. Marcel had bought Charisse's loyalty and quiet mouth. Not showering these latest whores with anything except orders to spread their legs, could possibly be buying him trouble if they talked to the wrong people.

"How much will we lose if we just do a streamed fight?" Marcel asked.

"According to the accountant, if we market it just right, we can actually make more from our online customers. We get payment up front, open it up to more guests and we could profit even larger."

At this, Marcel stopped pacing, his calculating

mind working over the figures. Just then the door opened and a busty brunette stepped in wearing nothing but a lace teddy. Marcel looked over and ordered, "Strip." The woman glanced at Jorge but quickly stripped naked. Marcel unzipped his pants and pulled out his engorged cock. "Suck," he ordered next. Again, the woman looked askance at Jorge, who just lifted an eyebrow and smirked.

She knelt on the floor and had no choice but to take Marcel in her mouth as he grabbed her hair and forcefully face-fucked her. Gagging, she kept going until he shot his cum into her mouth. Jorge, having witnessed many scenes like this in his life, prided himself on his steel will, but the thought of another dark-haired beauty kneeling before him had his dick painfully swelling.

Marcel pushed her back and zipped his pants up. Taking a deep breath, he said, "Now I can think." Glancing down at Jorge's erection straining his pants, he grinned. "Never knew this to affect you." Laughing, he grabbed the girl by the hair and ordered her to suck Jorge off as well. Forced to crawl over on her knees, she did just that until gagging once again.

Watching her slip out of the room, her clothes clutched in her hand, Marcel turned back to Jorge and said, "Now we plan. I want Charisse's sister. In my bed. In my home. I don't care if she is drugged to get her here. Once I've marked her, she'll have no choice but to stay with me. No one else will have her. I want this next fight planned. You think streamed only is the way to go? Fine, make it happen and it'd better make money. I want the goddamn cops off my back." Leaning down so that he was directly in Jorge's face, he continued, "I pay you a shit-ton of money to take care of me. You can't handle the job, I'll get someone else."

Jorge, his emotions never showing, just nodded. "What if we stage a fake fight scene? Let the word get out to the cops and they raid nothing. Then we can be somewhere else with just a streamed fight raking in the money."

Marcel sat down at his desk, his sharp eyes staring out of the window, his mind working the possibilities. Nodding, he turned toward Jorge, a smile on his face. "I like it. Make it happen."

"Got it boss." With that, Jorge stood and left the room, already planning his next move.

Marcel watched him leave and then he pulled his phone out again.

"Meet me in two hours. We have something to set up."

AFTER MEETING WITH their chief, Matt and Shane drove back to Tony's to see what else they had found. Settling around the conference table, Lily spoke first.

"I went back over the list of grads recently who might have had the skills to set up an online streaming with the ability to block any breach of security measures. While there are a number of people in the area who could have done it, BJ and I focused on the ones who did not have steady jobs or incomes. That list was very small; most people who graduate with a software engineering degree have no problem finding jobs. We narrowed it down to just a couple, and then I took that list and began looking at…um," she stopped, blushing. "Well, I looked into their bank accounts."

Tony looked over at her embarrassment. "Lily, that's what I pay you for, sweetheart. You find the things that don't readily show up."

"I know," she laughed. "It's just that I still feel like I'm going to get my hand slapped for snooping!"

"So did you find anything, baby?" Matt asked his wife.

"Actually, I did. From the names on the list that BJ gave me, I found one that hasn't had a steady job in several months and yet has had deposits of ten grand in his bank account each month for the past three months. I remember him though, from school. Nice enough young man. Not very vocal. Kept to himself. But seemed…I don't know…pleasant. It's hard for me to reconcile that he would have anything to do with this."

"You can never discount any suspect based on nice-ness," Gabe volunteered.

"Well, he's lived in Richland his whole life. I haven't had a chance to run a background on him, though. I was getting ready to do that when Tony called the meeting."

Matt and Shane took down his name. "Send us his info and we'll check him out as you see what you can find out also."

The group continued to conference for a few more minutes before BJ went by the safe room and picked up Suzanne.

"You guys come up with anything?" she asked.

"Still working the problem, baby, but don't worry. Between us and the police, we'll get em'."

Walking over and pressing her length against his, she purred, "Anything else you can think to come *up* with?" moving her hand down to grasp his crotch, loving the feel of it springing to life.

"Jesus, babe, you're killing me. I've got to work on something with Lily this afternoon but I'm gonna get you home first."

"When we get home, can't you stay just a few minutes?" she pleaded, looking up at him with a devilish smile on her face.

"Suzy, your pregnancy hormones are working over-time," he joked, pulling her hand from his crotch. "I'm not complaining, but I've gotta get my dick under control before we walk out of this room."

Twenty minutes later as they walked through the apartment door, Suzanne began stripping as she tossed clothes onto the floor on her way to the bedroom. BJ followed her lead, jerking his shirt over his head and adding it to the pile. Right on her heels, they just made it to the bedroom as they were both naked. She lay down on the bed, lifting her arms as she bared all for his eyes.

He stood for a second looking down at his woman. Ebony hair flowing across the pillows. Her lush breasts were already becoming larger while her stomach was only showing the earliest hint of roundness. The dark curls at the apex of her thighs beckoned him and as she spread her legs apart, her glistening sex had his cock painfully erect.

Sliding between her thighs, he latched on to her glistening sex with his mouth, licking until she was writhing beneath him. Plunging his tongue inside, he reached one hand up over her stomach, splaying his fingers out over their baby's resting place. His hand continued its path upward until he palmed her breast and began to roll the nipple.

She bucked up off of the bed as his warm mouth latched onto her clit, deeply sucking. The coil deep inside was tightening and as he continued to lick and suck, she felt herself fly apart, screaming his name.

His hand left her breast and he grasped her hips, lifting her as he lapped her juices. Moving over her, he was careful to keep his weight on his arms as his lips sought her nipples. Sucking deeply he nipped and soothed both equally, drawing them up to rigid points.

The electric jolt shot straight from her nipples to her womb causing it to contract from the contact. Moaning, she lifted her hips, desperate for him to be inside.

"I need you. Now," she pleaded.

He continued to tease her nipples, before sliding up to latch his lips onto hers. Plunging his tongue deep inside, he tasted her sweetness as he searched each crevice. Their tongues began to duel as though each vying for dominance. He slid his hand between her legs, not surprised to find her soaked for him.

"You know I'm ready. I'm always ready," she complained. "Hurry."

He answered her by moving the tip of his cock to her entrance. Looking down into her blue eyes, he smiled. *Fuckin' beautiful.* Sliding into her warmth, he leaned in to kiss her again, this time plunging his tongue with the same rhythm as he was plunging into her pussy. Her walls immediately began to contract and he knew her release was imminent.

She grabbed his ass with her fingers, digging in as though to force him to move faster, deeper. With only a few more strokes, she was thrown over the edge crying out his name. The orgasm rocked through her leaving her breathless.

He pulled out, much to her dismay, and rolled her to her side. Positioning himself behind her, he entered her from behind. Her body quickly welcomed him from this position and with his arms wrapped around her holding her breasts, he began pounding her again. His fingers tweaked her nipples and she felt herself climbing to the edge once more.

"You close, baby," he panted in her ear.

"Yeah, baby, yeah."

Plunging in as deep as he could go he felt his balls tighten, and then he pushed in to the hilt as his hot seed poured into her. Just as he was emptying himself, he felt her pussy walls clench around his cock, milking every drop from him.

They lay panting, trying to catch their breaths as he released her breasts and wrapped his arms around her body tighter. Pulling her back against his chest, he threw one leg over hers, cocooning her in his embrace.

When he could finally speak, all he could manage to get out was, "Damn girl."

Her giggles shook her body as it was tucked next to his. He felt her laughter through his chest. Kissing the top of her head he said, "Suzy girl, as much as I hate to do this, I've gotta get back to work. I promised Tony that I'd work with Lily this afternoon."

"Mmmm," was her reply.

"You take a nap and stay in. Got it?"

"Okay honey. I'm not going anywhere," she promised.

By the time he gathered his clothes dropped throughout the apartment and had gotten dressed, she was fast asleep. Tucking her in and kissing her forehead, he set the security system and headed out of the door.

Chapter 23

JORGE SAT AT the bar in Club Edge watching the door and checking his watch. "The bitch had better not be late," he muttered. The club was mostly empty, the cocktail hour had not started. Just then, he heard the front door open and in walked Charisse. Busty and leggy, in a dress that left little to the imagination, he knew exactly why Marcel had put her pussy on a pedestal. Fuckin' gorgeous and worked it well. If she could have stayed away from the coke, Marcel would've kept her in style for a long time. Probably set for life, even when her body was no longer young and beautiful. She would've had enough to set herself up somewhere real nice. But…hell, what did he care? She was desperate and he was just the man to use her for whatever he could get out of her.

He stood and barely nodded for her to follow, but she quickly acquiesced. Sliding into a booth, he motioned for her to sit across from him. She licked her lips but waited before speaking.

His eyes flickered to the strippers practicing on the stage then back to her. Her ample breasts looked natural spilling out of her top and she would be fabulous on the stage. The thought of getting her to perform flashed through his mind which was always on the lookout for more ways to make money. Lifting his eyes from her breasts he met hers, noting that she smirked at the knowledge that he was ogling her tits.

"You got something for me?" he growled.

"Yeah. My sister."

Seeing the interest flash through his eyes, she continued. "I hear Marcel wants a piece of my virgin sister. For his own. No way she can keep him interested. But the two of us? He could have us both. He can pound her tight pussy and have me to do all the things that he likes to do."

"I don't need you to get your sister. I can snatch her anytime I want and I'll let you know that Marcel is wanting her badly, so that's gonna happen real soon."

"She's street smart though. I can get her easy. Make a phone call. Tell her how sorry I am we parted on bad terms. She'll run right to me. Wherever I want to meet. No snatching her in a grocery store parking lot."

"I'm listening."

"You tell me where you want her, just don't make it an obvious dive. I'll get her there."

Jorge nodded. This was easier than he thought.

"And I want in as well," she added. "I want you to get Marcel to take me back too. Tell him he gets the sisters. Together. All the sister pussy he can handle."

"What makes you think your sister'll go along with this."

Charisse snorted. "I've seen some of the skanks around. Give them enough drugs and they'll fuck a dozen guys for the money." Looking away for a second, as though lost in memories, she suddenly turned back. "So we got a deal? You get Marcel's favor, he gets double pussy, and I get my position back."

"I need more than just Marcel's undying love," Jorge added sarcastically. "I want you to do something for me."

"What?" she asked.

"All you have to do is make a phone call. Do and say exactly what I tell you and I'll make sure you get all of Marcel's attention."

Licking her lips, this time in anticipation, she nodded emphatically. "Deal," she said triumphantly.

Standing, she walked around to his side of the booth and leaned over to kiss his cheek. One breast slipped out of her low top, leaving her distended nipple right at his face. Giggling, she tucked herself back in. Glancing over her shoulder as she walked away, she winked.

Jorge watched her as she left the building. *Fuckin' cunt tease. She'll learn. She'll learn.* Standing, he nodded to the bartender as he left the building as well. Time to set things in place. The next fight was going to bring him fortune. Devil's Spawn was ready and he had every intention of cashing in on his dog's blood lust.

CHARISSE PLACED THE call and begged Sherrie's forgiveness. "It just didn't seem like Christmas without seeing you at all," she complained. "Please meet up with me. I have a surprise I want to give you."

The next day found Sherrie driving to meet with her sister at a little café. Finding the address, she was surprised to be able to find parking right in front. Glancing around, she realized that there were few shops open with several in the area boarded up. Looking through her passenger window, she could see that the café was open and seemed to be in business.

Walking through the door, it took a moment for her eyes to adjust to the dim lighting. Seeing Charisse sitting at a table she walked toward her. Before she reached the table, she was grabbed from behind and felt a prick in her neck. Her struggles lasted for just a few seconds as her limbs began to feel heavy and she felt hands holding her firmly. Her last sight was seeing Jorge standing next to her sister smiling at her.

"Wha hav you done, Charisss?" she slurred before losing consciousness altogether.

"That feel good? Seeing sis on the floor?" Jorge growled in Charisse's ear.

Fighting to keep a smile on her face, she replied, "Sure. Of course." Her eyes darted back to her beautiful sister slumped unceremoniously on the floor of the dirty café, but the smile was no longer on her face.

Jorge barked at the man standing over her with a

hypodermic needle in his hand. "Bring her. And don't damage the merchandise." Then he turned and walked out of the door.

Charisse followed, but couldn't help but glance at the brute bending over to pick Sherrie up. "Be careful with her," she warned, suddenly filled with fear. Then she hurried out to follow Jorge. She had struck a bargain with the devil and Jorge was not a man to keep waiting.

BJ AND LILY were running the background checks on the names that Shane had given them as well as the software engineers that she had listed.

"Here's the one I was talking about. His name is Charles Ritchner. He had a job right out of college but it looks like he quit about four months ago. Since then, he's had no job but he's regularly putting in a lot of money in his bank account."

"What else have you got on him," BJ asked.

Continuing to search, Lily replied, "Um, let's see. He has a good credit rating, which is interesting since he has no official job. He's paid off his car. Has no student loans."

"Dig deeper. What about family?"

"His parents are both dead. He and a brother were raised by their uncle."

"Anything else? Anything at all that would give Matt and Shane a reason to question him?"

"Wow, this is interesting."

BJ turned from his computer and looked over her shoulder. "What is?"

"His uncle is a veterinarian."

Just then Tony walked in with Gabe. "You all found anything yet? Shane's on the phone and is chomping at the bit to get moving. He says they've run into a dead end with the names that you gave them but figured you have access to more data."

"She may have something. Charles Ritchner was raised by his uncle who was a veterinarian," BJ replied.

"Who is he?"

"Oh, Jesus." Lily turned her eyes up to the men standing around. "The uncle's name is Dr. Marker. He's retired but owns the ER Veterinary clinic right down the road from Annie." Continuing her search with shaky fingers, she added, "And his brother is Ralph Ritchner."

"Ralphie," BJ stated. "That's who Suzanne went to see. The one who blamed the clinic errors in filing the city's paperwork on Dr. Ketchum."

"Well, we don't know that he wasn't right, but I'm calling Shane right now."

"BJ," Lily said, turning her eyes up to him. "Dr. Marker has serious money problems. Creditors have been hounding him for the past two years. It looks like most of his money was gone until about three months ago and he's been adding some back into his account."

Tony had already relayed the information to Shane

and Matt. They were going to have Ralph and Charles brought in for questioning.

BJ quickly said, "I'm heading to Dr. Marker to see if I can get any information." Leaning over, he kissed Lily on the cheek. "Good work, darlin'!"

Tony looked down at Lily and smiled. "I concur with BJ – good work. Hate to dump more on you but can you try to see what intel you can get on the next fight?"

"On it, chief," she replied with a smile.

THE CLINIC HAD a busy morning as clients seemed to all want to be seen before the change of ownership. Suzanne had finished with her last client and was in the back completing a final inventory. Unfortunately for her, she was stuck with Phil's company. The details of the ownership transfer included Annie selling the entire inventory of equipment and supplies, so he and Suzanne were checking everything twice. As she moved around the lab, he couldn't help but notice how delectable she looked in her tiger-print scrubs.

"I guess you're about ready to move in and take over, aren't you?" she asked, trying to make polite conversation.

"Yeah, I'm ready. I've had a couple of interviews for staff and figure that by the first of January, I'll have a receptionist and a vet tech. That will do to get started." Looking over at her, he couldn't help but ask once again, "Are you sure you don't want to stay?"

Standing up and putting her hands on her hips, she was just about to retort when her cell phone vibrated in her pocket. Pursing her lips at Phil, she answered her phone.

"Is this Ms. McDonald?" a pleasant woman's voice sounded.

"Yes," she answered.

"I'm one of the workers at the Safe Haven House and I got your number from Dwayne Johnson. He and his brother are here and I thought I should try to get hold of someone."

"What's wrong? Why are they there and not with their mother?"

"She's at work and the boys showed up here. They said they wanted to play with the other children that they met here."

"Oh," Suzanne said, still confused. *I thought Tony had someone keeping an eye on them at the secure apartment.*

"And since he's been here, Chuckie has been throwing up. I can't get hold of his mother and Dwayne said that you'd be the next one to call. I really think that someone needs to come get them right away."

"Oh, of course. Yes. Um, tell them I'll be there as soon as I can," she agreed, disconnecting the call.

"Everything okay?" Phil asked.

"Um, no actually. I need to go and pick up a friend's child who has gotten sick." She turned around, then looked at him. "Oh my gosh, we were still inventorying."

"No, don't worry about it. You need to go."

"Oh shit. I didn't drive today. BJ dropped me off and is picking me up."

"I'll take you," Phil volunteered. "You need to go and I can't inventory by myself so I might as well make sure you get to your destination."

She eyed him suspiciously, but his face held nothing but sincerity. "Let me call BJ first and then I'll meet you out front."

Phil went to let Leon and Annie know what they were going to do while Suzanne tried to get BJ. His phone went straight to voicemail. Leaving him a message, she hung up. Grabbing her purse, she headed out front to meet up with Phil.

SHERRIE BEGAN TO come out of what felt like a deep sleep. She was vaguely aware of lying on something soft. Her head felt fuzzy and her mouth felt dry. It was hard to open her eyes, but she knew that she must. Forcing her body to sit up, she weaved a bit before being able to focus on her surroundings. *Where am I? What happened?*

Rubbing her hand across her face, she slowly began to remember. *The café. Meeting Charisse. Jorge! Oh my God. My own sister turned on me.* Looking around, she saw that she was in an opulent bedroom lying on a huge bed. Silk sheets had been covering her and she looked down in gratitude seeing that she was still wearing her clothes. Taking deep breaths, she tried to clear her head by forcing oxygen in and out of her lungs. Seeing what looked like a bathroom, she swung her legs over the side of the bed and came to a wobbly standing position. Slowly making her way to the bathroom, she was grateful to use the facilities and then drink a large glass of water. With each breath, moving around, and the water, her head began to clear.

Hearing voices in the distance she crept softly to the bedroom door and tried the doorknob. Much to her relief it turned. Opening it slowly, she peered out and saw a long hall with a well-lit staircase at the end. The voices were coming from downstairs.

Looking around, she realized that she did not have her purse or cell phone with her. She also did not see a land-line phone in the room. *Damn. I've got to get out of here.* She was about to go to the window, when she heard her sister's voice. *Charisse!*

"I did everything you asked. What do you mean that I'm not staying?" she screeched.

"I have no idea what deal you made with Jorge, but I'm telling you that you're not staying. I've got what I want and you are most certainly not part of the package."

"I brought my sister to you. I did that. Me. I hand delivered her right to Jorge. Just for you. But the deal was that you'd have both of us. Marcel baby, I want to come back and I know I can make you happy," Charisse whined.

The voices became lower and Sherrie had to strain to hear them.

"Do you know what is amazing to me, Charisse? You still don't get it. You didn't offer your sister up to me out of loyalty to me. You certainly have no loyalty to your own flesh and blood. No, you did this for your own selfish reasons. What did Jorge promise? Hmm? More coke? No more johns? A chance to be back at my house as my mistress? Whatever he promised, those words did not come from me. And I only reward loyalty."

"After everything I ever did for you?" she screamed.

"I thought you had class. That was what first attracted me to you, but you have none. I'm not having a junkie for a mistress. It seems that even Jorge is getting his own piece of class after seeing the likes of you parade around."

The voices were lower and Sherrie had to strain to try to hear what was being said.

The man's voice rang out again. "He's going after your sister's beautiful friend. The one that works at the vet clinic. We need to make sure she stays silent and Jorge's rewarding himself with her."

Sherrie could hear the sounds of scuffling as her sister screeched, "Get away from me." A door slammed and she couldn't hear her sister anymore. She heard the man's voice on the phone.

"Yeah. Get my pilot up. I'm taking a trip and I'll have a passenger for the private jet. A woman. Let me know when we can take off. I'll need about an hour at least to get ready and then it's about a thirty minute drive to the airport."

Oh Jesus. Is he talking about me? He's taking me somewhere? And Jorge has Suzanne. Oh Jesus, help me, I've got to get out of here!

She could hear him talking to another man. "Is everything ready for tonight? Good. Jorge has set up a fake fight and I've had that leaked. The police'll be raiding an empty warehouse." There was a pause and then a chuckle. "Yes, well the real one will be a surprise as well. I'll be in the air by that time. I have a trip to take and can't miss it. Right, see that it all goes as planned."

Sherrie's head pounded; whether from the drugs or fear she couldn't be sure. Turning to look at the bedroom windows, she quickly crossed over to them. She realized that they were actually French doors that led out to a balcony. Determined to escape no matter what, she tried the doors only to find them locked.

"You don't want to try that, my dear," a voice came from behind.

Whirling around, she came face to face with who she assumed was Marcel. Tall, dark. Cold, calculating eyes. He smiled, showing his pure white teeth and her heart pounded in fear, her chest heaving with each breath she took.

"What...what do you want with me? You can't do this, you know. You can't kidnap someone and get away with it."

"In a few hours, you and I will be on a plane. We're leaving this place and starting over somewhere. You'll live like a queen with the money I've made."

"I...what?" she asked. Her anger taking over her fear. "I'm not going anywhere with you. And if you do succeed to kidnap me somewhere, I'll certainly not stay."

"You are beautiful." His eyes swept the length of her. "Not as stacked as your sister. Not as tall, either. But you've got class. I like that," he said walking toward her. "It's going to be a pleasure being with you."

Before she could reply, his phone rang. Turning to leave the room, he said over his shoulder, "Do not attempt to leave. Those windows are secure; you won't get very far. And it would make me very...displeased."

She watched the door close behind him and began to shake. *Oh God, Charisse. What have you done?*

SUZANNE AND PHIL pulled up to the Safe Haven House. It was only about five thirty p.m., but the winter darkness had already set in.

"Thank's for driving me, Phil. I'll call Brad again to have him pick me up."

"No way. You get the boys and I'll take you wherever you need to go," he replied.

She was already out of the car and leaned down to answer. She hated to take him up on his offer but hadn't been able to get through to BJ. "I hate for you to go out of your way," she said, chewing on her lip in thought.

"Look, it's no problem. I'll make sure you get where you are supposed to –" He looked over her shoulder but before he could call out, a man approached Suzanne from behind and pulled her away from the car, slamming the door at the same time.

Phil jumped out of the driver's side yelling but was tased from behind. His body jolted and then he slumped to the ground. Suzanne watched in horror as his body fell but then she felt her muscles tense in pain before unconsciousness hit her as well.

The outside lights from the Safe Haven came on, but before someone could come out to see what was happening, Suzanne was dragged to a waiting car and its driver sped off.

BJ AND GABE pulled up to the modest home of Dr. Marker. The door was opened before they could knock and the distinguished elderly gentleman stood pensively looking at them.

"Gentlemen, may I help you?" he asked.

"Dr. Marker, we'd like to ask you some questions about your nephews," Gabe replied after he had identified him and BJ. "May we come in?"

Dr. Marker glanced between the two large men standing in front of him, wariness in his eyes. "What is this about?"

"We're concerned about some activities that both of them may be involved in and we think it leads back to you, sir. As I told you, we're not from the police but are working with the police in investigating some activities that we think your nephews may be involved in."

Dr. Marker's bravado held on only momentarily before his face crumpled and he hid his face in his hands. Gabe and BJ allowed him a chance to gain his composure and then followed him inside of his house.

Sitting in his small living room, they felt large on the small sofa but focused on the man in the chair in front of a roaring fireplace. While the fireplace gave off heat, it seemed to be the only source of heat in the house.

Dr. Marker looked at them and sighed heavily. "Have you ever suffered an addiction gentlemen? A need that grows so strong that you don't know if you can breathe without it." Without waiting for them to answer, he continued, "Well sirs, I have. I've had it so long, I don't even remember what life was like before it consumed me."

The snapping of the fire was the only sound in the room, before Dr. Marker sighed heavily again. "No, that's not true."

"What's not true?" BJ asked gently, noting the

older gentleman looked suddenly haggard.

Looking up at the two of them, he answered. "That I don't remember what life was like before the addiction. I had a wife. We were unable to have children and when my sister and her husband were killed in a car accident, we gladly took their two boys in to raise."

"Ralph and Charles?" Gabe prodded.

Nodding his head, Dr. Marker allowed himself a small smile in memory. "Yes, they were good boys and we had a good life."

"What happened?"

"I began gambling. At first it was just a simple pastime. Betting on a football game. Betting on other sports. It started so slow," he said, shaking his head. "So slow."

Again, the fire crackling filled the silence. "My veterinarian practice certainly made money, but I became consumed with what the extra money could buy. A huge house, vacations, an exclusive country-club membership. The more I won, the more I would gamble. And then when I lost, panic would set in. My wife begged me to stop. Sometimes I gambled away the house payment, car payments...," he said, continuing to shake his head as though he couldn't believe that he was talking about himself.

"Then, I did the unforgivable. I lost myself completely."

"What happened, Dr. Marker?"

"I was called to help with a dog that had been in a fight. I had never been to a dog fight and when I saw how injured the animal was, I was horrified. But I patched him up and the owner was so grateful that he paid me a huge sum. I know now that it was not only for the care I provided but it was also hush money. I also now see it as a form of gambling. I would treat some of the animals coming in and keep my mouth shut to the authorities and I made a lot of money."

He hung his head just as a huge sob tore from his body. Shaking with tears for a few minutes, the three men sat quietly. Taking a handkerchief from his pocket, Dr. Marker wiped his tears and nose.

"My wife of forty years died two years ago of cancer. It seems as though everything began to fall apart then. What money I made, I gambled…and lost. I lost my large house and had to sell my practice. I opened the ER Vet clinic, but it was at times a front for keeping the local dog fighting community treated and hidden from the authorities. Although," he added looking up, "it was a legitimate business and we did a lot of good for the community and saved a lot of pet's lives."

"So you hired Ralph and Dr. Ketchum to assist you in your illegal activities?"

"Dr. Ketchum? Phil?" Dr. Marker asked in confusion. "He was never a part of this. He's a legitimate veterinarian who knew nothing about Ralph and me hiding the attack reports."

Gabe and BJ looked at each other in surprise. BJ clarified, "So Dr. Ketchum was not the one hiding or destroying the reports that were supposed to go to the Animal Control?"

Shaking his head once again, Dr. Marker said, "No. Ralph kept most of them from him. If there was one that went through, there was a contact in Animal Control that would receive it and destroy it on their end."

"What about your other nephew Charles?"

"Ahh, Charles. He's very smart. A software engineer that can design anything," Dr. Marker replied with pride.

"How did they get involved with your activities?"

With that question, Dr. Marker's face fell once again, making him look much older than his years. Sighing again, he replied, "The boys knew that I was in financial trouble. They both wanted to help and since I was no longer able to help them financially, they were more than happy to jump in. Ralph had no real career path so hiring him to work at the clinic served both of our purposes. And Charles? He began working for the man who ran the dog fights and from what I understand, makes a lot of money doing it."

"You pulled your nephews into your world? The world you admit destroyed your life?" BJ asked incredulously.

"I didn't know what else to do. Don't you see?" Dr. Marker pleaded. "While I never attended a fight myself,

I received some warnings when I began to lose a great deal of money. Both boys offered to help and well…," his voice trailed off. Looking back up he said, "With Charles involved in some way with the fights and Ralph having knowledge of some of the dogs, I was back to making money betting again. It seemed so…harmless," he said, wringing his hands.

"You should know that both of your nephews are being questioned by the police and will most likely be arrested. You will also be questioned as well."

At that, Dr. Marker's eyes filled with tears again. "Oh no. I never meant for the boys to be this involved."

"They're adults. They made their choices and they'll suffer the consequences. Just as you will," Gabe said forcefully as he and BJ stood to leave. BJ was already on the phone to Lily and Gabe quickly called Shane.

Within hours, Ralphie had been questioned and arrested as well as the two Animal Control officers who admitted to destroying evidence.

Chapter 24

JORGE PULLED UP to a small building near one of the warehouses on the river. It was quiet, but that was to be expected. One of his jobs was to get to the fight location long before anyone else to make sure it was secure. And as the first of the crew would come, he was to oversee every step of the process. Turning, he pulled Suzanne out of the back seat wanting to get her inside as quickly possible. She was conscious but with a gag in her mouth and her hands and ankles taped, she was unable to put up much resistance.

"Come on in, doll baby. I've got to get things set up for tonight and then you and I won't have any interruptions."

He carried her into the dark space, turning on only a few light. "Mr. Hernandez?" a voice came from the other side of the pit.

Jorge noted the old dog trainer with several cages next to him. The dogs were muzzled, but ever alert.

"I brung 'em just like you said. Brought your dog, Devil's Spawn, as well as a couple of others I thought would do really well."

Jorge set Suzanne down on a metal folding chair

and walked over to the dogs. He looked on with pride at the dog he had specifically trained for this occasion. "Anyone know you were bringing him?"

"Oh no, sir. No one knows about him. He's a right smart fighter. He'll make you a lot a' money tonight, I'm sure of it. He'll sit here real tame like and then come out ready to kill."

Nodding, Jorge handed over a large roll of money. "You can leave, but come back in time to take him back to the farm when the fight is over. I still don't want anyone to associate my name with his right now."

The old man nervously glanced around at Suzanne and then bobbed his head as he slunk back to his truck.

Continuing to flip on a few more lights, Jorge prepared the area for the first of the workers to arrive. Glancing at his watch, he couldn't help but grin – the diversionary tactics of leaking out information to the police informants about another fight setting would be perfect. By the time the police arrived and figured out they had been duped, the real streamed fight would have taken place and the money made.

He looked over to Suzanne sitting in the chair staring daggers at him. Grinning he stalked toward her. Keeping away from her feet, he squatted in front of her.

"I've watched you a long time, beauty." He trailed a finger down her cheek and lifted her chin so that her eyes would meet his. "Keeping an eye on you was no problem at all."

Her eyes grew wide at that admission.

"Oh yeah, doll baby. I've been watching you ever since those little fuckers brought their dog to the clinic where you work and you took them home."

Her eyes grew wider as he leaned closer kissing her bottom lip, even with the gag in place. He took it between his teeth and pulled her lip out before letting it go. She tried to twist her head away, but her grabbed her hair and pulled it tightly back until she thought her neck would snap.

"You think you're too good for me, bitch. You've had that big man between your legs and think your pussy's too good for me. Well, baby when I get finished, you'll not only belong to me, you'll be branded for me." He leaned in for another kiss, licking her swollen lips while sliding his hand in her shirt squeezing her breasts. "Oh yeah, doll. You and me are gonna have some fun." As his hand slid lower it stilled on her slightly protruding stomach.

He jerked back, looking down at her in surprise. "Pregnant?" Throwing his head back, he roared with laughter. "This'll make that security boyfriend of yours absolutely crazy. What a perfect revenge for all the shit he and his cop friends have caused."

Continuing to laugh, he stood and moved over to the door, waiting for the first of the crew to appear. Looking at his watch, he pulled out his phone to place some calls.

CHARISSE STOOD IN her small apartment, looking around as anger poured off of her. Jorge promised. He'd promised that Marcel would take her back. *Jesus, I'm such an idiot. Why did I ever listen to him?* She flopped down on her sofa, her mind racing. Running her blood-red, manicured nails through her hair, she thought of Sherrie. As angry as she could get at her sister for not understanding her choices, she couldn't help but think of them as children playing together. *We were so close.* In high school, Sherrie had been the smart one. The good one. She remembered the first time she scored under the high school bleachers. She'd wanted to buy more pot but had spent all of her money. And the seller took one look at her huge tits and offered to let her have the bag for a quick fuck. It had been so easy.

She couldn't remember the faces of the constant line of men after him, but she remembered that first one. His face, void of any emotion as he pounded into her finally throwing his head back as he came. He zipped his pants up and tossed the bag of marijuana at her saying if she'd do that some more, he'd keep her supplied.

She leaned her head over and held it in her hands as she forced the memories to the back of her mind. Even though her sister was younger, Sherrie had always tried to protect her. Sighing deeply, Charisse stood up and walked into the bathroom, staring at the reflection in the mirror. *Oh my God, what have I done? I just sold my sister into a life of depravity. Oh Jesus.*

Rushing out of her building, she knew she had to go to Marcel. Somehow convince him that he was wrong. That what he was doing was never going to work. Somehow, she had to try to save her sister.

THE S.W.A.T. TEAM was in place. Matt and Shane were ready. The police chief walked over to them, finalizing the details.

"This place it too quiet," Shane said, his eyes narrowed in suspicion as the S.W.A.T team rushed the old warehouse. The call quickly came back that it was empty except for one woman. Hurrying in, Matt and Shane approached the lone woman being escorted down the stairs.

Shaking her beautiful blonde head, she cursed, "I should've know that slick shit would pull something like this sometime."

"What are you doing here?" questioned Matt.

The statuesque bombshell eyed him speculatively before answering. "I'm here for the same reason you are, big boy. I'm looking for Marcel Washington."

"You're Charisse," Shane stated, already knowing who she was from the surveillance photos on Marcel. "Marcel's woman."

Giving an undignified snort, Charisse shot him a glare. "Was. Was Marcel's woman. He tossed me aside like yesterday's garbage." She stood silently for a moment deep in thought before giving a huge sigh. "Look, I came here to talk to Marcel. Don't know where he went but I will tell you he kidnapped a woman. My sister." Leaning in, poking a long, manicured nail into Shane's chest, she continued, "And I want that son of a bitch taken down. He fucked with me and I may have led him to my sister, but I won't go down like that. I want him the fuck away from her!"

"Where does he have her?" Matt bit out with Shane already on the phone.

Charisse pursed her lips before answering. "He did have her at his house, but I'm sure she's no longer there." Suddenly tears sprang into her eyes at the enormity of what she had done and a sob ripped from her. "Oh Jesus, I sold my sister into his hands. You gotta find her," she pleaded.

At the chief's nod, Shane placed the call to Tony. "Tony, Marcel Washington's kidnapped a woman. Sherrie Mullins. Get BJ and Lily on any surveillance they can pull up on his house and see what they can find. Yeah, the bust here was a set-up. The real fight must be taking place somewhere else."

As the police took Charisse away for more questioning, Shane and Matt looked at each other. *So where is Jorge and the real fight?*

TONY TURNED TO his crew and began to bark out orders, his military leadership taking over. "Lily, BJ.

Get on your computers and pull up anything you can from Marcel Washington's house. I know you were working on tapping into the security system we installed for him, so see what you can find. It appears that he's kidnapped Sherrie Mullins, the sister of his former mistress."

At this, BJ's head swung around from his laptop to Tony. "That's Suzanne's friend."

Tony and Gabe looked at him. "They know each other long?"

"No. Sherrie appeared at the clinic a couple of months ago and a friendship started then."

The silence was deafening as the ramifications began to set in.

"Fuck!" BJ bit out. "Do you think Sherrie was a plant for Marcel to keep an eye on the clinic and any of the fighting dogs that might have come in?"

Tony was back on the phone to Matt and Shane in an instant. Relaying the information to them put Shane on high alert since Annie was his wife. Tony kept Matt on the phone while Shane called Annie, finding out that she was fine and at home.

Within a few minutes, Lily shouted, "We've got something." She and BJ pulled their chairs round her laptop and began showing Tony, Gabe, Vinny, and Jobe what they were looking at. "I can't get visual right now, but I can get sound from the office area of his house. BJ's also got records from his cell phone for the past twenty-four hours."

"What are we looking at?" Tony barked out.

BJ replied, "He's made some calls to a small airport strip outside the city. Looks like he may be trying to leave the area or possibly the country."

Tony jotted down the information on the airport, while Lily continued with her report.

They listened in horror to the conversation that Marcel had with Charisse. Lily turned to BJ saying, "He's got Sherrie and if your information is correct, then he may be trying to get both of them away."

Then the rest of the conversation came over the speakers on the laptop. About Sherrie's friend. About Jorge having Suzanne.

The silence in the room lasted only an instant before pandemonium broke out. BJ jumped out of his seat, trying to call Suzanne but it went straight to voicemail. Tony was on the phone to Matt once again. "Jorge's got Suzanne. BJ's coming to you. The rest of us will get to the airport at the coordinates that Lily pulled up from the phone calls."

Gabe growled that he was going with BJ, surprising no one since he considered Suzanne to be like a little sister. As a former military medic, he also knew his skills may be needed.

Shane called Tony back before BJ left. Tony looked over at him and quickly said, "Fuck. Got it." Turning to BJ he said, "BJ, they just got word that Phil Ketchum is at the hospital. He was tased outside of the Safe Haven House. He'd just dropped Suzanne off there. He's told the police that she received a call from someone saying they were from the Haven and that the Johnson boys were there and needed someone to keep them until the mother could be reached. He saw someone approach her from behind but he was tased before he could yell out."

BJ stumbled back, slamming into a hard object that reached out to steady him. Hearing Vinny's voice behind him saying, "Hang on, man. She's gonna need you clear headed."

BJ pulled out his cell phone noticing a voicemail. Quickly hitting the code, he held the phone to his ear, listening to the sweet voice of Suzanne.

"Hey sweetie, I got a call from the Safe Haven saying the boys showed up there and Chuckie is sick. Phil is driving me over there since I don't have my car. I know he's not our favorite people, but I'll be fine. It's just about a five minute drive anyway. I'll call you when I get home. I love you."

He did not realize that the phone was still in his hand until Gabe reached out and took it from him, clicking it off. Gabe moved around into BJ's line of vision and got in his face, while grabbing him by the upper arms.

"BJ, hang on. We'll get her. We'll get her back."

Tony looked around at the men he trusted with his life. Too many military operations had occurred successfully for him to doubt his team. With Vinny's medic skills and Jobe's speciality of being able to take out the enemy, he was comfortable that the three of them could handle the situation.

"Vinny and Jobe with me, going after Marcel and hopefully Sherrie. Gabe and BJ – you head to the station to meet up with Matt and Shane. Lily?" he added looking down at her pale face. "You work it from here, darlin'. Keep all of us up on what's going on at both ends and keep working the information. See what you can get for me about the pilot and for BJ, where the fuck Jorge would have gone. We clear?"

Nodding, she immediately turned back to her computers. She heard the sound of the men getting ready and leaving the office behind her, but she was totally focused on finding her friend.

WITH SOME FRANTIC phone calls to Matt, BJ and Gabe headed to the river's docks to an area about three miles from where the earlier false raid was held. Having received more intel from Charisse, the police had an idea where the real fight could be and had begun raids on a few more of Marcel's business fronts including Club Edge. They began picking up several of Marcel's men who were surprised to find out that their leader was leaving the country. It didn't take long for them to begin rolling over on each other.

BJ listened to Matt as Gabe drove as quickly as he could to their destination. According to Matt, it appeared that another fight location was set up, but whether it was real or another decoy they didn't know. But it appeared that if Jorge wasn't found anywhere else, this was as good a place to start as any.

BJ stared straight ahead, the only illumination coming from the street lights in the inky night. He could feel Gabe's eyes cutting over to him but couldn't find it in himself to talk. All he could focus on was Suzanne. Getting to her. Getting her back. Her…and the baby. Closing his eyes tightly for a moment, he felt his chest tighten. The pain sliced through his heart.

"You gonna be okay, man?" Gabe asked, already knowing the answer.

BJ opened his eyes, rubbing his chest. "Yeah. When she's back in my arms."

Nodding, Gabe continued to speed through the night.

TONY, VINNY, AND Jobe raced to the outskirts of town to a small, private airport. With pictures of Marcel Washington and a description of Sherrie, they hurried to the place where Lily was able to determine the phone call to the unknown pilot had come to. Turning off the main highway, they made their way along several consecutively smaller and smaller roads, following the GPS but noting that there were signs for the small Richland County Municipal Airport.

"He's using a legit airport to store his plane," Jobe commented.

"Yeah, if he uses it for business trips and counts it as a tax deduction, he has to claim it and the storage facility," Tony responded.

"Taxes? You think he pays taxes?" Jobe asked incredulously.

"Sure. Someone like him knows he has to keep the legit side visible to try to hide the illegal activities. He claims his mansion. His cars. Probably claims Club Edge as well. He'll have accountants who will make sure his legit businesses and assets are well accounted for to keep the IRS off his ass."

Jobe just nodded as Vinny took a quick look at the GPS. "We're getting close. Says the airport is only about one mile ahead. Turn here and this little dirt road will take us around to the side. Looks like there are trees for cover as well."

For the last several hundred yards. Tony turned off the headlights, slowly following the small road toward the lights of the airstrip. Coming to a stop in a clump of trees, they donned their equipment and weapons. Former military, they were trained in search and rescue. Alert, Tony took one last quick look at the picture of Sherrie. Not that he would forget her. *Beautiful. Drop dead gorgeous. Long blonde hair, crystal blue eyes. Clear complexion.* He'd read the dossier that Lily had pulled up. Sherrie and Charisse Mullins could not have been more different as sisters. Charisse had been picked up by the police for hustling, shoplifting, and prostitution. She'd made it into Marcel's stable and then as one of his strippers at Club Edge where she attracted his attention and became his main mistress for the past year. Sherrie on the other hand, graduated with honors and just completed her degree for becoming a paralegal. And from what he could tell had been cleaning up after her sister for years. *And look where it got her? A one-way ticket to Marcel's hell.* One last look at those mesmerizing blue eyes that seared straight into him and he slid the picture into his camo pocket.

Looking up at Jobe and Vinny, he gave the silent order to proceed. Making their way to the fence surrounding the airport, they quickly cut their way through after ascertaining that there was no perimeter alarm system in place. Making their way toward the only building with lights, they saw the small Cessna aircraft out of the hangar. Nodding to each other, Jobe moved toward the aircraft while Tony and Vinny moved toward the building.

Glancing inside, Tony saw Marcel talking with another man as he heard Jobe through his earpiece say that there was one pilot in the aircraft. Knowing Jobe would be able to easily take out the pilot, he turned his attention to the individuals in the doorway of the hangar.

Marcel was looking over papers that had been handed to him, including what appeared to be several passports. Wanting to locate Sherrie before moving against Marcel, he maneuvered around to the side of the building to a small door. Slipping inside, he was hidden from sight behind huge stacks of barrels and crates. From this angle he could see her lying on a small cot in the corner, mouth gagged and hands and feet tied.

Jobe came across his earpiece again, this time with the simple two words **Pilot eliminated.** Tony smiled at Vinny as they silently acknowledged the former military lingo. He knew that Jobe had not killed the pilot but that he had eliminated the threat of the pilot. Turning his attention back to the drama in front of him, he stealthily made his way closer as Vinny moved to the other side of the hangar.

When Tony was close enough, he stepped out with this weapon raised. "Stop right there, Marcel." The man in front of Marcel whirled around to Tony's voice, stopping in his tracks with his hands in the air giving up immediately.

Marcel dove behind the man while pulling out his gun, training it on Sherrie. "Go for it big man and she's a goner."

"No worry of mine," Tony lied. "I'm just here for you. Another one of your women won't get in my way."

Marcel's eyes flickered indecision as he realized that Sherrie wouldn't be a deterrent since no one knew who she was. That second of indecision was all Tony needed. With the sound of his weapon discharging echoing through the cavernous hangar, he hit Marcel in the shoulder, rendering his firing arm useless. Howling with pain, Marcel began to scream and curse. The man with him began to turn away when Vinny appeared, halting his retreat.

Tony ran over to Sherrie, whose eyes were wide with shock and fear. Gently bending down, he cradled her as he spoke assurances that they were there for her. He gently pulled the gag from her swollen mouth as he pulled out a canteen of water. Holding it for her to drink, he wiped her mouth when the water dribbled over both of them.

She tried to speak but the words came out in a croak. Turning her frightened gaze to her rescuer, she could not seem to stop shivering.

He pulled out a knife and noticed her jerking back as he tried to cut her hand and feet bindings. "Shhh, honey. I'm just going to cut your restraints." With an expert flip of the knife he had her hands and feet free in an instant. Knowing her limbs would be numb, he began to rub them to restore the circulation. Staring down into those crystalline blue orbs, he suddenly felt lost. He couldn't seem to look away. He could hear Jobe in the background calling the police, but his attention was totally focused on the beautiful woman in front of him.

Her shivering brought him back to his senses and he realized that he had no idea the extent of her injuries or abuse at the hands of Marcel. Vinny knelt by them, quickly assessing her injuries.

"Wounds looks superficial. Probably drugs in her

system. Needs attention stat." Vinny lifted his gaze and noted the special interest his commander had in his eyes as he held the woman in his embrace.

Tony picked her up in his strong arms, cradling her against his massive chest. Looking down, knowing she was in shock, he just wanted to get her out of there as quickly as possible. He heard Jobe call out that the police and rescue squads were about five minutes away.

"You're gonna be fine Sherrie," he said softly, not wanting to frighten her more, but she did not answer.

Sherrie stared up at her rescuer as his arms were holding her tightly. *Someone came. Someone came for me.* She could not take her eyes off of the warmest caramel eyes she had ever seen. She tried to lick her parched lips, but her tongue felt swollen. Her rescuer had offered her water but dribbling was the best she could do. As he placed her on the stretcher in the ambulance she couldn't take her eyes off of him. Tall, dark, olive skin with pure white teeth in a gorgeous smile. He had a stubble of a beard on his square jaw, looking at though he just hadn't shaved recently but on him it looked good. And those eyes. Staring at her as well.

As she was loaded into the ambulance, she mouthed **Thank you**, just before they closed the doors. Pulling away, she realized that she didn't even know her rescuer's name.

Chapter 25

JORGE LOOKED AT his watch one more time, then re-checked his phone. Knowing that something was amiss, he quickly walked back down the stairs to the pit he had arranged. Devil's Spawn was already in place at the side of the pit...hungry, angry, and ready. Jorge glanced at the dog before swinging his eyes over to Suzanne, still strapped into a chair.

His mind began to work furiously. *What the fuck is wrong?* He knew that by now Charles should have been there to set up the cameras and computers. Even though Charles had gotten very efficient at his job, it still took some time to get the equipment in place. Besides Charles, the early guards of Marcel's should have arrived as well. For a brief flash, he wondered if he had the right location, but immediately dismissed that thought since he had the text from Marcel himself.

Has it been canceled? Did something go wrong with the other decoy site? He quickly dismissed those thoughts as well, knowing that Marcel would let him know if something had changed. *Or would he?* Suspicion began to slowly worm its way into his consciousness. His calls to Marcel went immediately to voicemail. He then tried calling several of Marcel's goons. Nothing.

The suspicion began to grow as Jorge began to wonder if he had been set up. *Fuck Marcel. If that bastard found out I was betting on the side…Goddamnit, if he set me up I'll kill him.* With that thought, he walked over to Suzanne whose exhausted eyes looked at him warily.

"Come on bitch. We're getting outta here." He leaned down and roughly grabbed her upper arm, hauling her out of the chair. His anger, out of control, almost had him not paying attention but his life on the streets kicked in and he suddenly shoved her back down. Running to the wall, he killed the lights inside the warehouse and looked outside seeing what looked like a complete armory coming for him.

Goddamn Marcel set me up. Looking around quickly for a chance to escape, he knew his time was limited. His gaze landed on Suzanne and his eyes glittered.

OUTSIDE OF THE warehouse, the police and Tony's men saw the lights go off. BJ's heart pounded, knowing that Jorge must be inside and that he now knew they were there. The S.W.A.T. team surrounded the building to keep Jorge from escaping but his focus was entirely on Suzanne.

Donning night vision goggles, the men moved to the doors of warehouse. As the police moved into the building, BJ and Gabe were right behind. What they saw stopped them in their tracks.

The lights suddenly came on and they pulled off their goggles as everyone blinked in the light. Suzanne was tied to a chair, gagged and sitting in the middle of the dog fighting ring. Several knife cuts had blood trickling down her arms and legs. Her blouse was opened and Jorge was crouched behind her with his arm reaching around holding his knife to her abdomen. The sound of growling came from a large dog barely restrained in a cage only a few feet away from Suzanne. His cage appeared to have a remote held in Jorge's hand.

The rescue team leader immediately barked the order for no one to proceed. Matt took the lead by calling out, "Jorge, you know this is it for you. Let the hostage go."

Years of living on the street had Jorge just smiling at the police. "You think I don't know I won't get out of this alive. You sure as shit aren't taking me alive, so this is only going to go one way. And I'm not going alone."

The men hesitated, quickly deciding how to take Jorge out without harming Suzanne.

"Hey big man," he called out to BJ. BJ stepped forward, his hands in plain sight. "Yeah, you. Been watching your girl for a long time. Ever since those fuckin' kids brought that dog to her and she got nosy." Sliding his free hand around to her throat, he gave a squeeze causing Suzanne to jump. "Decided I wanted her for myself. Imagine my surprise when I found out she was knocked up." At that, he dug the tip of his knife into her stomach just enough to cause a small trickle of blood to ooze out.

BJ stared coldly at Jorge, his eyes boring straight into the man who BJ vowed to kill with his own hands.

Devil's Spawn smelled the blood on Suzanne and his fight training to kill caused the huge dog to tear at his cage. Growling fiercely, the dog bared his fangs as he fought to get loose.

The police eyed the dog warily, before Matt spoke again. "Don't do this man. It doesn't have to end this way."

"You think I haven't figured out Marcel set me up? Everything I did for that prick and he set me up as his fall guy. Hell no. I'm nobody's fall guy. Look at this. You can't shoot me without the bullet going straight through her. You come after me, my knife ends her life and cuts straight into big man's baby. And that dog that's ready for blood? One click of my finger and he's out of the cage and on her before you can stop either of us."

BJ focused on Suzanne, meeting her eyes. He saw her body begin to shake as tears rolled down her already tear-streaked face. *Hang on, baby. I promise...promise I'll get you out of this.* He willed his thoughts to channel straight into her soul and noted when a light flickered in her eyes as though she knew exactly what he was saying.

With an earpiece set to the frequency of the police, he could hear the S.W.A.T. team leader setting up the snipers – one for Jorge and one for the dog. Refusing to look anywhere else but at Suzanne, he prayed the others around him did their jobs.

Jorge leaned in closer to Suzanne's ear and whispered, "My whole fuckin' life was living on the streets until I made it into Marcel's camp. All I wanted was one thing that was clean and pure and mine. I saw you, beauty, and that's what I wanted. I could've given you the world. Now, we can go out together." With that his knife made another small cut on her abdomen. Her eyes wide in terror searched out BJ's again.

A slight sound to the side had Jorge jerking his head around, pressing on the remote at the same time. Devil's Spawn shot out of the cage leaping the few feet in the air onto Suzanne, it's mouth open and fangs bared as it hurled itself onto her.

A muffled scream erupted from Suzanne as she saw the beast within inches of her body, saliva flinging from its mouth and eyes boring into hers as it went for the kill.

Several shots rang out simultaneously, one hitting Jorge in the head spraying blood all over Suzanne as her body was caught between his and the bloodied dog that lay partially on her legs, his head shot as well.

BJ bolted over to her, unable to discern what blood was hers and what belonged to Jorge or the dog. She continued to cry as Gabe stepped over Jorge's body to quickly release her hands and feet, allowing her to slump forward into BJ's arms. He quickly picked her up and sprinted away from the carnage. Gabe, right there with him, reached around and deftly sliced off the gag from her mouth.

BJ fought the EMTs, who tried to get him to place her in the ambulance, but climbed in himself while not letting her go. They headed to the hospital as the others climbed into their vehicles to follow. Shane called Annie to let her know Suzanne was alive and told her to stop by Tony's to pick up Lily and head to the hospital.

Gabe placed a call and found out that Tony's team was successful. Reporting to Matt and Shane, he said that Tony was already at the hospital with Sherrie.

Glancing back at the carnage in the middle of the pit, Gabe flashed back to his days as an Army medic. Shaking his head, he walked out into the clear, cold night meeting up with the others, and headed toward the hospital. Giving no more thought to the dead, his focus was on his friends and the living.

Looking down at the bloodied woman lying in his arms, BJ felt tears stream down his face. Terrified she was losing the baby, he wondered how she would survive another loss. "Baby, I'm here," he said, rocking her in his arms. The EMTs worked around him, convincing him to place her on the stretcher while allowing him to stay right by her head. He pushed her hair from her face and grabbed a towel and tried to wipe some of the blood from her forehead.

"It's okay baby, whatever happens, I'll still be here. We'll face it together. We'll always face it together. Trust me."

THE HOSPITAL WAITING room was filled with concerned friends and family. Once at the hospital, the staff would not let BJ go back with Suzanne until he explained that he was the fiancé and the father of her baby.

To his relief, when she was finally cleaned, they found that the majority of blood was from Jorge or the dog and not hers. There were still multiple lacerations, some requiring stitches. Bruises in the shape of fingers were on her neck and upper arms.

"Doctor, there's vaginal bleeding from the patient," a nurse's voice rang out.

BJ jerked his eyes downward from her face and saw the nurse between Suzanne's legs look up in concern.

The ER obstetrician was called and BJ was whisked away and taken back to the waiting room. Beginning to put up a fight, Gabe grabbed him by his arms and held on to him.

"Let 'em do their job, man. Hold on. Just hold on."

BJ slumped into a chair, feeling as though his legs were going to give out. Lily left Matt's side and sat next to him. "BJ, we're all here," she said between tears, reaching over to hold his hand.

Annie, tears already falling, felt a sob rip from her.

Shane, sitting next to her with his hand on her swollen stomach, pulled her closer. "Babe, gotta get a grip. This isn't helping Suzanne and it's not good for our baby." At that, she tucked her face into his chest and let his warmth soothe over her.

Jobe and Vinny sat in the room, having heard about the take-down from Gabe, each wondering what hell Suzanne must have endured.

Tony sat to the side. He had checked on the condition of Sherrie when he arrived at the hospital, finding that she had been treated for bruises and cuts and was soon to be released. She had been interviewed by the police, where she told them all she knew about Jorge.

As the doors to the ER treatment rooms opened, everyone's eyes looked up but disappointment filled as it was not a doctor coming to tell them about Suzanne. Tony's eyes however, stayed on the person walking into the room. Sherrie. Pale, bruised, terrified. Her eyes glanced around the room before landing on Tony's. Blushing, she looked away as she began to walk toward the outer door. Tony stood and quickly walked over to block her path.

She was forced to lean her head way back as he was so much taller than she. Licking her chapped and still swollen lips, she nervously asked, "How is she? Suzanne? I heard she was here."

"They're still checking her out. Maybe losing the baby," Tony answered in his usual clipped tone but focusing on her blue eyes.

Pulling in her lips, her eyes filled with tears as she began to sidestep him to leave.

"You should stay. You're a friend," he added.

Her eyes glanced around the room nervously. Slowly she shook her head as a tear escaped and slid down her pale cheek. "No. I...I don't belong. I...," her sad voice drifted off. Taking a deep breath, she began to leave again.

"Do you have a ride home? Are you okay to go home by yourself?" he asked, suddenly not wanting to lose the contact.

Giving him a sad smile she replied, "I've been alone for a long time. I'm used to it." With that she stepped to the automatic doors and began to walk through. Turning, she looked into his caramel eyes one last time. "Give Suzanne my love. And tell her...I'm sorry." With that she disappeared into the night.

Tony stood for a moment, the desire to follow warring with the need to stay. Shaking his head, he turned and went to the seat next to BJ.

The ER doctor then came out and called for Brad Evans. He stared for a second before feeling Lily squeeze his hand and he jumped to his feet. Following the doctor through the doors, he spared a glance at the room behind him filled with friends and feeling the vibes of hope flooding the room.

They walked into the ER bay where Suzanne lay still and quiet. Turning to the doctor with questions in his head, he just stared numbly.

"Her wounds were mostly superficial and only a few required stitches. There was no head injury. We have her mildly sedated since her heartrate was fast and blood pressure was elevated. We believe that is due to the trauma of what she experienced. We'll move her to a room upstairs and you can be with her. As soon as she awakes, we'll have the hospital psychologist speak with her."

"And the preganacy? The baby?" BJ asked haltingly.

The doctor smiled and said, "Right now, everything is fine."

BJ's eyes jerked to the doctor's face in question.

Nodding, the doctor continued, "There was some minor vaginal bleeding. It's stopped. An ultrasound was completed and the fetal heartbeats are strong."

BJ stood stoic, letting the words of the doctor slowly sink into his consciousness. *She's going to be fine. The heartbeats are fine. Heartbeats? What the fuck?*

His eyes jerked back to the face of the smiling doctor who nodded to BJ's unspoken question.

"Yes, Mr. Evans. You are going to be the proud father of twins." The doctor left the room, leaving BJ leaning over the bed staring at the woman he had loved his whole life.

Brushing the hair from her forehead, he planted a sweet kiss on her lips. "Baby, we're gonna have twins. You gotta get well and you gotta get strong. And I'm gonna spend the rest of my life taking care of you and our children. You and me, Suzy girl. Always."

Her eyes fluttered open and she gave him a lazy, slightly sedated smile as she looked into the face that had filled her dreams forever. "Twins?" she whispered.

He only nodded, finding that he was unable to speak. He kissed her once more before the nurses prepared to move her to a room in the hospital. Taking a quick moment to rush back to the waiting room, he announced his news to the ever growing crowd that now included Suzanne's parents, Bernie and Mac, as well as her brother and his wife, Rob and Laurie.

From her bed down the hall, Suzanne could hear the roar of cheers coming from the distance. Smiling, she placed her hand on her slightly swollen abdomen. "Babies," she whispered as a tear slid down her face just before she slid back into a peaceful sleep.

Chapter 26

(2 months later)

"I NOW PRONOUNCE you man and wife. You may kiss your bride."

This time the words of the minister were said over Suzanne and BJ and had barely left his mouth before BJ took her mouth in a kiss felt down to her toes. The clapping from the assembly of friends and family had her blushing as her eyes took in the man standing before her. The only man she had ever loved. The man now her husband.

The wedding ceremony had only lasted a short while and the pictures were finally finished. The large barn that had held many holiday gatherings was now decorated with flowers and streamers in ivory and pink. The guests had finished their meal and the bride and groom had just finished their first dance as man and wife. As their friends swarmed around on the dance floor, BJ led Suzanne off to the side to have a chance to get off of her feet. They sat with Shane and Annie, who at two months further along in her pregnancy was no bigger than Suzanne. Shane, uncharacteristically nervous, hovered over Annie who finally told him to go find some men to hang out with if he couldn't leave her alone.

"Not doing it babe."

Annie huffed as she said, "Shane, I'm pregnant, not an invalid."

"Both of you women have worked too hard to get the new clinic up and running and I'm not taking any chances. So sit back, relax, and get used to being pampered," he retorted.

Hearing laughter behind them, Leon and his wife came over to congratulate the bride. Soon the tables around them were full of their friends. Matt and Lily, recently married themselves, along with Gabe, Vinny and Jobe and their dates rounded out their table.

Pamela, Dwayne and Chuckie walked over giving the couple a hug. They had found a new apartment in a nice neighborhood with a park nearby and the boys had adapted well. The boys blushed as Suzanne ruffled their hair and exclaimed, "You two are so handsome!" BJ offered his handshake to them and Suzanne could not help but notice the boys standing a little taller with huge smiles on their faces. She and Pamela smiled at each other knowing that with all of Tony's men around, the boys would not lack for male role models.

Suzanne's little niece, the flower girl, came bounding around the table and threw herself in Suzanne's lap. "Caroline!" her mother admonished. "Be careful." Rob scooped up his daughter as he leaned down and kissed his sister's cheek. "Love you, Suzy," he said, as she tearfully looked into her big brother's face knowing he accepted BJ into the family.

Sherrie walked over, a nervous smile on her face as she was greeted enthusiastically by Suzanne. Sherrie still felt guilty about her part in what happened to them but with Suzanne's help, she was coming to terms with what all she had tried to do to help her sister. After Suzanne had been released from the hospital, one of the first calls she made was to Sherrie. The two friends met and began the first of weekly get-togethers. It took Sherrie awhile to move forward from the poor choices her sister had made that fateful day, but she finally began to understand that they were her sister's choices, not hers. Suzanne held no animosity toward her and with time, she learned to forgive herself. She had not seen her sister since that day and doubted if she ever would again.

The others at the table welcomed Sherrie as well, but as her eyes slid over to Tony's she noticed that while his warm eyes were on her, he never made an attempt to talk to her. Nodding slightly, she made her excuses to leave early, promising to have lunch soon with the new bride. Slipping out of the side door, she allowed herself a glance backwards only to find Tony still staring at her, a slight nod from him as her only acknowledgement.

The DJ called for the next dance and Suzanne was helped to her feet by BJ, who kissed her soundly. Mac puffed his chest out as he walked to the center of the floor taking Suzanne by the hand for the father-daughter dance. He led her in a circle, showing off his pride and joy before taking her in his arms to the sounds of *I Loved Her First* by Heartland. Her ebony hair was swept up in soft curls falling down her back with her lace veil floating around. At five months along with twins, her wedding dress allowed for her expanded body and soft layers of silk and lace swirled around her as they danced.

Looking into the blue Irish eyes of his only daughter, Mac felt the tears come. "You know you'll always be my little lass," he said, trying to keep the smile on his face.

Suzanne, losing the battle to the tears, replied, "I know, daddy."

They both glanced to the side to see BJ standing next to his parents, an arm around both of them swaying to the music as well. BJ's grandparents stood next to them, arms around each other. Helen's expression was one that she knew this day would come.

"He's a good man," Mac admitted. "I've known him since the day he was born." He chuckled as they continued to move back and forth across the dance floor. "In fact when you were born, Bill and Wendy and your mom and me all decided that you two should grow up together and get married."

"I love him daddy and he loves me too. I think we always have."

As the music came to a stop, Mac kissed his daughter's cheek and led her over to where BJ was standing. Tall, strong, looking handsome in his black tuxedo. Mac placed her hand into BJ's outstretched one and held both of theirs for just a moment. "Take care of her, Brad," Mac said.

"Always," came the heartfelt answer. As BJ took his bride back to the floor to gently sway her to the music, loving the feel of her in his arms, he continued, "You can trust in that."

Epilogue

(Five years later)

BJ GENTLY ROCKED his body into Suzanne's as they lay in the bed early on a Sunday morning. He held his hands on her abdomen, swollen with his child, as he took her from behind. Ever aware of her comfort, he had placed a pillow between her knees. Her pregnancy hormones had her usually coming quickly and today was no exception. Her pussy clamped down on his cock and he felt the baby move slightly against his hands. Knowing that they were about to enter the time when they would stop having sex before this child came, he savored the feeling of her warm body pulling on his.

With a few more strokes he felt his balls tighten and he held her firmly as he poured himself into her, allowing her to clutch him greedily. He slid one hand up to cup her enlarged breast as the other hand continued to massage her stomach. Leaning around, he kissed her mouth as she met his lips.

Hearing the rumblings from the room across the hall, BJ reluctantly pulled out, laughing as she mewed from the loss of contact. "Gotta get the twins," he said. "You lay here for a minute and I'll get them."

She pulled herself out of bed and grabbed her robe from across the footboard. Before she knew it blond-headed James and dark-haired Katherine bounded into the room, followed closely by their father with socks still in his hands. The children jumped into the bed with their mom, careful to hug her without pouncing on her stomach. They quickly kissed her good morning and then leaned down to kiss her belly, saying good morning to their soon-to-be born brother.

Looking up at BJ with the socks that had never made it on to their children's feet, she laughed as she held out her hand. He tossed her James' while he grabbed Katherine's feet and tickled her as she squealed with delight. She slipped her son's socks on, then sent him on his way to comb his hair and brush his teeth. Katherine bounded from the bed, ready to do whatever her brother did as well.

BJ leaned over and gently pulled Suzanne to her feet. *A mother of twin four-year olds and soon to be mother of another baby...and still the most beautiful woman I have ever seen.* "Suzy girl, do you feel like going to the picnic today?"

She knew her fatigue showed and smiled indulgently at her husband. She reached up to smooth her hand over his stubbled jaw, loving the feel of it under her fingers. "Yeah," she replied softly. "I wouldn't miss it for anything."

It was the annual pet adoption fair that Annie's clinic held every year and it became time for all of their friends to gather, help with the animals and then culminate in a huge barbecue picnic. Besides Annie and Shane, Matt and Lily and their friends from Tony's would all be there. Good food. Good friends. And family.

As she turned to walk into the bathroom, BJ called softly, "I love you, you know."

She stopped and walked back into his arms, looking up into his slate blue eyes. "I know."

He held her in his warm embrace, saying, "I've loved you since I was sixteen years old."

"And I've loved you forever," she said, feeling their new child kick against his body as he held her close.

Kissing her sweet lips in a kiss that promised everything, he replied, "I will always love you till the end of time. You can trust in that."

The End

Books by Maryann Jordan

Thank you for reading this book. I hope you enjoyed it! If so, please leave a review. Reviews are the life-blood for an indie author. I also hope that you will check out some of my other books. Each is a stand-alone book (no cliffhangers). And of course, alpha males and the strong women they fall in love with!

The Fairfield Series
Laurie's Time

Emma's Home

Carol's Image

The Love's Series
Love's Taming

Love's Tempting

Love's Trusting

Coming 2015
Alvarez Security Series
Gabe

Tony

Vinny

Jobe

Other Authors Of Interest

MJ Nightingale

Andrea Michelle

Andie Long

Emma Shorthall

A.d. Ellis

Victoria Brock

ML Steinbrunn

Jen Andrews

Sandra Love

Kristine Raymond

Anna Mychals

42312910R00236

Made in the USA
San Bernardino, CA
01 December 2016